LOST
INNOCENCE

Books by Jannine Gallant

The Siren Cove Series

Buried Truth

Lost Innocence

The Born to Be Wilde Series

Wilde One

Wilde Side

Wilde Thing

Wilde Horses

The Who's Watching Now Series

Every Move She Makes

Every Step She Takes

Every Vow She Breaks

LOST INNOCENCE

JANNINE GALLANT

LYRICAL PRESS
Kensington Publishing Corp.
www.kensingtonbooks.com

LYRICAL PRESS BOOKS are published by

Kensington Publishing Corp.
119 West 40th Street
New York, NY 10018

All Kensington titles, imprints, and distributed lines are available at special quantity discounts for bulk purchases for sales promotion, premiums, fund-raising, educational, or institutional use.

Special book excerpts or customized printings can also be created to fit specific needs. For details, write or phone the office of the Kensington Sales Manager: Kensington Publishing Corp., 119 West 40th Street, New York, NY 10018. Attn. Sales Department. Phone: 1-800-221-2647.

Lyrical Press and Lyrical Press logo Reg. U.S. Pat. & TM Off.

First Printing: July 2018
ISBN-13: 978-1-5161-0376-8
ISBN-10: 1-5161-0376-9

eISBN-13: 978-1-5161-0377-5
eISBN-10: 1-5161-0377-7

10 9 8 7 6 5 4 3 2 1

Printed in the United States of America

To Tara, my smart, strong, determined,
wonderful daughter.
Your commitment to everything you do will take you far.
I wish you nothing but the best!

Chapter One

The day she'd dreaded had arrived.

The roar of a diesel engine blasted through the tranquility of a May morning and sent the mother robin perched on her nest into flight. Nina Hutton dropped her paintbrush onto the ledge of her easel and scowled. Rarely did a vehicle venture down her dead-end street, let alone one emitting puffs of exhaust into the pristine coastal air and creating enough noise to frighten away the wildlife. Spinning on her stool, she rose to her feet and stared in the direction of the disturbance. Not that she could see squat from the seclusion of her backyard.

Finally, the rumble of the engine died, doors slammed, barking erupted, and a high-pitched squeal pierced the sudden silence. "Daddy, look! Our new house matches my dress."

A deep male voice responded, too low for Nina to make out the words over excited yelps and the clatter of metal against metal. She softly swore. The For Sale sign planted in the yard of the run-down Victorian across the street had disappeared the previous month. Apparently, the new owners had arrived. So much for peace and solitude . . .

Since the subject of her current painting was winging its way through the brilliant blue sky, there was little reason not to satisfy her curiosity as the voices faded in and out. Openly gaping at her new neighbors wasn't an option, not when she could spy on them from an upstairs window. After cleaning her brushes and stowing her paints, Nina left the easel where it stood near the big madrone tree with its nest of baby robins, crossed the yard to the back deck, then entered her house through the open sliding door.

Sunlight pierced the high windows in the main room, catching dust motes in the beams. She sniffed the aroma of beef stew slow cooking in the Crock-Pot as she skirted around the green suede couch and climbed the stairs to the second floor. Entering her bedroom, she dropped down onto the padded window seat, then adjusted the blinds to peek out.

A big yellow moving van stood in the middle of the cul-de-sac with a loading ramp leading from its rear to the ground. Beyond it, a dark blue pickup was parked in the driveway of the house across from hers. Two men in uniform shirts struggled to haul a tall armoire up the steps of the wraparound front porch, while a third man wearing a black T-shirt stretched tight across his broad back followed them, carrying a large box labeled *Books* in bold red marker. A series of expletives from one of the movers—unsuitable for the ears of the small girl running in circles on the weedy patch of lawn, chased by a white and tan ball of fur—drifted upward on the breeze.

She wondered where the child's mother was. *Probably inside, trying to figure out where to put the furniture.* The girl couldn't be more than six or seven, all arms and legs in a princess dress of pink tulle that was indeed the same color as the house. Blond hair had been pulled back in a ratty ponytail. Despite the girl's high-pitched shrieks, which complemented equally shrill canine yapping, Nina smiled.

The man in the black T-shirt emerged from the front entrance a few moments later—minus the box—and raised his voice to be heard. Thankfully, both the child and the dog piped down. When he reached the street, he fisted his hands on his hips and glanced in Nina's direction.

Nina quickly ducked out of sight. *Gorgeous* was the word that sprang to mind. The short sleeves of his T-shirt clung to well-defined biceps, while brown hair with a hint of a wave topped the most handsome face she'd seen outside a movie theater. Silvery eyes narrowed against the sun above a straight nose and strong chin. The man reminded her of Clint Eastwood back in his spaghetti Western days. All he needed was a battered cowboy hat, a poncho, and a cigar clamped between those white teeth.

"Wow. Just wow." She settled more comfortably against the cushions as her new neighbor disappeared into the moving van only to return a few seconds later carrying a white painted headboard in one hand and a box labeled *Kitchen* in block letters beneath the other arm. If she had to sacrifice the peace and quiet she'd enjoyed since the last tenant—a rock-n-roll wannabe who'd spent most evenings practicing on his drums—moved out, at least the new owner of the dilapidated Victorian was easy on the eyes. *Very easy.*

Best of all, she could enjoy his beauty with no internal pressure since he was obviously a family man and unavailable. She clenched her fist around the edge of the windowsill. Over the last six months, she'd honestly tried to put herself out there on the social front, only to wind up disappointed and aching . . . missing Keith. Accepting the fact that she was happier alone was easier on her and any potential suitors who invariably failed to live up to her unrealistic expectations.

When her cell phone chimed, she pulled it out of the pocket of her jeans, happy to escape her thoughts, and glanced at the display. A smile formed as she answered. "Hey, Leah."

"Hey, yourself. What do you have going on today?"

"I was working before my subject flew away. Why? Aren't you at school?"

"Recess. Can't you hear the kids screaming in the background?"

"Not over the commotion next door."

Nina glanced out the window as a string of oaths blistered her ears through the open window. One of the moving men stood at the end of the ramp next to a carved oak bookcase, rubbing his right shin. Thankfully, the girl and dog had disappeared, presumably ordered inside out of hearing range.

"What's going on next door?"

She returned her attention to the conversation with one of her oldest and dearest friends. "The people who bought the Victorian are moving in this morning. I can barely hear myself think over the ruckus, let alone focus on painting."

"Oh, yeah? What are they like?"

"The man is drool-worthy, probably a little older than us, and his daughter is cute but loud. Their dog is small and yappy. I haven't seen the wife or girlfriend or whoever yet. She must have gone inside before I set up watch from my bedroom."

"You're spying on them?"

"Of course. Wouldn't you?"

"I'd probably walk across the street and introduce myself. Did that thought ever occur to you? Maybe welcome them to the neighborhood."

"The guy's too busy flexing his muscles." Nina gave the hottie an appreciative stare as he hauled a rolled-up rug slung over one shoulder into the house. "Literally, since he's busy unpacking a moving van. I'm sure his partner is equally occupied. There'll be plenty of time to meet them later."

"I suppose so, but not this afternoon. The bridesmaid dresses finally arrived. Can you meet me and Paige at All Dressed Up for a fitting? Three o'clock sharp."

"Says the woman who's chronically late. Of course I can." She leaned an elbow on the windowsill. "I can't believe you and Ryan are getting married next month. The time has flown by since he proposed last fall."

"I know, right? I can't wait to say *I do*. Oh, crap, the bell is ringing. I need to herd the little monsters back into the classroom. See you this afternoon, Nina."

The phone went dead before she could respond. Sticking it back in her pocket, Nina glanced down as the movers finally maneuvered the bookcase inside. Spying was getting a little old. Maybe the mother robin had returned to her nest, and she could get back to work on the painting Miss Lola had commissioned. Sliding off the window seat, she headed downstairs but stopped when she reached the deck door.

The munchkin hadn't gone inside after all. She stood with her hands clasped behind her back in front of the easel while her furry companion sniffed the base of the tree before squatting to pee. Sliding open the screen, Nina stepped out onto the deck.

The child turned to regard her. "How come you didn't finish the picture? The bird's feathers look funny."

"Because the robin flew away when your moving

truck drove up." Nina crossed the yard to the young girl's side. "Does your mom know you're over here?"

Her uninvited guest rocked back and forth on pink tennis shoes. "Daddy says my mommy watches me all the time. She always knows where I am."

While Nina struggled to imagine any mother turning a child who couldn't be much more than six loose in an unfamiliar neighborhood, she didn't argue. "I'm Nina. What's your name?"

"Keely. It means beautiful. My daddy says I was a very pretty baby, but a mean boy in my kindergarten class told me I look like a giraffe because I have long legs."

"Calling people names is definitely not nice, but giraffes are graceful and majestic."

"Majestic. I like that word." She gave a little hop and a skip. "Where did Coco go?"

"Your dog?" When Keely nodded, Nina turned her to face an upended rump as the dog sniffed a clump of ferns, tail wagging. "There she is. She's very pretty, just like you."

The girl smiled. "Coco's a paplon. I love how the fur hangs off her ears. It's soft."

"You mean a papillon?"

"That's what I said, a paplon. Come on, Coco. Let's go."

"It was nice meeting you, Keely. Tell your parents I'll stop by to introduce myself sometime soon."

She opened her mouth, then shut it, and ran off without another word to disappear around the side of the house. After giving the ferns a final sniff, the dog followed.

When a chorus of cheeping erupted above her, Nina glanced up and smiled. The mother robin had returned, and the babies in the nest were making it clear they were on the verge of starvation. She settled at her easel and resumed work. Not that painting birds was her true passion, but sometimes artistic zeal took a back seat to paying the bills. Miss Lola was a steady customer and bird enthusiast with deep pockets, and Nina had learned the hard way you did what was necessary to survive.

Two hours later, she put the finishing touches on the painting. Shading the orange of the mother robin's breast and adding a protective gleam to her eye. Instilling a sense of urgency in the gaping mouths and stretched, scrawny necks of the hatchlings. Curling the edges of the thin bark peeling away from the madrone tree. Satisfied with the results, she cleaned her brushes, put away her paints, and then rose from her stool.

As she headed straight to the kitchen, her stomach rumbled. Probably because she'd had nothing but a yogurt for breakfast, and it was well past noon. After making herself a turkey sandwich on wheat, she peeked out the kitchen window. Silence reigned next door. Apparently the movers were on a lunch break since the truck was still parked in the street, blocking her view. No matter. She could squeeze her Mini Cooper around it. Maybe she'd drive down to the beach for a run before she met her friends for the dress fitting.

Biting into her sandwich, Nina climbed the stairs two at a time to her room, where she tossed her paint-stained shirt and jeans into the hamper before sorting through her dresser drawer for a pair of shorts and a tank top. She finished eating while tying on her running shoes, then paused downstairs at the kitchen sink to chug a glass of water.

Heading outside, she stopped at the end of her driveway and surveyed the limited stretch of pavement between her front lawn and the van through narrowed eyes. The Mini Cooper was small, but not that tiny. Backing out would seriously endanger either the car's shiny red paint or her grass. She rounded the end of the truck at a fast clip and smacked straight into a hard, T-shirt-clad chest. Her nose mashed against the pulse beating at the man's throat, and when she drew in a breath, a woodsy scent teased her nostrils. Strong arms closed around her as they both wobbled and swayed before her new neighbor steadied her and took a step back.

"Sorry about that." He assessed her from the top of her head to her running shoes, and a hint of appreciation entered those silvery eyes. "You make quite an impact."

"I guess I should look where I'm going." Her slightly breathless tone annoyed her no end. Getting flustered over a married man, no matter how hot he might be, was pointless. "I'm Nina Hutton." She extended her hand. "Welcome to our little corner of the neighborhood."

A warm palm gripped hers. "Nice to meet you. I'm Teague O'Dell." When he released her hand, he waved toward the thick woods surrounding them. "I love the seclusion here. It's the reason I bought this place. A far cry from the Southern California suburbs."

"You moved to Oregon from Los Angeles?"

"We lived in Encino, which is in the L.A. area. After . . . well, I wanted a complete change, small town instead of urban sprawl."

"Siren Cove certainly offers that."

"This house needs a lot of work, but I don't mind." He regarded her steadily. "I just want a safe place where I don't have to worry about my daughter if she wants to play in the yard."

"You found it." She gave him a quick smile, wondering if he was always so serious. "Uh, I'd love to meet the rest of your family, but I was on my way out for a run on the beach. Do you think someone could move the truck?"

"Of course. Sorry, I didn't realize we were blocking

your driveway. I'll go get the keys, and hopefully we'll have the van unloaded and out of here in another hour or so."

"No worries. Nice to meet you, Teague, and good luck with the unpacking. I don't envy you that task."

"I'm sure we'll be hip-deep in boxes for weeks."

He hurried away, presumably to retrieve the keys, and Nina climbed into her car to wait. A minute later, the truck engine fired up with a roar, followed by a shout from Teague. Her gaze was glued to the rearview mirror as he raised the metal ramp, biceps bulging beneath the weight, to slide it into the truck before the driver pulled forward out of her way.

After backing to the end of the driveway, she returned her new neighbor's wave, then accelerated down the street. "Oh, my. Mr. Hottie O'Dell is eye candy with a capital *C*." She couldn't help wondering what Keely's mother looked like. *Probably Malibu Barbie.*

Turning at the corner, she pressed harder on the accelerator to send her little car flying down the coast road south of town. One thing was certain, she needed to stop salivating over attached men, no matter how hot. Since pulling off a relationship seemed beyond her capabilities, for now, she'd simply run off her frustrations.

Nina parked in the half-full lot above the beach and followed the winding trail down to the water's edge, then ran facing into the wind. Her shoes pounded the sand in a steady rhythm as the salt spray off the waves dampened her arms and legs. Out near the breakwater, the three monolithic rocks that gave Siren Cove its name stood sentinel over the town. Her breathing came in harsh pants as she passed a handful of young women watching toddlers build castles with buckets and shovels. She recognized a couple of the mothers and nodded in greeting but wasn't tempted to join them.

If Keith hadn't died, maybe I'd be part of that group. Or not.

She shook off the painful thought and ran faster past a woman bundled in a jacket bent over a tide pool to poke something with the tip of a stick while a blond girl sat alone on a nearby rock. Farther up the beach, a couple strolled hand in hand, their laughter drifting on the breeze. Sweat dripped down Nina's face and neck to pool between her breasts. Slowing to a stop, she braced her hands on her knees and forced air into her labored lungs.

What an idiot she was, letting her emotions get out of control and running like a woman possessed. Now she'd have to go home to shower before she could try on her dress for the wedding. Which meant she'd better head straight back to her car. Turning down the beach, she jogged to cool off and smiled at a fellow runner in a bright pink T-shirt going in the opposite direction. The young girl had left her rock to stand ankle-deep in water while the tide surged away from her bare feet. Up ahead, the group of preschoolers had abandoned their castles to chase seagulls, screaming like banshees as the birds flew away with equally harsh cries.

When a scrap of paper blew across her path, Nina bent to grab the piece of litter and thrust it into the pocket of her shorts, then picked up her pace again. The cool breeze off the ocean dried her sweat and soothed her soul. By the time she reached the trail up to the parking lot, she'd gotten over her attack of self-pity.

Until the next time.

Where had she put the lottery ticket? She turned the pockets of her jacket inside out but found only a few coins and a small clamshell, then searched through the open bag on the bench by the kitchen door. Bits of sand stuck to her fingertips as she pulled out the miscellaneous assortment that had accumulated since she'd last cleaned out her tote bag. Relief filled her when her fingers closed around a piece of paper, but it wasn't the magic ticket, only an old grocery receipt she wadded and chucked in the trash.

The lottery ticket must have blown away while she was on the beach, but she didn't have time to spare looking for it right now. Not if she didn't want to be late.

What were the chances her numbers would be the winning ones, anyway? She'd played those same numbers for years to no avail, but this time she'd felt lucky. Her lips tightened. Obviously not. The underlying feeling of nervous anticipation keeping her on edge must be due to summer drawing near. Memories of that humid day had become more insistent and dominated her dreams. She glanced toward the small head bent over the picture books open on the table.

The day of reckoning was almost here.

Chapter Two

Teague stared across the sea of boxes at his daughter lining up stuffed animals on the sofa. He pressed the fingers of one hand to his temple while clutching his phone tighter in the other. "You want me to start work *this* Saturday? I was counting on an extra week to get settled and find childcare for my daughter."

The voice of the fire captain on the other end of the line explained calmly but firmly that they were short-handed due to an on-the-job injury. His new boss's appeal may have been couched in the form of a request but in actuality was a direct order.

"Fine, I'll make it work and report for duty Saturday morning. Thanks for the call." He disconnected and stuffed his phone in his pocket. Times like these, the ache of missing Jayne was nearly unbearable. The weight of the world pressed down on him and threatened to crush his spirit, but he didn't have time to wallow in self-pity. Instead, he needed to find a reliable babysitter without delay.

Avoiding boxes, he reached the kitchen where the real

estate agent had left a packet of local information on the counter. Sorting through takeout menus, he found the promised list of daycare facilities, summer camp programs, and vetted babysitters available to work weekends and evenings. A live-in nanny would be more convenient, but after the last fiasco, hiring another one wasn't an option.

Pulling out his phone again, he started making calls and counted himself lucky when three potential candidates agreed to meet him for a brief interview that afternoon. Hopefully at least one of them would pan out.

Teague headed back to the living room and froze. The assortment of animals still occupied the black leather couch, but Keely was nowhere in sight. He cocked an ear for any hint of sound upstairs, but the house was suspiciously quiet. A box labeled *Art Supplies* stood open next to the coffee table, and a container of crayons and one of chalk had been left on its polished surface.

"Keely." His shout echoed back at him. When his heart rate accelerated, he took a calming breath. This was why he'd left the city, so he wouldn't have to worry about his daughter every time she disappeared from view. Hurrying past clumps of furniture, he reached the front door and stepped out onto the porch.

"Keely!"

A bark sounded, slightly muffled, followed by high-pitched laughter coming from the direction of his neighbor's house. Relief filled him. As he descended the steps, Nina Hutton cruised up the street in her bright red Mini Cooper and pulled into her driveway. By the time she stepped out of the car, he'd reached her side.

Dark hair cut short and wispy framed perfectly symmetrical features and pure green eyes. A sweat-dampened purple tank top was plastered to her curves, and spandex running shorts showed off legs that could easily have graced the cover of a *Sports Illustrated* Swimsuit Issue. The woman was stunning.

"Can I help you with something?"

He forced himself to stop staring. "Uh, Keely and Coco went missing. I'm pretty sure they're in your backyard."

"I found them there earlier. Maybe she went back while I was at the beach."

"Do you mind if I check?"

A smile curved the edges of Nina's pink lips. "Since I'm not in the habit of collecting children, of course not. Come on through."

He walked at her side across the patch of lawn separating her small, two-story cabin from the single-car garage, following a series of drag marks he feared were his daughter's doing. He gave his new neighbor points for not saying anything about the trail of uprooted grass as they passed flower beds bursting with blooms behind brick borders.

"I'll make it clear to my daughter she's not to visit you without permission anymore."

"I honestly don't mind."

"Well, I do."

He halted abruptly when they rounded the corner. Keely stood in front of her red and blue plastic easel, painting with big splashes of color on a large sheet of paper clipped to its surface. Beside her stood a much taller, wooden easel holding an oil depiction of a nesting robin on a square canvas. The picture looked like the work of a professional.

His daughter glanced over her shoulder and waved her brush. "Look, Daddy, I'm painting."

"So I see. How did you get that easel over here?"

"I pulled it behind me." She turned back to her painting. "Isn't my picture pretty?"

"You have an eye for detail." Nina stepped closer. "I can easily tell those flowers are hydrangeas."

They looked like lavender blotches to Teague. "Very nice, but we have to go home."

"I'm almost done."

"Keely." His voice held a note of warning.

"Please can I finish my picture, Daddy?"

"I need to shower and leave again for an appointment, but I don't mind if she stays a little longer."

Teague glanced from his daughter's pleading eyes to the understanding in Nina's and nodded slowly. "I suppose so, but we're going to have a serious talk about boundaries later, right after I repair those drag marks in the lawn."

Keely added swirls of green around the lavender blobs. "What are boundaries?"

"Something you don't know much about." He bent to stroke Coco's head when the dog left the hydrangea bushes to lean against his ankle. "You need to finish up quickly. I'm interviewing babysitters, and the first one will be here soon."

"Maybe Nina can watch me instead."

When his neighbor's eyes widened in what looked like horror, Teague held back a grin. "No, she can't." His tone was non-negotiable as he met the woman's gaze head-on. "If you need to get ready to go somewhere . . ." He took another quick look at those incredible legs.

She glanced at the watch strapped to her wrist. "I have a dress fitting for a wedding. You have real talent, Keely. I'd be happy to help you with your painting when I have more time."

His daughter stood a little taller. "You'd do that?"

"Sure. I'll show you a few basic techniques . . ." Nina glanced his way. "If your dad doesn't mind?"

"Of course not, but don't feel obligated."

"I don't." With a quick smile, she headed across the backyard to the large deck and disappeared inside.

Teague tried to dismiss the sexy image of long legs imprinted on his temporal lobe. The woman was getting married soon, and salivating over her extremely fine ass seemed somehow wrong. He turned back to his daughter. "I need to get a tool—if I can find the right box in that huge mess we call a living room—to fix Nina's grass. Don't move from this spot while I'm gone."

She tilted her head at an angle before adding a yellow sun to the top corner of her picture. "I won't."

Five minutes later, he gave up the search for the box marked *Garden* and pulled the divot repair tool out of his golf bag instead. It would take longer than using a hand rake but would still do the job. His daughter had finished her painting, and he was making serious progress on the drag marks when Nina strolled out of the house and stopped beside her car. The sweaty running clothes had been replaced by a sleeveless shirt and shorts only marginally longer than the ones she'd previously worn. She still looked extremely hot.

"You don't have to do that." She glanced over at Keely, who was turning cartwheels in the front yard.

He focused on her face. "Yes, I do. The next time the sprinklers go, the grass should perk up again."

"Well, thanks for your due diligence, but I wouldn't have lost sleep over those marks." Nina opened her car door. "Good luck with your babysitter search."

"I appreciate that . . . and your compassion for my daughter." He kept his voice low. "She's acting out a bit, hiding her insecurities over this move with boldness. I'm trying to set a course between understanding and a strict adherence to our rules."

"Seems to me you're doing just fine. She's a sweet kid, funny and bright. As I said, I don't mind if she visits me."

"Thank you, but I'll try to keep a tighter rein on her."

With a nod, she climbed into her car, started it, and backed down the driveway. Maybe he should have investigated his neighbors more thoroughly before buying the old Victorian. He hadn't been this attracted to a woman since Jayne, and his hormones had shifted into overdrive.

He glanced away from the now-empty street when Coco strolled over to his side. "Not very smart."

The dog cocked her head and gave him a curious look.

"Getting all hot and bothered over a woman headed off to try on a wedding dress. Bad form." His life was problematic enough. He didn't need any more complications.

Leah pressed her hands to her cheeks, and her brown eyes grew wide. "Oh, my God! You two look stunning."

Nina studied her reflection beside Paige's in the mirror and smiled. "We do, don't we?"

"Absolutely." Paige fluffed the chiffon material of her skirt, which hit her just below the knees. "We're opposites in every way, but this aqua color looks fabulous on both of us. Your eyes look even greener than usual, and mine are bluer."

"That's because the color sort of shifts when we move." Nina glanced over her shoulder to assess her bare back. "I need to even out my tan. I have pale marks from running in a tank top. I was just down on the beach an hour ago."

"Maybe so, but strapless was definitely the right choice

for style." Leah walked in a slow circle around her two bridesmaids. "Wow! Definitely worth waiting for them on backorder."

"Nina would look spectacular in a sack." Paige's tone was matter-of-fact as she sucked in her breath and fingered the band around her waist. "If I lose two pounds, it'll fit perfectly, but we need to take up the hem at least three inches."

The seamstress scribbled in her notebook, then placed a couple of pins in Paige's skirt. She glanced at Leah over the top of her bifocals. "Is this the length you want, a couple inches above the knee?"

"I think so. That's where Nina's dress falls right now, so we can't go any longer."

"I'd kill for her legs." Paige stood on her toes and twirled. "Even in heels, I'm short."

Nina grinned. "I have giraffe legs, just like my new neighbor."

"Huh?" Paige stopped moving when the seamstress touched the wide band at her waist.

"If it's tight, I can let it out a half inch."

"No, I'm going to lose those two pounds instead." She glanced back at Nina. "What new neighbor?"

"The people who bought the Victorian across the street moved in this morning. They have a little girl who made herself at home in my yard. She's blond and adorable like you, but on the gangly side. She told me a mean boy said she has giraffe legs."

"I hope she punched him."

"She just might have since she seems pretty self-confident."

Leah broke off her conversation with the seamstress. "Did you get a look at the girl's mother yet?"

"Nope, but I've had a couple of conversations with her dad. Very intense and a little stressed out, but friendly enough." Nina waved a hand in front of her face. "He's even better-looking up close. On a scale of one to ten, the dude's a thirteen."

Paige turned to stare. "This I want to see. Does he have a name? I'll stalk him online. He must have a profile on Crossroads. Everyone does."

"Teague O'Dell. They moved here from the L.A. area. Uh, Encino, I think he said."

"I'll check him out." Paige eyed the bride-to-be. "You don't get to since you're a soon-to-be married woman."

"I'm engaged, not dead. Ryan knows he's the only man I'll ever want, but there's no harm in just looking, right?"

"Good point." Nina held out her arms when the seamstress pinched the fabric together at her sides. "You make me feel better about checking out the extremely fine behind of a man who is obviously taken. 'Look but don't touch' will be my motto whenever he saunters by."

"Words to live by." Leah frowned. "I'd say we need to take the bodice in about an inch on Nina's dress, Marge. Other than that, it's perfect."

The seamstress pinned the fabric, then stepped back and nodded, her gray curls shaking. "Be careful you don't poke yourself when you take off that gown." She turned to face Leah. "I should have the alterations done in two weeks."

"Great. Thanks so much, Marge. Go change, you two, and then maybe we can have a cocktail together."

"The intrepid trio rides again." Paige headed toward the fitting room. "Just like old times."

In the back of the shop, Nina unzipped her dress and

eased out of the silky material. "I miss you guys. Lately, Leah is always preoccupied with Ryan and wedding details."

"And I've been gone a lot, gearing up for my usual hectic summer, scouring the countryside for antiques to fill my store." Paige peeked around the partition. "I've another estate sale to go to this weekend."

"I need to get a life. I spend all my time painting, and sometimes I go days without talking to anyone. That can't be healthy."

"We should make a point of hanging out more often, even if Leah's too busy to join us." She ducked back into her own curtained cubicle, and her voice was muffled beneath the fabric of her dress. "Also, you should get to know your new neighbors. The mother of the little girl would probably welcome any overtures on your part since she probably isn't acquainted with anyone in the area."

"True." Nina hung up the gown and finished dressing. "I'd be doing both of us a favor. Good idea." She slung her purse strap over her shoulder and headed out to the main room. When Paige appeared a few moments later, they thanked the seamstress and left the shop.

Leah glanced at her watch as they paused outside the door. "It's after four. Do you want to head over to Castaways for a drink and appetizers?"

Nina nodded. "I'll leave my car here since it's only a couple of blocks. Did you walk, Paige?"

"Yep. Grab your bike, Leah, and let's go."

They strolled up the sidewalk, with Leah pushing her pink cruiser, chatting about the dresses and how wedding plans were progressing.

When they reached the bar, Nina held open the door,

then glanced over at Leah as she lifted her bike into the rack. "You don't have plans with Ryan this evening?"

"He's in Portland at a board meeting for Crossroads. I guess they're planning more effective advertising strategies for website users who want to target specific groups."

"I like the sound of that." Paige smoothed back a strand of blond hair that had come loose from her upswept twist. "Small businesses would definitely benefit from the ability to target interested clients. Lately, I have more and more online customers searching for specific pieces."

Nina let the door shut behind them as she followed her friends toward a table near the wall of windows with a panoramic view of the ocean. "Old Things is a success because you're a smart businesswoman, Paige, and Ryan is a genius when it comes to coding and social media strategies."

Leah pulled out a chair and sat. "You've got that right. My future husband is brilliant, period. He was smart enough to propose to me."

"Good point." Nina smiled as their cocktail waitress approached. "What are we having, ladies?"

"How about a bottle of your house chardonnay." Paige glanced at the appetizer menu. "And stuffed mushrooms to go with it. Does that sound good?"

"Perfect," Leah answered. "Bring me the bill, please, Janice. This is my treat since you two were good sports about a last-minute dress fitting."

"You've got it." The older woman tucked her order pad in her apron pocket. "How are wedding preparations going?"

"Pretty smooth, all things considered," Leah answered.

"Good to hear. I'll be right back with your wine."

After their waitress hurried away, Leah planted her elbows on the table and glanced over at Nina. "So, other than acquiring new neighbors, what have you been doing?"

"Painting. Mostly seascapes for the art fair coming up in July, but today I completed another bird study for Lola Copeland."

"That woman is a birdbrain, if you'll excuse the pun." Paige wrinkled her nose. "She came into my shop the other day and picked out a cookie jar shaped like a chicken, then was all flustered when she realized she'd left her wallet at home. Her granddaughter—at least I assume it was her granddaughter—looked mortified. Since it wasn't expensive, I sent the jar home with her and told her to pay me later."

Nina leaned back in her chair. "She's good for it. I could use more clients like her."

Leah stopped searching through her oversized purse to glance up. "I thought your sales were on the rise."

"Actually, they are, but you never know when the economy will tank." Nina pointed to the printed sheet of paper her friend laid on the table. "What's that?"

"The band we're using for our reception sent me a playlist. Ryan and I are supposed to pick the songs we want. You two can give me your opinions."

By the time they'd weeded out a few disco classics that set Nina's teeth on edge, along with a couple of old standards, they'd consumed all the mushrooms and most of the bottle of wine.

Paige pointed with one polished nail. "What's wrong with 'Fly Me to the Moon' and 'Moon River'? You have something against lunar songs? I bet your grandma and the other older guests would love them."

"Those two remind me of the con artist who scammed Gram last fall, and I don't need any memories of that nightmare. I kept 'My Way' and 'Some Enchanted Evening' for her generation." Leah shoved the marked-up paperback in her purse. "One more job I can cross off my to-do list. Thanks for your help."

"Happy to be of service." Nina topped off their wine-glasses, then set the empty bottle on the table. "As long as Ryan won't mind that we didn't ask his opinion."

"Are you kidding, he's thrilled when I deal with this stuff."

Nina smiled. "Did you know you glow every time you mention your fiancé?"

"That's because I'm crazy in love with the man." Leah glanced from Nina to Paige and back. "I want that kind of love for you two."

Paige took a healthy swallow of her wine. "Maybe one of these days. Stranger things have happened."

Nina didn't respond. She'd had her shot at happiness, but a land mine had blown it away five long years ago. She glanced out the window across the cove to the endless stretch of sea. Maybe there was another man out there she could love, but the way her life was going, she didn't like her odds of finding him.

Chapter Three

Teague ushered the young woman to the door. When she sneezed again, he winced. "I'm sorry the position won't work out for you. I guess I should have mentioned Coco over the phone."

She glanced up at him as she stepped out onto the porch. "That would have been nice, but I should be fine once the allergy pill kicks in."

Ignoring the hint of sarcasm in her tone, he forced a smile. "I hope so. Again, I apologize."

"Good luck finding someone else." The woman bolted down the steps and pulled out of the driveway a few seconds later.

Running a hand across the back of his neck, he turned to go inside. Two down, and only one interviewee remained. He crossed his fingers and sent up a prayer.

"Can I let Coco out now?" Keely shouted to be heard over the shrill yipping of their imprisoned pet.

"Please. I can't take much more of that racket."

"She didn't like being locked in there."

When his daughter opened the door off the back hallway, Coco pranced out, shook, then trotted toward him. Rising on her hind legs, she planted front paws on the screen and peered outside.

"Your quarry escaped." He narrowed his gaze on the dog. "It's almost like you knew she had allergies."

"Why did you send the first lady away?" Keely joined them in the entry. "She seemed to like you."

Teague hesitated for a moment. "I don't think she would have worked out." *Mostly because the woman eyed me the way Coco did a bone.* He'd been down that road before and didn't need a repeat trip. "Maybe we'll get lucky with the next one."

Keely rubbed a spot of mustard on the sleeve of her princess dress. "If the third one starts sneezing, Nina could watch me. Coco didn't bother her."

"Our new neighbor isn't a babysitter."

"She could be. You said the most important qualcation is common sense."

When did I say that? He stared at his daughter, who was way too bright for his own good. Lately, she'd morphed into a sponge that absorbed every word out of his mouth. "Qualification. I'm sure Nina has another job." At least he assumed she did.

"She said she'd help me paint. I bet if we asked her nicely—"

"Is that a car? Maybe the last applicant is early." He pushed Coco out of the way and glanced through the screen door.

Not the prospective sitter. Nina's little red Mini Cooper pulled into her driveway. After a moment she got out and glanced his way. He ducked out of sight since he didn't want her to think he had nothing better to do than watch her comings and goings. Not that her *goings* weren't worth watching. He pried his gaze away from the sway of her extremely fine ass as she disappeared into her house.

"Not the sitter. Maybe I should order a pizza while we wait. There's no way in . . . uh, no way I'm going to cook tonight."

"We didn't go to the store yet, so we don't have any food."

Good point.

"I meant to go earlier, but . . ."

He wondered for the hundredth time if this move was a huge mistake. At least in Encino they'd been organized and had a routine to follow. Not to mention his parents had only been an hour away and available to watch Keely in emergencies. But the negatives had far outweighed the positives.

"We'll stock up on supplies after I interview the next woman."

"I hear something." Keely pressed her nose against the screen.

A loud rumble echoed through the deepening twilight. "A motorcycle? That can't be the babysitter."

A black Honda bike with dual exhaust pipes turned into the driveway and stopped behind his pickup. When the engine died, silence settled before booted feet hit the pitted pavement.

"Maybe it is." His daughter grinned up at him. "Cool."

The rider pulled off her helmet, then smoothed a cap of rumpled silver hair with a gloved hand. She swung a leg encased in black leathers over the seat, tugged off gauntlets and draped them across the saddle beside her helmet, then turned to head in the direction of the house. The woman had to be past sixty. Lines radiated from the corners of sky-blue eyes, and her neck was creased above the open collar of a red leather jacket.

"Not your typical grandma," Teague muttered.

"What, Daddy?"

"Nothing." He opened the screen door. "You must be Stella Lange. I'm Teague O'Dell, and this is my daughter, Keely. Welcome."

She shook his outstretched hand in a firm grip before glancing downward as Coco sniffed her boots. "And who might that be?"

"Our dog, Coco. Are you allergic?"

The woman turned her gaze on Keely. "Not in the least."

"That's good. The last lady had a sneezing fit."

She chuckled softly. "No fear of that happening with me."

Teague stepped back and nudged Coco aside. "Come on in. The place is a disaster since we just moved in today."

"I'm not a stranger to messes, and I'm not intimidated by work." She eyed Keely up and down. "You're a very pretty young lady. Is Aurora your favorite princess?"

Keely touched her pink satin skirt, then twirled in a circle. "Belle is, but my yellow dress is too tight."

"Maybe I can loosen a seam."

"Stella?" Teague interrupted.

The woman glanced over at him. "Yes?"

"You're hired. Any chance you can sit for us starting this weekend? I have to work Saturday, and I haven't had a chance to organize day camps for Keely yet."

"I'd be delighted to." She offered a broad smile. "Don't you want to contact my references first, though?"

"If you'll leave me a list, I'll get back to you, but I expect they'll check out since you were recommended."

"Great." Stella pulled a typed sheet out of her pocket and handed it over. "My rate is at the bottom." She patted Keely's shoulder. "I'll see you on Saturday."

"Can we fix my Belle dress then?"

"You bet." She backed up a few steps and pushed open the screen door. "I'll look forward to your call, Mr. O'Dell."

He glanced at the figure she'd handwritten under the list of names with contact information. Stella didn't work cheap. "Uh, Teague, please. Thanks for coming over on such short notice."

"Not a problem. I do have other clients I currently sit for, but I don't expect working you into my schedule will be a problem. Good luck with the unpacking."

"Thank you. I imagine we'll need all the luck we can get." After Stella headed down the walk, he shut the door and turned to face his daughter. "What did you think?"

"I liked her."

"Good." He glanced over his shoulder as the motorcycle roared away. "Let's just hope our schedules mesh and those references check out, because I'm short on options."

Keely took his hand and skipped beside him as he headed toward the kitchen. "I'm six and a half. I could always watch myself."

A sputter of laughter escaped. "Nice try, but that's not happening."

"Even though I know not to turn on the stove or answer the door when you're not home?"

"Even though." He searched through the takeout menus the real estate agent had left. When a rap sounded at the door, setting Coco off in a barking frenzy, he frowned. "I hope Stella didn't change her mind."

"I'll go see." Keely raced off, and a moment later, the door creaked open. "Hi, Nina."

Teague dropped the menu. *Nina?* He pictured those short shorts of hers and swallowed as he hurried toward the entry.

Their neighbor stood in the doorway holding a Crock-Pot and a loaf of bread. The delicious aroma of herbs and meat wafted through the house as she broke off her conversation with his daughter.

"Nina brought us dinner." Keely slammed the door shut after their guest stepped inside. "Doesn't it smell good?"

"Extremely. That was awfully nice of you."

Nina met his gaze and offered a hesitant smile. "I figured you didn't have much time to shop or prepare a meal. I made a huge batch of stew this morning and am happy to share."

"We were going to order pizza." Keely danced around her. "But I like stew when it doesn't come out of a can. That kind is sort of gross."

"I have to agree. Where do you want me to put this?" Teague stepped forward. "I can take it."

"Don't. It's hot."

He jerked his hands back. "Oh." *Duh, that's why she's wearing oven mitts, idiot.* "Uh, you can bring the Crock-Pot into the kitchen. The counters are the only flat surface not covered in boxes."

"I'm sure you'll get everything sorted out soon enough."

He wished he had her confidence. Pushing aside the takeout menus, he indicated a spot on the Formica countertop. "Set it there."

She did as he suggested and laid the loaf of bread wrapped in foil beside it. "There's butter and garlic on the bread, but you'll need to heat it."

"Wow, I really appreciate this. You went above and beyond—"

"Can't she stay to eat with us, Daddy?"

Nina glanced between them. "You're obviously not set up for guests, and I'm sure your wife—"

His fists clenched along with his heart. "Not an issue."

Her cheeks turned pink. "I'm sorry. I just assumed . . . When I mentioned her mom earlier, Keely . . . Never mind. Open mouth, insert foot. I'm going to leave now."

"But I want you to stay." His daughter rushed over to block the doorway. "Please?"

Teague tamped down on the jolt of pain zinging through him and forced a smile. "Of course you're welcome to have dinner with us. We'd both enjoy your company."

"I don't want to impose."

Keely grabbed her hand. "Do you want to see my flower painting?"

"I'd love to . . ." Nina glanced his way. "If you're certain—"

"Absolutely." This time he actually meant it. "But you can admire the painting after we eat. Keely, go wash your hands."

She held them behind her back. "They aren't dirty."

He pointed toward the doorway. "Go, now, and use soap. I put a bar in the bathroom earlier."

Her pink tennis shoes thumped against the hardwood floor as she left the room.

Nina faced him head-on, her clear, green gaze direct. "I'm sorry. I didn't realize Keely's mother wasn't here. Your daughter mentioned her mom keeps a close watch on her, so I just assumed . . ."

Pain returned to burn in his chest, but he wouldn't let it pull him under. "Keely meant her mom watches her from heaven. That's what I told her after my wife died."

"Oh, God, I'm so sorry." She pressed a hand to her mouth. "I wouldn't have said anything if—"

"It's been two years, and Keely has adjusted. Probably a lot better than I have, but we don't avoid talking about Jayne. I want my daughter to have strong memories of her mother."

"I'm sure you do. If you'd like me to go, I'll make up an excuse when Keely returns."

"I don't. Please stay and have dinner with us." His voice rang with conviction as he realized just how much he wanted her company. "Maybe you can give me the insider scoop on Siren Cove."

"All right, I will." She waited a beat. "But I should probably go wash my hands, too, before we eat."

"Only if you've been grubbing around in boxes and petting the dog." He glanced down at Coco. "Speaking of whom . . . I should probably find her food bowl along with dishes for us to use."

"Your packing boxes all seem to be labeled. I can look for them."

"My hands are clean." Keely ran into the kitchen, waving her fingers in the air. "Can Nina look at my picture now?"

"After you help her find our dishes, and I feed Coco. I'm almost positive I put the dog stuff in the laundry room."

"I think the dish box is on top of the table." Keely's chest puffed out. "I can read at least half the box labels." She grabbed Nina's arm and tugged her out of the kitchen.

Left alone, Teague closed his eyes for a moment. Explaining why Keely's mother wasn't in the picture was a drawback he hadn't considered. Everyone from daycare employees to school officials to coworkers would undoubtedly ask. He'd damn well better get used to answering without letting the explanation tear him up inside. Squaring his shoulders, he left the room with Coco following at his heels.

Twenty minutes later, the three of them sat on the couch with bowls of stew and pieces of bread in front of them on the coffee table while Keely chattered away about the next picture she planned to paint.

"Could I sell mine like you do and make enough money to buy ladybug rain boots? Daddy says they're ridiculously expensive."

Teague paused with the spoon halfway to his mouth as his daughter's comment sank in. "Wait a minute." He held up a hand for silence as he glanced over her head at Nina. "You're a professional artist? Painting isn't just a hobby?"

"Not since I graduated from art school. I may not sell like Picasso, but I get by."

"I'm impressed."

"No reason to be." She blew on a bite of stew. "What do you do?"

"Daddy fights fires. He got a special commendation for saving two little boys when their house burned down."

Nina set down her spoon and met his gaze. "Sounds like your daddy is very brave."

His cheeks heated. "I was just doing my job."

"If you say so." She glanced down at is daughter. "Is something wrong with your stew, Keely?"

She pulled her fingers out of her mouth. "No. My tooth's loose. It feels funny when I bite my food."

Teague frowned. "Don't play with your tooth at the table."

"This isn't a real table."

"Whatever." He turned to face Nina. "I have two days

to get this place into some semblance of order before I report for work on Saturday. I can't live like this for long."

Her sympathetic gaze met his. "You mentioned interviewing babysitters. Did you find someone?"

He nodded. "An older woman named Stella Lange. Do you know her?"

"The name doesn't ring a bell. Maybe she hasn't lived in the area long."

"Stella rides a motorcycle and said she can fix my Belle dress." Keely slurped a spoonful of broth. "I like her."

Nina smiled. "A woman of many talents."

"As soon as I check her references, we'll be in business." He lost his train of thought when his gaze locked with eyes fringed by thick dark lashes. The woman was strikingly beautiful in a way that probably turned most men into wordless morons. He was no exception. With an effort, he focused his attention on the bowl of stew in front of him. "Uh, hopefully I can sign Keely up for some fun summer camps, but I'm not sure when they'll start."

"I want to take swimming lessons. How many days would I get to go to camp, Daddy?"

His daughter dominated the conversation for the rest of the meal, which was fine with Teague. Nina was getting married shortly, so even if he was ready to start dating again—and that was a big if—she wasn't available. Best not to even think about the soft curve of her cheek, let alone her other curves. The last thing she'd want was her new neighbor gawking at her every time they crossed paths.

"Daddy."

"Huh?" He jerked out of his thoughts when Keely jiggled his arm. "What?"

"Nina said she needs to go, and your knees are blocking us in."

He rose to his feet as his face heated. "Sorry, I was trying to figure out the best way to tackle this mess."

Nina stood, then glanced around. "My suggestion would be from the top down. You can't very well organize this room until you get everything out of it."

"Good idea. Also, the upstairs needs less work. The kitchen and living area will be a war zone for a while once I start remodeling this place."

"You plan to do the job yourself?"

"Most of it. I paid my way through college working construction."

She stepped around him. "Well, you certainly have plenty to keep you busy. To my knowledge, the previous owner hadn't done any work on this house in decades."

"Which was why I could afford this place. Anyway, I'm looking forward to the project." He followed her as she headed toward the door. "Thanks again for the terrific meal. Do you want to take your Crock-Pot home with you?"

"You can keep the leftovers and return it later."

"I appreciate that. Nina?"

She stopped with her hand on the doorknob. "Yes?"

"You've made Keely and me feel welcome in a strange new place, and that means a lot. If I can ever help you out with anything at all, just let me know."

Those amazing eyes darkened before she smiled. "I'll keep that in mind. Have a good night, Teague."

"You, too." He stepped out onto the porch and walked to the railing to better observe the sway of her fabulous ass as she crossed the yard. A couple of the boards creaked and groaned as he shifted, bringing him back to reality. Replacing them was another job to put on his to-do list. Not until her front door shut with a click that echoed in the night did he finally go back inside to face the unpacking job awaiting him.

She stared in disbelief at the winning numbers displayed across the TV screen. Surely it was some sort of mistake . . . or maybe she was seeing things. She blinked twice, but her special numbers were still there, bold and taunting. 7-1-75-6-30-5. The date her baby was born, and the horrible day nearly five years later when she thought she'd lost her forever. But she hadn't. Lynette had come back to her. Again and again and again.

Of all the times to lose her damn ticket. Fate couldn't be so cruel.

She'd bought sandwiches to eat on the beach, along with the lottery ticket, at the convenience store late that morning. She'd stuffed her change and the ticket into her coat pocket before hurrying outside and hadn't thought about it again until after they'd returned home.

Hell and damnation, she needed that money. Over three million dollars. With such a huge windfall, she wouldn't have to worry about financial security ever again. There'd be no reason to risk leaving Lynette home alone.

She pictured herself on the beach, poking through tide pools to discover an unbroken clamshell. She'd dropped it into her pocket and glanced up when a woman ran past, a tank top plastered to her back with sweat. Had the ticket blown out when she'd reached into her pocket? She'd recognized the jogger on her return trip up the beach. She'd been pretty sure the artist hadn't noticed her, only Lynette wading in the surf. Nina Hutton had bent to pick something up off the ground, then shoved it into her pocket and run on.

Could it have been the lottery ticket?

The mantel clock ticked loudly in the silent room. Maybe the woman wouldn't check her numbers right away. It was possible she wouldn't even realize what she'd found. Her hands clenched and unclenched at her sides, fingers stiff. There was still hope she could recover the ticket, but she wouldn't risk asking for it straight out and drawing attention to herself.

Waiting for Nina to leave her house before searching for her rightful property was a far better plan. She'd find the ticket, collect her winnings anonymously, and then she and Lynette could continue with their lives.

Or move on to the next one.

Chapter Four

Nina tossed the load of laundry in the washer, shut the lid, then hurried into the kitchen when her phone rang for the third time. The landline, not her cell. *Odd.* With a shrug, she answered. "Hello."

Nothing. Apparently the caller had hung up before the answering machine clicked on.

It was likely just a robocall—probably best since she didn't have time for a conversation, anyway. The sun had finally broken through the marine layer, and she needed to hustle out to the bluff before the fog rolled back in. With any luck, she could still paint for a couple of hours in decent light.

Fifteen minutes later, she'd loaded her paints and easel into the passenger seat of her Mini. A tight squeeze, but she had the angle down just right. With the window open, the breeze blew short wisps of hair around her face as she headed into town, then drove north along the coast. A giant cypress stood sentinel on a point accessed by a dirt track off the main road. She'd started on the project several weeks before but hadn't had time to finish the painting.

After setting up her work area, she painted with quick, sure strokes, capturing the magnificence of the ancient tree alone on the precipice with waves crashing in the background. Lost in her art, she painted until the fog crept in to blur the stark lines of branches and trunk. Disappointed, she packed up to leave.

She'd have to include the final touches another day. Normally, time wasn't an issue, but as the Summer Art Fair approached, every day was critical if she wanted to complete another half dozen pictures to sell. The fair always provided a healthy boost to her income in addition to spreading her reputation among West Coast art enthusiasts who attended the annual event. After stowing her gear, she turned the car in a circle, bumped back down the track, then accelerated onto the highway. As she approached Leah's driveway, on a whim she slowed and turned down the gravel track to stop behind the used Volkswagen Bug her friend had bought after her old car was totaled.

She'd barely had a chance to climb out when Barney raced around the corner and leaped up to plant dirty paws on her chest. "Down, boy. No, don't jump on me. Where's your mama, huh?"

"I'm back here!" A shout came from the far side of the carport.

With the big mutt frisking along at her side, Nina headed toward the garden.

Leah waved from between two rows of peas. "Hey, want to help me pick these? You can have some for dinner since I seem to have an overabundance all of a sudden."

"Sure." Her sandals sank into the earth as she joined her friend. "Isn't Ryan back yet?"

"He should be home from Portland soon. I can't wait to see him. A week alone seems like forever."

Nina dropped a handful of peas into the bucket on the ground. "I won't stay long, then. I thought I'd stop by to say hi since I was in the neighborhood and figured you'd be home from work by now."

"Yep. I don't know who'll be happier to see the school year end, me or the kids." Leah glanced over. "How are your new neighbors settling in?"

"Okay, I guess. Lots of activity hauling away boxes over the last couple of days. They're in an unpacking frenzy right now since Teague starts work tomorrow."

"Is his wife nice?"

Nina's hand stilled on the vine. "That was my mistake. He isn't married, at least not anymore. His wife died a couple of years ago. I made a fool of myself based on a comment from his little girl."

"Wow, sounds rough, moving to a new town with a daughter to care for and no support. Or does he have family here?"

"I don't think so because finding childcare seemed to be his number one priority. I've made myself scarce since the first day, so I'm not sure."

"Why?"

Nina turned to frown. "What do you mean, why? He's busy, and I did my neighborly duty the day they arrived by bringing them a meal."

"You said the man is hot, and he sounds like a good guy, if his daughter is his top priority. Do you have something against dating men with kids?"

"Of course not, but—"

"So get to know him. Maybe you two will hit it off."

Her toes curled as she pictured Teague hauling a stack of packing boxes to his truck, his T-shirt riding up to expose a strip of tanned skin above the band of his shorts as he heaved the boxes into the cargo area. "I'm not going to throw myself at the man, no matter how good-looking he is. Geez!"

"Don't throw. Have a conversation. To my knowledge, you haven't been on a date in a couple of months. Or am I wrong?"

"You're not wrong, and he does seem like the solid, dependable sort—in addition to being hot. I guess I could put myself out there a little. Test the waters."

"You certainly could." Leah squeezed her shoulder before she returned to picking peas. "What else is new?"

"Nothing, really. I'm just painting as much as possible to get ready for the art fair."

"I'll be on my honeymoon at the end of the month. I can't wait."

"I bet." Nina eyed her up and down. "You look disgustingly happy."

"Probably because I am, but I won't nag you about dating anymore right now." Leah dropped another handful of pea pods into the bucket. "You said Teague has to work on Saturday. What does he do?"

"He's a firefighter."

Her friend staggered backward in a fake swoon. "You live next to a single, hot firefighter, and you're standing here talking to me? What's wrong with you?"

Nina grinned. "Well, when you put it like that . . ."

Her friend picked up the bucket and thrust it toward her. "Take your peas and go. I'll pick more for me and Ryan."

"Fine, I will." She stepped carefully toward the edge

of the garden. "See you later, Leah, and thanks for the peas."

"You're welcome. Why don't you share them with your neighbor? You have plenty."

"Maybe I will."

A short time later, Nina pulled into her driveway and glanced across the street as she stepped out of her car. Despite the fog hanging low in the trees, music drifted from the open upstairs window of the old Victorian. Sixties folk music. *Interesting.* She would have taken Teague for a classic rock kind of guy.

After pulling her easel out of the passenger side, she hauled it up to the front porch and fished her keys out of her pocket. When she pushed the door open, a draft of air blew through the house and knocked one of the bills she'd left on the entry table to the floor. Stepping over the envelope, she headed straight upstairs to her studio, propped the easel against a wall, then ran back down to unload the rest of her gear. On the second trip upstairs, she shivered and wondered where the cool air was coming from. After setting down her box of paints along with the still-damp canvas, she went outside a final time to grab her purse and the bucket of peas.

The Simon and Garfunkel hit had segued into smooth jazz. Apparently Teague's taste in music was as eclectic as her own. Maybe she'd shell the peas and take them over to him. *Just to be neighborly.* Squaring her shoulders, she went back inside. The fact that simply looking at the man turned her knees to overcooked pasta had nothing to do with her burst of generosity.

The cold draft was worse when Nina entered the kitchen. Goose bumps pebbled her skin as she glanced toward the window over the sink. Firmly closed, exactly the way she'd left it. She set her purse and the bucket down on the counter, then snapped her fingers. Damn, she'd left clothes in the washer in her rush to leave earlier. Hopefully they wouldn't smell musty yet.

Rounding the big refrigerator-freezer on the way to the laundry room, she stopped short. Glass littered the folding table next to the dryer. The window above it was shattered and had been raised to a fully open position. Her heart thumped a painful rhythm as she pushed aside the empty laundry basket. Avoiding the jagged shards, she peered through the opening. The screen lay on the ground below.

"Oh, my God!"

Spinning, she ran back through the kitchen and stopped in the middle of the living room. Her TV and laptop were still where she'd left them. Obviously, they hadn't been after electronics. Money or jewelry? She'd had her purse with her . . .

After sprinting up the stairs, she entered her bedroom and glanced around. Nothing seemed to be out of place. The lid to the jewelry box sitting on her dresser was closed. She flipped it open and sorted through a few chunky stone necklaces and bracelets. Most of them weren't terribly valuable, and she was pretty sure none were missing. Nor were there any empty spaces on the earring tree next to her jewelry box. If not jewelry, then—

"Oh, no." Nina pressed a hand to her chest as she turned around. The framed landscape of lupine alongside a country road still hung over her bed. Her pulse thrummed painfully as she entered her studio and crossed to the stack of canvases leaning against the wall. Holding her breath, she counted all thirteen pieces she'd stockpiled for the fair.

"Thank God." She sagged in relief and pressed a hand against the wall to steady herself. She might not sell like

Picasso, but each painting was worth around five grand and represented hours and hours of work.

When a knock sounded downstairs, she nearly jumped out of her skin. On shaking legs, she left the studio and slowly descended the stairs as a second series of raps rattled the door.

"Pull it together, Nina. Robbers who break windows don't come back and knock." With a grim smile, she opened the door a few inches and met Keely's innocent gaze. Gripping the frame in relief, she opened the door wider. "Hi, Keely, how are you?"

"Okay. Daddy says I'm only to invite you for dinner, then come straight home. He's grilling chicken and says we owe you a meal." She frowned. "Actually, I'm not sure if I was supposed to say the last part."

"I need to ask your dad something, so I'll come back with you now, if you don't mind." Nina stepped outside and closed the door.

"Sure." Taking her hand, Keely skipped beside her down the steps. "Do you like barbecued chicken? I do. Did you know Daddy's painting my room? Guess what color."

Nina sorted through the barrage of questions. "Uh, yes, I like chicken. Let's see, is your room pink?"

"Nope. Purple." She stopped at the end of the driveway. "Hey, where did Coco go? She was with me when I came over."

Nina spotted the dog trotting around the side of the house where her laundry room was located. "There she is. I hope she didn't cut her paws or destroy evidence."

"Huh?"

Nina bent and scooped up the dog. As Coco squirmed to get down, she felt each paw before releasing her. "She seems fine."

Keely ran ahead and threw open the front door. "Daddy, Nina wants to talk to you," she shouted.

Upstairs, the music cut off. A moment later, Teague ran down the central stairway. Faded jeans sported a lavender brush mark across one thigh, and his white T-shirt was speckled in the same color. Somehow, he didn't look any less masculine, even with purple trim.

"Hey, Nina, did Keely invite you to dinner?"

"She did, but there's something I needed to ask you." She glanced down at the expectant face of his daughter. "Why don't you take Coco back outside. Her paws look dirty, and I saw a hose curled up next to the driveway."

"Okay. Come on, Coco."

After the door slammed shut behind them, Nina turned to face Teague. "Sorry to take charge like that, but I have a reason."

He crossed his arms over his chest. "Problem?"

She dragged her gaze away from the mist of purple paint that tinged the hair on his muscled forearms. "Yeah. Someone broke the window in my laundry room. I assumed their intent was to steal something, but nothing seems to be missing. Did you notice anyone out on the street earlier this afternoon?"

His eyes darkened to the color of storm clouds. "No, but I've been painting for the last few hours. I was just finishing up when I sent Keely over to your house."

"Should I ask your daughter? I didn't want to say anything if it would upset her."

"Nothing much disturbs Keely, but she was having a marathon tea party in the backyard with her stuffed animals, so she wouldn't have seen anyone on the street."

Nina's brow creased. "Unless she wandered away, as she tends to do."

"Her bedroom faces the rear of the house, so I was

keeping a pretty close eye on her. You can ask her if you want."

"No, I won't say anything." She ran the toe of her sandal along a seam in the wood floor. "The whole thing kind of creeped me out. I guess I should report the break-in to the police, even though nothing was stolen, then call about getting the window replaced."

He studied her for a moment. "Do you know the size to order?"

She shook her head. "I can measure it, though. How hard can it be?"

"How about if I do it for you? I actually know where my tape measure and other tools are now since I unpacked that box this morning."

Before she could answer, the door burst open, and Keely skipped inside, her wet tennis shoes squeaking on the wood floor. Coco followed, leaving a trail of water behind her.

"Her feet are clean now."

"I bet." Teague pointed. "Go straight to the laundry room and dry her with one of the old towels stacked on the washer. I have to help Nina with something, but I'll be right back."

Keely let out a deep sigh. "I don't see why—"

"Go."

Nina couldn't help grinning as the girl disappeared down the hall. "Sorry about your floor. My suggestion, designed solely to keep her busy, wasn't the best choice."

"You lack experience with six-and-a-half-year-olds." He laid a warm hand on her arm. "Let's go measure that window."

He detoured to the shed beside the house and came out with a silver tape measure, then crossed the yard beside her.

"Thanks for your help. I appreciate it."

"No problem. That's what neighbors are for."

"True, which is why you don't have to pay me back for the meal I brought over."

He stopped for a moment before continuing up the driveway. "I didn't mean my invitation that way. If you have other plans . . ."

"I don't, and I'd be happy to have dinner with you and Keely. Right after I cover that broken window with some cardboard to keep out the cold." She opened the front door and gestured him inside. "This way. The laundry room is through the kitchen. Oh, I have fresh peas to contribute to the barbecue."

"Huh?"

She pointed to the pail on the counter. "Straight from my friend's garden. I'll bring them over for dinner."

"Sounds great." He stepped into the laundry room and frowned. "Wow, it definitely looks like whoever broke the window did it near the latch so he could unlock it."

"That's what I thought. The screen is lying on the ground outside."

"But nothing was taken?"

"Not that I could find. Pretty strange."

He pulled out a length of tape to measure the opening. "How'd they get back out again?"

She frowned. "I'm not sure. The front door was still locked when I got home." Leaving him, she hurried back through the kitchen, then tried the sliding door onto the deck. It opened effortlessly.

A shiver slid through her as she shut it.

Teague walked up behind her and handed over a sheet of notepaper. He'd written numbers across it in bold lettering. "Give the guy at the glass company this information. They should be able to get a replacement window fairly quickly."

"That's good news. Thank you." She stepped back. "Apparently the culprit left through the slider into my backyard. At least he didn't break that door."

Teague nodded. "A slider would have cost a heck of a lot more."

"When are you planning to have dinner?"

"Six thirty, if that works for you."

"Great. That will give me plenty of time to report this to the police and to my insurance company, clean up the mess, and shell those peas. Thanks again for your help."

"You're welcome." He gave her an indecipherable look. "Definitely call the police to report this. Right now, I'd better get back to Keely and Coco. God knows what they're doing, left to their own devices."

"With your daughter's imagination and initiative, it could be almost anything."

"True. I'll see you in a couple of hours."

After the front door closed behind Teague, Nina forced herself into action and checked the rest of the house for anything out of place, including the contents of her medicine cabinet. The prescription pain meds left over from a sprained ankle three months before were still on the shelf, so the thief hadn't been after drugs. Standing in the bathroom doorway with fists clenched on her hips, she surveyed her bedroom. The dresser drawer where she kept her running clothes was slightly ajar. Had she left it that way?

Frowning, she slid it open. Clothes that had been neatly stacked were askew. Pulling open each drawer, she found nightgowns and underwear disturbed from their orderly piles.

"Eww!" *Some freak touched my bras and panties.* "Sick pervert!"

She practically ran out of the bedroom and down the stairs. As she paused in the main room to pull herself together, the desk in the corner caught her eye. The file folder of invoices she'd left on its teak surface was horizontal instead of vertical. Sucking in a deep breath, she pulled open the drawers to discover all her paperwork in disarray.

"Oh, my freaking God!" Had the creep been after financial data in addition to a cheap thrill? She did all her banking online, so that information was safe, but her last credit card statement was in a folder that looked like it had been searched. She'd have to cancel the card and get a new one. One more thing to do . . . right after she called the police.

This day just kept getting better and better.

Chapter Five

Teague sat across the dining room table from Nina, drinking pinot noir over the remains of their barbecue dinner and discussing the state of the local economy. From the living room, Keely's laughter accompanied the high-pitched voices of the Muppets on the TV. He'd done his very best to keep the conversation on neutral topics, but the whole evening had been a little too comfortable, considering the woman smiling at what he hoped was a witty remark was soon to be married. He couldn't help wondering where her fiancé was and why he hadn't been on hand to measure her broken window.

"Earth to Teague." She swirled her wine in the bowl of the glass. "Did I bore you into a stupor?"

"Huh?" He blinked twice and realized he'd lost the thread of the conversation. "No, of course not. Actually, I was wondering why I hadn't seen your fiancé around. Is he out of town?"

Something resembling pain flashed in the depths of her green eyes. "I don't know what you mean."

"I'm sorry. Did I say something wrong? The first day

we met, you mentioned trying on a dress for your wedding."

The emotion in her eyes cleared. "Not my wedding. My friend Leah's wedding. I'm co-maid of honor along with my other best friend, Paige."

A burst of satisfaction filled his chest with warmth. "You aren't getting married?"

"That would be a good trick since I'm not even dating anyone."

He couldn't seem to stop staring at the perfection of her face. "You're kidding, right? Are the men around here blind or just stupid?"

That earned him a broad grin.

"Thanks. I appreciate the vote of confidence. I guess I'm having a hard time getting back into single life after . . ." Her voice trailed off, and she bit her lip.

Reaching across the table, he laid a hand on her arm. "You don't have to explain anything to me."

Her gaze rose to meet his. "You'd probably understand how I feel better than most since you've lost someone." She drained the wine remaining in her glass. "I was engaged, but Keith died in Afghanistan a little over five years ago. People say I need to move on, that I've mourned long enough. Easier said than done."

His heart ached for her. "We all recover from tragedy in our own way, in our own time frame." He tightened his grip. "There's no right or wrong way to go about it. That's the best piece of advice I took from my grief counseling group after Jayne died."

"I know, and I actually believe I'm finally ready to start feeling again. Maybe I just haven't met anyone to suit me lately . . . or I'm too picky for my own good."

"The way you look, you can afford to be as choosy as you like. I'm pretty sure guys would line up to date you."

She smiled. "The same is true for you. Once the single women of Siren Cove realize there's an unattached fire-fighter in town who's possibly a thirteen on a scale of one to ten, you'll be inundated with help getting settled in."

He laughed out loud. "Beautiful with a dry humor guaranteed to entertain. Definitely a winning combo."

"Daddy. Hello! I asked if I can have ice cream."

"What?" He tore his attention away from Nina to focus on his daughter, who stood in the doorway wearing an impatient expression.

"We bought rocky road. Remember?"

"Sure." He pushed back his chair. "I'll get it for you." When his phone rang, he glanced at the display and recognized his new boss's extension at the fire station. "Just as soon as I take this call. It's work."

"I'll get the ice cream for her." Nina stood and herded Keely toward the kitchen.

"Thanks." He shot her a grateful glance before raising his cell to his ear. "O'Dell here. What can I do for you, Captain Barker?"

"We have a fully engaged house fire near the east end of Pine Avenue. It's an all-hands-on-deck situation to keep it from spreading. I'll throw your bag of gear in my truck if you can meet us at the scene."

A siren blared in the background, and Teague raised his voice to be heard. "Of course. That's close to my home, so I'll be there in a few minutes."

"Great." The connection went dead.

He tightened his grip on the phone. Keely. *Shit.*

"Is there a problem?" Nina stood in the doorway with his daughter at her side, holding a bowl of ice cream.

"Unfortunately, yes. I don't officially start work until tomorrow, but there's a house fire. They need me now. Is there any way you could watch Keely for me?"

"Of course. Go. We'll be fine here."

"Thank you." He pulled his keys out of his pocket and hurried toward the entrance. "I really appreciate this."

"That's what neighbors are for, remember?"

"I remember." He dropped a kiss on the top of Keely's head in passing. "Be good for Nina. Bed at eight-thirty, okay?"

"Do I have to?"

"Yes, you do."

"Teague?"

He glanced back at Nina and met her wide-eyed gaze as he opened the front door. "Yes?"

"Stay safe."

"You bet."

He hurried down the steps and ran to his truck, thankful he'd taken the time to study a map of Siren Cove the previous evening. He knew exactly where he was going since his destination was only three blocks away. A siren wailed in the evening dusk as he approached the turn onto Pine Avenue. He stopped to let the ladder truck roar past with a blare of its horn, then turned in behind the fire captain's vehicle. Parking out of the way of the blazing structure, he approached Barker as the man stepped out of his truck dressed in full gear.

"Quite an initiation to the team, O'Dell." He tossed him a large duffel bag. "I'm glad you stopped by the station yesterday to get outfitted. Suit up then find me." He took off at a run, shouting orders to his men as they unrolled hoses.

Teague scrambled into his gear before joining the captain, who was speaking to an older man with gaunt cheeks and watering eyes.

"My dog is in there, probably hiding in the bedroom

closet." He coughed and drew in a ragged breath. "You have to get her out."

The captain glanced toward the two-story home as a downstairs window exploded, showering glass onto the ground. "Mr. Murphy, I can't risk lives for a dog, but we'll do our best."

"Then let me go back in, damn it! My room is in the upper right corner. It's not burning yet since the fire started in the kitchen on the other side of the house, but the smoke—" He broke off in another coughing fit.

Teague nudged the captain's arm. "If we put a ladder up to the side egress window, I can go in. That section of the structure still looks stable."

He nodded. "Only take a quick look then get back out. I'd say we have about ten minutes before that corner goes." Raising his voice, he shouted, "Rod, I want a ladder at the northeast second-story window."

Teague lowered his helmet and adjusted the ventilator as two men moved the ladder into position. When the captain gave him the go-ahead, he ran up with each rung vibrating beneath his boots, broke out the screen, then slid open the window. A gray haze filled the room as he crawled over the sash and dropped to the carpet. Rounding the bed, he hurried toward the open door in the corner and felt his way to the back of the closet. At floor level, eyes gleamed in the dark, and a low growl greeted him.

"Easy, girl. Don't make this hard for me."

The air down low wasn't too thick with smoke yet. Grabbing a flannel shirt off a hanger, he scooped the dog up in it and held the quivering bundle against his jacket, thankful the animal wasn't any larger than a sack of potatoes. Timbers creaked and groaned as he headed back toward the window. Below him, more glass blew out in a piercing blast, and the smoke creeping in around the door grew heavier.

Reaching his goal, Teague thrust his burden through the opening to one of the crew who had scrambled up the rungs behind him. He stepped out onto the ladder as flames licked in under the bedroom door. Hurrying down, his booted feet hit the ground with a thud.

"Good work getting out of there fast." The captain thumped him on the shoulder. "Move that ladder out of the way, then go string some caution tape out on the street. We've got downed power lines across the driveway. Keep the looky-loos back out of harm's way. I think half the neighborhood is out there now."

"You got it."

An hour later, they were mopping up the smoldering ruins when one of his new coworkers approached. "O'Dell, isn't it?"

He nodded and held out his gloved hand. "Teague O'Dell."

The other man shook it. "Mateo Torres. Hey, can you go door to door and spread the word to the neighbors the power company will be back out in the morning to restore service once the scene has cooled down." He nodded toward the truck with the electric company logo on its side as the vehicle turned around in the street. "Their technician told me the box on the pole is a main breaker, and they can't turn it back on safely until they get those downed wires off the driveway. There should only be a handful of houses affected by the outage."

"I'll take care of it and deliver a safety speech while I'm at it."

"Thanks, and welcome to the team."

Teague left the charred wreckage that had once been a kitchen and flipped up his visor to take a deep breath of air not saturated with smoke once he reached the end of the driveway. The fog from earlier in the afternoon had receded, and stars shone in the night sky. Turning on his flashlight, he approached the nearest house affected by the outage.

The residents of the first four homes he visited answered their doors before he could even knock, obviously keeping a close eye on the proceedings. After explaining the power situation and cautioning each family to stay clear of the burned-out home, he moved on. Pine Avenue, like all the streets in the area including his own, ended in a cul-de-sac that backed onto forest land. His boots thumped against the asphalt as the shouts from the fire crew faded. Rounding a slight curve, he stopped in front of the final two homes on the street.

A Honda motorcycle he recognized stood in the driveway of a ranch-style house. The beam of his flashlight reflected off the shiny chrome. Smiling, he knocked on the door then stepped back. When it opened moments later, Stella Lange faced him holding a fat orange candle clutched in her fist.

He lowered his flashlight. "Hi, Stella. I didn't realize you lived so close to me."

"And I didn't realize my newest employer would be working for our fire department. How is Hank Murphy doing?"

"Just a little smoke inhalation. His house is a total loss, I'm afraid."

"Who's at the door?" A young girl's voice echoed, high and tinged with a hint of fear, from somewhere inside.

Stella turned. "One of the firemen. Go back to bed, hon. Everything's fine."

"I can't sleep."

A hint of frustration flashed in her eyes. "I'll be there in a minute."

"I won't keep you." Teague gave the woman a sympathetic smile. "Hearing all those sirens can be frightening for a child."

"Especially since she's timid to begin with. Her parents are going through a rough patch, which doesn't help, but my plan is to buck up her courage while I'm watching her."

"I hope you succeed." He backed up a step. "Anyway, I came to tell you your power won't be restored until morning. Make sure you and your guest stay well clear of the wreckage when you leave the house tomorrow."

"We certainly will. Thanks, Teague."

He pointed toward the residence opposite hers with the beam of his flashlight. The house was similar in style to his Victorian and possibly in worse shape, if the sagging shutters were any indication. "Do you know if anyone is home next door?"

"Probably. The woman who lives there with her daughter doesn't socialize with any of the neighbors, but she's usually around."

"Thanks. I'll see you tomorrow."

"I plan to drop off my charge and be there bright and early. Good night, Teague."

After Stella shut the door, he crossed the street to approach the front porch of the neighboring house. He knocked on the door and waited. When no one answered, he knocked again with the same results. Shrugging, he headed back down the walkway. It was nearly ten, so maybe the residents had gone to bed, despite the commotion on their street.

When he glanced over his shoulder, a flicker of movement and light upstairs drew his attention. Curtains parted, and he caught a quick glimpse of a face framed by pale hair before the material twitched shut. Apparently, the homeowner didn't care to hear an update on the power situation. Or maybe she didn't trust strangers knocking on her door this late in the evening.

He didn't blame her.

Returning to the scene of the fire, Teague went back to work on the cleanup, and it wasn't until well after midnight when he finally pulled into his own driveway. Exhaustion weighed his steps as he shut the car door with a click, then trod up the path to the front porch. Using his key, he unlocked the door and entered the dimly lit house. The glow of a single lamp illuminated his way to the living room where he stopped just inside the doorway.

Nina was stretched out fast asleep on the couch, covered with the dark blue afghan his grandma had crocheted when he moved away to college. At her feet, Coco raised her head and gave a low woof, then jumped to the floor and trotted over to his side. After he reached down to scratch her ears, she scampered up the stairs, her tags jingling with each step.

After a moment, he headed to the laundry room where he stripped off all his gear and dumped it in a stinking heap in the corner. Pulling a pair of sweatpants and a T-shirt out of the basket of clean clothes, he quickly donned them and shut the door behind him. Moments later, he was back in the main room, feeling a little like a voyeur as he gazed down at Nina.

Dark lashes fanned perfect skin above high cheekbones. The woman was so beautiful, his heart ached a little just looking at her. Her full lips were open slightly, and movement behind closed lids indicated she was dreaming. He couldn't help wondering what about. Did she still long for her dead fiancé, even in sleep? The nights he woke from dreams of Jayne came less often lately. He wasn't sure if that was a good thing or not.

Before he could step away—or bend to wake her—Nina's eyes slowly opened. The confusion in their depths cleared after a few seconds, and she struggled to sit up.

"I guess I fell asleep."

"It's late. I'm glad you did."

She pressed a hand to her mouth to cover a yawn. "I assume the fire is out. Where was it? I heard sirens right after you left."

Too tired to stand, and feeling awkward staring down at her, he moved around her knees to drop onto the leather cushion beside her. "On Pine Avenue, Hank Murphy's home."

"Oh, no. He owned the hardware store before he retired. His son runs it now. I think he's been living all alone since his wife died a few years ago."

"Just him and his dog. I got the poor little thing out before the house was fully engaged."

Nina reached over to lay her hand over his. "I'm sure he was thankful." She studied him for a moment. "You look exhausted. You should get some sleep."

"I will in a minute. Right now, I'm too comfortable to move." He let out a sigh. "Did Keely give you any backtalk about going to bed?"

A smile curled those full lips. "Only a little. She was asleep by nine. I like your daughter, Teague. She's funny and bright. You're doing a great job raising her."

He turned his face sideways to meet her gaze as warmth stole through him. "Thank you. That's the best compliment you could give me."

"It's the truth. Anyway, I enjoy her, so don't hesitate to ask me to watch her in an emergency. I'm usually home."

He blinked, trying to keep his fuzzy brain focused on the conversation when all he really wanted to do was lean his head against soft-looking breasts cupped by the silky material of her shirt. Only the knowledge that he stank of smoke kept him from giving in to the impulse.

"I appreciate that. I made it clear to the captain before I took this job I can only work day shifts, but when there's a situation that requires more manpower, I'll be called in no matter what the hour. The department here is a whole lot smaller than the one I worked for in Southern California."

"I bet, so please feel free to reach out when you need help."

When she tried to pull her hand away from his, he turned his palm up and held on. "I got incredibly lucky moving in next to you."

She kept her tone light. "As I mentioned earlier, all the single women in town will line up to help you out."

"Nina?"

"What?" Her voice was breathless, and the fingers he held quivered in his grasp.

Everything below his waist kicked into gear. "I really want to kiss you right now, but I smell like an ashtray. If you're not interested, maybe this would be a good time to go home."

"I'm interested . . . in a kiss. I'm not sure about anything else."

The seconds ticked by as he held her gaze. "I'm okay with that. For now."

"Okay, then." Her breath escaped in a rush. "I don't care how you smell. Just kiss me so we can both stop wondering what it'll be like and go get some sleep."

"You're sure?"

She nodded and scooted closer until their thighs pressed

tightly together. He used his free hand to cup her chin and looked into her eyes.

"You're unbelievably beautiful, but I like what I see inside you even more."

A rush of moisture entered those green eyes before she leaned forward and took away whatever words he might have said next. Teague opened his mouth over hers and kissed her with the pent-up need of someone who hadn't let himself be attracted to a woman in a very long time. The taste and heat of her was addictive. When she caressed the back of his neck and feathered fingers into his hair, he nearly came unglued. Finally he was forced to pull back in order to breathe.

"Wow, I guess you satisfied my curiosity . . . and then some."

He leaned his forehead against hers. "Sleep might not be an option after all."

"You really do need a shower." Her tone held a hint of humor. "Make it a cold one."

"I'll have to." After a moment, he forced himself to his feet, then pulled her up after she untangled the afghan wrapped around her legs. "Good night, Nina, and thank you."

"You're welcome." She flipped her wrist to indicate the couch. "We'll have to do this again."

"Yeah?" Her smile made his heart stutter.

"Yeah. Good night, Teague."

Chapter Six

"Thanks for the update, Chris. I appreciate it." Nina folded a T-shirt while holding the cell phone against one ear with her shoulder. "Or should I call you Officer Long?"

His snort of laughter made her smile.

"We've known each other since we were kids. I don't think we need to be formal. Anyway, I'm just sorry my news isn't better, but without identifiable prints or any other similar incidents to go on, we'll have a tough time finding the person who broke into your house. I realize that's frustrating."

She stared at the heaps of clothes piled on the laundry room floor. "I'm just glad he didn't take anything. Granted, spending my day washing every stitch of clothing I own wasn't my original plan, but I can't stand the thought of wearing anything that pervert touched."

"I get it, believe me. Did you speak to your credit card company?"

"Yes, and there was no unusual activity." She folded a pair of shorts from the load she'd washed the previous day, then frowned when something in the pocket crackled. "I canceled my card, and they're sending me a new one. So whatever the reason this creep looked through my paperwork, it wasn't so he could go on a spending spree at my expense."

"I'm glad, because disputing charges can be a hassle sometimes." His voice faded, then grew stronger as he spoke in a rush. "I'll give you a ring if anything turns up, but I'm not terribly optimistic unless he strikes again."

"Let's hope not. Thanks for calling. Bye, Chris."

She set down the phone and stared at the small square of paper she'd pulled out of her pocket. Whatever writing had been on it had faded in the wash. Strange. It looked like a lottery ticket, but she hadn't bought one in ages. She wadded it up and tossed it in the trash can beneath the broken window currently covered in cardboard and duct tape.

Thankfully, the glass company had promised a replacement window by the middle of the following week. She just wanted everything back to normal with no reminders her home had been invaded by a pervert. After she folded the rest of the load, she hauled the basket of clothes upstairs to put away.

She had enough on her mind, thinking about the kiss she'd shared with Teague the night before. He was far more dangerous to her composure than a dozen broken windows. Kissing him had reminded her of all the excitement missing from her life over the last five years. Not to mention passion. She hadn't wanted to pull away when the kiss ended, but taking the next step was a risk.

Heading back downstairs, she paused to glance through the glass panes at the top of the front door. Teague's truck was gone, and a black motorcycle stood in the driveway. The new babysitter. She'd been outside collecting her paper when the woman arrived shortly before eight. Nina didn't know her, but the older woman looked vaguely familiar. She'd probably seen her around town.

She hoped Keely was having fun. The night before, the girl had mentioned Stella had promised to fix her Belle dress. Any woman who was old enough to be a grandmother and could both sew and ride a motorcycle had to be an interesting character.

When the dryer buzzed, she headed back to the laundry room to start another load. Unfortunately, folding clothes was a brainless chore that left her plenty of time to think. She paused with a bra dangling from her fingertips.

Having a fling with Teague, no matter how tempting, wasn't an option. Not only would she have to see him on a regular basis—or plot out a complicated schedule to avoid him once the affair was over—but Keely's feelings had to be taken into consideration. Maybe she was finally ready for a new relationship, but if she discovered a few weeks down the road that she wasn't, she and Teague wouldn't be the only ones affected.

Her lips pressed tight. Obviously, they needed to have a conversation in the near future, before she made herself crazy with pointless speculation.

When her doorbell rang, relinquishing her thoughts was a relief. She dropped a nightgown back into the basket and hurried to the entry to throw open the door.

A stout woman with a cloud of silver-gray curls framing her wrinkled face stood on the doorstep. She grinned broadly. "Well, don't keep me in suspense. Where's the latest masterpiece?"

Nina smiled in response. "Come on in, Miss Lola. Your painting is ready to go."

"I can't wait to see it!" She breezed past, leaving a trail

of her signature lilac fragrance in her wake. "My accountant told me I need to cut back on my art purchases, so this picture may be my last until he gets a few investments straightened out. I hope it lives up to my expectations."

"You and me both," Nina mumbled as she led the way into the main room where the framed painting of the mother robin was propped against the couch cushions. "What do you think?"

"Ooooh, it's a beauty." Planting her hands on broad hips clad in pink stretch pants, her patron cocked her head to one side to study the paining. "You've outdone yourself, Nina. The detail in the nest and tree bark is superb."

"Thank you. I'm glad you like it."

"Not like, *love*. I intend to put this one in the guest bedroom where my granddaughter can enjoy it since she'll be here for most of the summer. The oranges on the robin's breast will complement the décor in there."

"That's great." Nina lifted the painting. "I'll wrap the frame in heavy paper to avoid damage on the drive home."

"No need. I brought a blanket. But you can carry the picture out to my car for me."

"Of course." She nodded toward the envelope she'd left on the end table next to the couch. "That's your invoice."

Lola scooped it up and took a peek inside. She pursed her lips. "My accountant isn't going to like this. Uh, my checkbook is in the car."

"Great." Nina paused in the entry. "Can you get the door for me?"

"I've got it!" Feet pounded up the porch steps before Keely pulled open the screen. Her curious gaze darted from Nina to the older woman. "Is this the lady who bought the robin painting?"

Lola followed the two of them down the steps. "I am, indeed, and who might you be?"

"Keely. I live next door." She jumped to the walkway, then twirled in a circle as her yellow satin skirt flared around her ankles. "I came to show Nina my Belle dress. Stella fixed it."

"You look very pretty." Nina shifted the painting in her arms. "Do you mind opening the rear door of the car?"

"Sure." Keely swung the door of the Lincoln wide then grinned.

"Thanks." Nina glanced down at Keely. "Hey, you lost your tooth."

"It came out in a bite of waffle this morning. The tooth fairy will come tonight and leave me five bucks."

Lola grunted. "In my day it was a dime."

After wrapping the picture in the blanket left on the seat, Nina turned around and smiled. "I think we call that inflation. Keely, this is Miss Lola."

"Oh." The girl eyed the woman, who had pulled a checkbook out of her purse. "Aren't you too old to be a Miss?"

Nina raised a hand to her lips and tried to turn a burst of laughter into a cough that ended in a strangled rush of air. "Uh, that's not very polite."

"It's honest." Lola ripped off the check and held it out. "I suppose you could call me Mrs. Copeland, but I've always been Miss Lola, despite having outlived three husbands."

"That's a lot."

"Three too many, in my opinion." She turned to face Nina. "I'll be in touch about an owl I saw in the woods the other day . . . once my accountant turns loose the purse strings."

Trying to keep a straight face, Nina took the check and stuffed it in the pocket of her shorts. "I'll look forward to hearing from you. Enjoy the rest of your weekend."

"You, too, dear." Lola nodded at Keely. "It was nice meeting you, young lady." She slid onto the driver's seat, started the engine, and backed up with a jolt as her rear tire hit the edge of the lawn before she drove away.

Nina winced at the tire marks left on her grass, then shrugged off her irritation and turned to face Keely. "Your dress isn't tight at all now. You look perfect."

"It's short, but Stella said she can add lace to the bottom."

"Good for Stella. I'm glad you came over to show me."

"I have to eat lunch. Then we're going on an adventure walk in the woods. Want to come with us?"

"Sounds fun, but I have a lot of laundry to do."

"Oh." Keely skipped backward. "Maybe tomorrow or the next day."

"I'd love to. I'll talk to you later."

"Okay." The girl spun and ran back to her house. The front door swung shut behind her with a bang.

Nina headed inside to the piles of clothes awaiting her. Hours later, she was putting away the final load when a revving engine caught her attention. A glance out the bedroom window told her she'd missed hearing Teague return but not Stella firing up her Honda. Keely's sitter backed the bike down the drive and took off with a roar.

Silence settled over the cul-de-sac, disturbed only by the screech of a seagull circling in the cloudless sky. Taking the empty laundry basket with her, she ran down the stairs. When a quiet knock sounded, Nina detoured to the entry and pulled open the door.

Teague stood on the porch, his eyes shadowed with fatigue. He smiled but shook his head when she gestured him inside. "I can't stay. I just came over to thank you again for helping me out last night." He nodded toward the empty basket. "Anyway, you look busy."

"No, I finally finished washing all the clothes that creep touched. Mission accomplished, but I wasted an entire day on the chore." She set down the plastic basket and leaned against the doorframe. "You look tired."

"I am. The whole crew at work was dragging after only five hours of sleep."

"I bet. The captain is a good guy. I imagine you'll fit in just fine with that group."

"I expect I will. They already invited me to join their Monday night poker club. Too bad I had to turn them down."

"Why? Do you suck at bluffing?" Nina asked.

"Maybe, but bringing Keely along with me would probably cramp their style."

"I could always—"

He laid a hand on her arm and squeezed. The heat from his fingers on her bare skin sent warmth straight to her core.

"I'm not going to ask you to watch my daughter so I can go out drinking with the boys."

"What if I offered?"

"Honestly, I'd rather take you to dinner than play poker." He finally pulled his hand away and slid it into his pocket. "I like spending time with you, Nina, but I'm not free to date whenever the mood strikes."

She crossed her arms over her chest. "Are we talking about that extremely hot kiss now?"

"I figured we should." He stared at his feet for a moment before lifting his chin to meet her gaze head-on.

"I'd like nothing more than to start something with you, but I'm not ready to explain to Keely why you're sleeping over."

"I don't recall ever saying I planned to sleep with you."

A hint of color darkened his cheeks. "No, you didn't, and I'm not presuming anything. But we're both adults, and the attraction between us was . . . is . . . ."

"Combustible?"

"An apt word. If anyone is going to get burned, I don't want it to be my daughter. You're her new idol. Since my wife died, she tends to cling to women she admires, like her kindergarten teacher and the occasional babysitter. I don't want her to have unrealistic expectations about you."

"And you don't think we'd last together for more than a quick fling." Her tone made it a statement rather than a question.

"We only met a few days ago, so it's a little too soon to say. I'm just being cautious, despite the fact I currently have a raging hard-on just looking at you in those shorts."

Her gaze drifted downward. "You're nothing if not direct. I kind of like that."

"I don't play games, and I'm not going to pretend Keely isn't my top priority. There are times when I don't always get to do what I want."

"I can respect that. How about if we start as simply friends? I haven't had sex in nearly six years, so I can probably curb any urge to throw myself at you since my self-control is clearly amazing."

"Six years?" His voice rose.

She smiled. "Since Keith was deployed to Afghanistan. I'm not one to sleep around, although lately I've been thinking the idea has merit."

He slowly pounded his head against the support post on the porch. "You're killing me. Don't say stuff like that."

"Hey, you brought up the subject of sex."

"Obviously a big mistake." His breath came out in a rush. "Fine, we'll be friends without benefits, more's the pity. I'm glad we cleared that up. Excuse me while I go home to take another cold shower."

"Think of it as a way to lower your power bills."

"Funny. I'll talk to you later, Nina."

"Sure. Have a nice evening."

She stood without moving until he entered his house, then finally turned to go back inside. Even though she'd basically come to the same conclusion, her heart ached. The hell of it was, she felt as if she'd just lost something precious. Something she'd never really had to begin with.

The local news blared on the old TV squatting on the corner cabinet in the living room. She could afford a new one, but they'd built them to last in the good old days, and she enjoyed the nostalgia of a happier time. Lynette sat on the rug in front of the screen, dressing her Barbies. She wasn't addicted to electronics the way other kids were. Not that she had a choice. Lately, though, she complained more and more. The whining grated on her nerves.

Her attention swung back to the TV screen when the anchor introduced the next story. Cameras flashed to a live shot of a reporter standing in front of the convenience store in Siren Cove. Her grip on the remote tightened as she turned up the volume.

"The Lottery Commission has confirmed the winning ticket worth over three million dollars from Wednesday

night's drawing was purchased right here in the store behind me." The perky brunette threw out a hand to point to
the Gas 'n Go sign above the door. "So far no one has
come forward to claim the prize. For now, the mystery of
who in this community is a millionaire will remain just
that, a mystery. Back to you, Fred."

"It could have been a tourist who bought the ticket,
you brainless bimbo," she muttered.

But the good news was Nina hadn't cashed in her
winning numbers. Not yet, anyway. She'd searched the
woman's whole damn house, looked through every pocket
in every pair of shorts in her room. She'd sifted through
piles of clothes to make sure the ticket hadn't fallen out
into one of the drawers. She'd checked the laundry basket
downstairs, but it had been empty, as was the hamper in
her bedroom. Then she'd scoured Nina's desk and searched
the kitchen counters just in case the precious square of
paper was lying around out in the open. She'd even
looked in her paint supply boxes in the room set up as a
studio to make certain the artist hadn't stuffed the ticket
in with her brushes. But the key to her peace of mind was
nowhere to be found.

Her gaze darted back to the blond head bent over the
dolls, then rose to the portrait hanging above the mantel.
Lynette, holding a striped kitten in her arms, her face so
joyous and carefree. Tiger had been dead for decades, but
not her precious one.

Pain shot through her temples. She dropped the remote
and pressed her hands to her head. The image in the picture blurred, and light blue eyes changed to silver in her
mind. The long, blond hair was exactly the same, as was
the eager expression. The happy laughter had drawn her
like a magnet, and a deep-seated exhilaration filled her

when she'd discovered the source. Fate throwing her a bone after her fruitless search of the artist's home.

Soon she would have her heart's desire back where she belonged instead of the sullen impostor who rarely smiled anymore. The day of reckoning was near.

First, though, she needed to reclaim her ticket to financial freedom. Then and only then would she and Lynette be safe. If the lottery ticket wasn't in Nina's home, maybe it was in her car or her purse. She'd find it eventually. That much was a given.

Chapter Seven

Teague used a crowbar to rip out a series of rotted planks, then carried the armload to the dumpster. With a grunt, he heaved them over the side. All he needed was two more uninterrupted hours, and he'd have the porch floor repaired. Wiping sweat off his brow with his T-shirt sleeve, he turned around and frowned.

"What the heck are you doing?"

Out on the patchy front lawn, Keely's feet wavered over her head before she went down with a thump. "Trying to stand on my hands."

"You almost landed on Coco." Teague returned to the porch to rip out the next section.

"I'm bored." She sprawled on the grass beside the dog and banged her heels against the ground. "And hungry. When's dinner?"

He let out a sigh. "Can you eat a snack? I'd really like to get some more work done before I fix a meal."

"Maybe Stella should have cooked dinner."

"It's only five thirty. Can you please stop pounding your feet like that?"

She paused with her heels off the ground and glanced over. "You're making way more noise than me. I bet you're bugging Nina with all that racket."

He rolled his eyes as she tossed one of his more frequent comments back at him. "You're the only one I hear complaining. I'm sure you can find something to do to alleviate your boredom if you put your mind to it."

"What does *alleviate* mean?" She sat up straighter. "Hey, here comes Nina now."

Teague glanced across the street as Nina left her house and headed toward her car, her long, toned legs displayed to perfection in running shorts. He swallowed against a suddenly dry mouth. "She's leaving, not coming over here."

Keely scrambled to her feet, setting Coco into a barking fit. "Nina! Hey, Nina! Where're you going?"

Turning in their direction, she smiled. "Down to the beach for a run."

"I want to go to the beach. I haven't been a single time since we got here." His daughter braced her fists on her hips and scowled. "Why can't we ever do anything fun?"

Teague let out a sigh. "Not this evening, Keely. I want to finish fixing this porch."

Nina strolled down the driveway and stopped at the edge of the lawn. "I can take her with me if you want."

"Can I, Daddy? Please?" Keely jumped up and down while Coco ran around in circles, barking. "Please? Please let me go."

He met Nina's amused gaze. "If she takes you, she won't be able to run."

"That probably wouldn't be the end of the world."

He crossed his arms over his chest. "I don't want to put you out."

"I offered. I wouldn't have if it was an imposition."

In the face of her determination, Teague caved. "Fine. I'll get the booster seat for you."

"Yay!" Keely raced toward the truck, apparently afraid he might change his mind. "I'll get my seat."

He met Nina at the end of the driveway and lowered his voice. "Are you sure you don't mind? She can be a handful sometimes."

"I think I can manage one small girl." She glanced down. "And a dog. My guess is they're a package deal."

"If you're up for it."

"Sure. We said we're going to be friends, right?" She held out her arms. "This is me, making a friendly gesture. Anyway, I like Keely. We'll have fun."

"Well, thank you. I appreciate this because I really do want to finish repairing the porch this evening."

"You're welcome." When his daughter appeared around the side of the pickup with her booster seat, Nina patted his arm. "I'll see you later. Maybe we'll bring back pizza or something."

He couldn't help taking her hand in his to squeeze. "You rock."

"I know. See you later, Teague."

After a minor struggle to get the booster and Coco into the back of the Mini, the pair drove away with Keely hanging out the window, waving. He waved back. He'd rather be going to the beach with them than working on the damn porch. On the other hand, he didn't want someone punching through the rotted boards, so the repair was a must.

After finishing the demolition, Teague began replacing the boards and screwing them down, thankful the understructure had been treated and was still sound. As the evening shadows stretched across the yard, his pace slowed, and he glanced up more frequently. When the hair on the back of his neck rose, he scrambled to his feet to scan the yard and street. Nothing in the quiet cul-de-sac appeared out of place, but the juncos in the trees had stopped twittering. To the west, a bank of fog was rolling in, chilling the moist evening air.

I should have told Keely to take a jacket.

He resisted the urge to call Nina. His daughter wasn't going to freeze, and she'd be disappointed if he cut her outing short. He needed to work on tamping down the over-protective streak that had emerged after Jayne's death. Moving to a quiet, *safe* town had been a proactive step. Letting go of his anxiety was proving more difficult and was undoubtedly the cause of his current paranoia.

A squirrel eyed him from the walkway, its bushy tail twitching, before it scampered away. Somewhere in the woods behind him, a blue jay squawked. After taking a final look around, he went back to work. If someone had been in the vicinity, they were gone now.

Nina zipped the fleece jacket she'd had the fore-thought to bring with her up to Keely's chin, then rolled the sleeves until her hands were visible. "There, that should keep you warm."

"Thank you." She stroked one hand down the front. "It's soft."

"And cozy. Do you want to walk farther, or are you getting tired?"

"Let's keep going." The girl waved toward the mono-lithic boulders out in the cove as they followed Coco up the beach. "Look at the fog on those rocks. It's kind of spooky."

Nina smiled. "Those are the Sirens. Legend has it they were once mermaids who lured sailors toward the shore where their ships smashed against the rocks beneath the surface. There's one old wreck way out in the cove, and people swear they've heard the ghosts of the drowning men who went down with the ship."

"That's so cool!" Keely danced in a circle and flapped her arms. When she smiled, her missing tooth added charm to an already expressive face. "Have you heard them?"

"I'm afraid not."

"That's too bad. What happened to the mermaids?"

"Lightning struck them, and they were turned to stone. Maybe the gods were angry at their impudence."

"What does *impudence* mean?"

"It means they were bold and naughty and didn't care about others."

Keely nodded solemnly. "Like the mean boy at school who called me a giraffe."

"Exactly." When Nina's phone rang, she pulled it out of her pocket to glance at the display. "I need to discuss something with my friend Paige for a minute. We keep leaving each other messages."

"Okay. Can I go talk to that girl over there?"

Nina glanced in the direction of Keely's pointing finger to a small figure some distance away. The girl ran across the sand toward the water, while a woman in a hooded jacket picked her way down the cliff trail to the beach.

"Sure, but stay out of the surf." Nina followed Keely and Coco at a slower pace as she answered her phone. "Hey, Paige. Thanks for calling me back."

"Sorry I didn't reach you sooner. We *so* need to finalize plans for Leah's bachelorette party. I can't believe her wedding is in three weeks."

"Exactly. Will the end of this week still work to pick up the party stuff along with my art supplies in Portland?"

"I'm afraid not. There's a two-day auction at an estate sale in Idaho I really want to attend. I heard they have some excellent pieces. I can make the trip tomorrow or Tuesday if you're free."

"Damn, I can't." Nina frowned. "I have a guy coming to replace my broken window Tuesday, and tomorrow is supposed to be sunny again, so I need to paint."

"How'd you break a window?"

She flinched just thinking about the creep who'd searched through her underwear drawer. "Long story, and I don't have time to explain right now. Don't worry about the trip to Portland, Paige. I can go on my own."

"Are you sure?"

"Positive. We talked about having a theme for the party. Any brilliant ideas yet?"

"Actually, yes. Since Leah's style is totally flower-child retro, what about a sixties theme?"

"You *are* brilliant! That'll be a lot of fun."

Paige laughed. "I know, right? Also, I confirmed the stripper."

"A critical part of any bachelorette party." Her gaze strayed up the beach to where Keely had reached the other girl. The two stood ankle-deep in the surging tide. "I talked to the owner of Castaways, and he agreed to the stripper on the condition he doesn't show up before midnight."

"I'll make sure our guy knows. Is there anything else we need to take care of?"

"I don't think so." When a large wave rolled in, she raised her voice. "Don't go in any deeper, Keely."

"Who's Keely?"

Nina returned her attention to her conversation. "My new neighbor's daughter. I brought her down to the beach with me."

"That was nice of you."

"She's a cute kid, and her dad was busy. Anyway, I'd better go."

"Okay, I'll talk to you soon."

"Have fun at your auction. Bye, Paige."

Nina disconnected and returned her phone to her pocket, then glanced up the beach. The woman stood at the base of the path, beckoning to the other girl. After a few moments, the child bent to pet Coco before she left Keely's side to plod through the sand. When Keely and the bedraggled dog ran back along the shoreline, Nina grimaced.

"Looks like Coco got soaked by a wave."

Dripping wet and covered in sand, the dog shook twice before scampering out of Nina's reach.

Keely stopped beside her and spoke between deep breaths. "I told her to stay back, but she was being bad and didn't listen."

"Good thing I keep a beach towel in the car. We should probably head back now."

"Okay." Keely took her hand as they turned around. "That girl was nice."

"Yeah? Maybe you can see her again over the summer. Is she in your grade?"

"She's eight, and she said she's homeschooled. That sounds really boring."

Nina glanced down. "We all like different things."

"Lynette said she doesn't have any friends."

"That's too bad."

"I was going to tell her where I live so she could come visit me, but then she had to leave." Keely frowned. "I don't know any other girls here to be friends with."

"Your dad mentioned summer camp. I'm sure you'll meet plenty of kids your age."

"I hope so." She skipped a couple of times to keep pace. "I'm hungry."

"Let's order a pizza to take home. I don't think your dad will have time to cook dinner tonight."

"Okay." She laughed out loud, her shrill giggles carrying on the breeze. "Look at Coco. She's rolling in that pile of seaweed."

Nina let out a sigh. "Perfect. My car will probably never smell the same again."

Convincing Coco to rinse off in the ocean was a challenge, but Nina finally got her up to the car with most of the sand removed, then wrapped the shivering dog in an old beach towel. It was well after seven before they picked up their pizza and headed toward home. She parked in her driveway and let Keely carry the pizza while she wrestled the booster seat out of the back.

Teague shut his shed door and hurried to take the seat from her as they approached his pickup. "Good timing. I was just putting away my tools. How did everything go?"

"We had *so* much fun." Keely danced in a circle, clutching the pizza box. "I met a girl on the beach, then Coco rolled in seaweed, and we got a pizza with pepperoni and olives because Nina let me pick the kind I wanted."

"Sounds like quite an adventure." He returned the booster to the truck, shut the door, and faced her. "It looks like Nina let you borrow her jacket. Did you thank her?"

"Of course I did. Geez, Daddy."

Nina smiled. "Keely was very well-behaved. Coco, not so much. She's kind of a mess."

"I'll clean her up later. Thanks for getting the pizza. I'll pay you back, but let's go eat it while it's hot."

"Don't be silly. Dinner, such as it is, is my treat." Nina walked beside him up the porch steps. "Wow, it looks like you finished replacing all the damaged boards."

"I still need to stain them, but I'm happy to have gotten this much accomplished." He waited until Keely disappeared inside with the pizza. "Thanks again for helping me out."

"I enjoyed it. Honestly, I haven't spent a lot of time around kids since . . . well . . . I was one, but your daughter is entertaining." Nina glanced down at Coco as she preceded them through the doorway. "The jury's still out on your dog."

"She's a work in progress."

When he put a hand to the small of her back to usher her into the dining room, she forgot all about Coco as the warmth from his palm spread downward. With a sharp mental reminder that they weren't going to pick up where they'd left off after the last meal they'd shared, she stayed quiet while they ate, content to enjoy Teague's interaction with his daughter. The man was patient and supportive yet firm, allowing Keely to chatter about their beach trip without letting her interrupt. Nina couldn't help being impressed.

When they finished the pizza, Teague sent his daughter upstairs to get ready for bed, then leaned back in his chair to study Nina. "You didn't have much to contribute to the conversation."

"I was just thinking you're a great dad. Keely is very lucky. You actually listen when she talks."

"Don't most parents?"

"You'd be surprised. My friend Leah teaches fifth grade, and she says parent disconnect is a huge problem. They can't put their phones down for two minutes to interact with their kids."

"What's the point of having children if you don't enjoy them? Granted, everyone has an off day and needs a little time to themselves, but—"

Nina laid a hand on his arm. "You're a good man." Releasing him, she pushed back her chair. "I should go." *Before the temptation to stay proves irresistible.*

He walked with her to the door then out onto the porch. They both paused to gaze up at the star-strewn sky.

"The fog cleared out again." His arm brushed against hers. "It's a beautiful night."

"A perfect evening to . . ." Nina spoke in an even tone, despite the way her heart rate had accelerated to warp speed.

He brushed a wisp of hair off her cheek. When he stepped closer, his breath fanned her face. A trace of stubble around his firm mouth was visible in the glow of the porch light.

"A perfect evening to give your dog a bath. You and Coco in the starlight. Doesn't get much more romantic than that."

He grinned. "Funny." The silver of his eyes darkened. "You are so damn beautiful."

Placing a hand against his chest, she pushed him back a few inches. "Friends, remember? That's what we agreed is best. I didn't take Keely to the beach with the intention of starting something."

"I know, but I'm only human."

"Let's not complicate things." Rising on her toes, she kissed his cheek. "Good night, Teague."

"Fine, you win." He turned to grip the porch railing in front of him. "Good night, Nina."

As she walked away without looking back, she didn't feel like a winner. She felt the way she usually did . . . alone. The difference was, she was no longer certain her own company would be enough to satisfy her.

Chapter Eight

Teague paced up and down the patch of withered grass in front of his house and held his phone a little tighter. "You want me to send Keely alone on a plane? She's only six." He forced himself to breathe.

His ex-mother-in-law spoke in a reasonable tone, in sharp contrast to his current frame of mind. "It's a short flight from Portland to San Francisco. You put her on the plane with all the attendants making her feel like the special girl she is, and Sterling and I will pick her up at the gate when she lands at SFO. Simple. That's why they allow unaccompanied minors on direct flights. And don't worry. We'll pay for the ticket and extra fees."

The expense wasn't his greatest concern, not by a long shot. "You want her for over a week. She's never been away from me for longer than a couple of days."

"I realize it'll be an adjustment for you both, but we won a family vacation for four to Hawaii, and we want to take our two youngest granddaughters with us on the trip. Sterling and I miss Keely, and she'll have a great time playing on the beach with her cousin. How long has it been since she spent any quality time with Hallie?"

"A while," he admitted.

"Carol is all for this trip."

Jayne's older sister was divorced with four kids. She was probably thrilled not to have to deal with her youngest for a week.

"I'm sure they'll both have a great time." He pressed a hand to his chest. "What day do you want her?"

"Thursday."

"That's only three days from now." His voice rose. "Why such short notice?"

"We had limited booking options to claim our prize, so we took a cancellation. Better right now than after the kids are back in school. Anyway, I already checked flights, and there's one out of Portland on United that leaves shortly after three. It gets in close to the same time as Hallie's flight from Denver, so we can make one trip to the airport to pick up both girls. They'll spend the night with us before we fly to Hawaii on Friday morning."

"Sounds like you have it all figured out." He stopped pacing when Nina's car cruised up the street and turned into her driveway.

"I do. You'll have to check in at the counter rather than online so you can accompany Keely through security to the gate. Make sure you get to the airport early."

"Fine. Email me the details. Luckily I have Thursday and Friday off this week."

"How's everything going since the move?"

"We're managing."

"That's good to hear." Her forthright voice softened a hint. "I'll let you go, Teague. Please don't worry about Keely. We'll take excellent care of her and make sure she has the time of her life."

"I'm sure you will. Bye, Doreen." He hung up, then rubbed the back of his neck as tension took hold.

"Is everything okay? You look stressed."

He faced Nina when she stopped at the edge of the street holding a bag of groceries.

"Yeah, life is just peachy."

She ignored his sarcasm. "If I can help . . ."

"I'm afraid not. Keely's grandparents want to take her and her cousin to Hawaii for a week plus additional travel days. Letting her go will be tough but probably good for both of us."

She gave him a sympathetic smile. "That's not so long, and I'm sure she'll have a wonderful time with your parents."

"Jayne's parents. Of course I want them to remain an active part of my daughter's life, but nine days . . ." He let out a sigh. "I expect she'll be beyond excited when I tell her."

"Lying on a white sand beach and swimming with turtles sounds like heaven. I'd be overjoyed, too."

He smiled. "Maybe I'm just jealous. I haven't been anywhere tropical since my . . . uh, in years." His heart ached a little as he pictured the private beach in Costa Rica where he and Jayne had spent their honeymoon. But the twinge of pain was nothing like it had once been. Apparently time was finally doing its job of healing.

"You'll be fine, and so will Keely. When does she leave?"

"This Thursday. I'm putting her on a plane in Portland to meet her grandparents and cousin in San Francisco."

"Oh, yeah?" She shifted the bag in her arms. "I was actually planning a trip to the city the end of this week. There's a terrific shop where I get my extra-large canvases and framing materials. I have a couple of big projects planned before the Summer Art Fair."

"Couldn't you just order everything online?"

"Yes, but shipping is expensive. I also have a few things to buy for Leah's bachelorette party. My friend Paige intended to go with me and make a day of it, but she had to bail. She's out of town for an estate sale, and I don't want to wait until next week to go."

"We could carpool if you want." The words were out of his mouth before he paused to consider the consequences. Hadn't he been the one to tell Nina they needed to keep their relationship casual? Keely wouldn't be around for the three-hour drive home . . .

"Actually, that might work out well for me if you're cool with a couple of extra stops. Paige had planned to drive her van, and I was wondering how I'd be able to fit everything into my car."

"The Mini Cooper isn't the most practical vehicle for an artist."

"I know, but I love that car." Her smile lit up her face. "I have an open trailer I hitch to it for short trips to events in town, but I wouldn't want to pull it all the way to Portland and back."

"Well, I'm happy to offer you a ride in my truck." *Probably more so than I should be.*

"Thanks." She took a step backward. "I'd better go put these groceries away before my ice cream melts. See you later, Teague."

"Sure." He told himself to head straight inside to deliver the big news to Keely. Instead, he appreciated each step Nina took, wondering if the woman ever wore anything but shorts that displayed her amazing legs to perfection. Not that he was complaining . . .

When the door shut behind her, he pried his attention away. Time to put on a bright smile and tell his daughter she was going to Hawaii without him.

Nina was pretty certain every woman in the terminal had her gaze glued to Teague. Maybe because he was better-looking than every other man in the vicinity. Maybe because his confident stride and the way he filled out his jeans was pure sexy. Or possibly because the sadness shadowing his silvery eyes spoke of a tragic hero who needed saving. When he reached the bench where she was waiting, she stood but didn't offer any platitudes, just took his hand and squeezed it.

"Ready to go?"

She nodded. "Are you okay?"

"I will be. Watching my daughter walk down that boarding tunnel to the plane was harder than I expected, and I didn't think it would be a piece of cake." His grip on her hand tightened. "She's all I have."

"I know, so I won't give you a lot of statistics about air travel being safer than driving in your own neighborhood. You'll miss her. Maybe you can look at this as practice for when she goes away to college."

"Are you trying to make me feel worse?" He smiled. "Fine. No more whining."

They left the terminal to dodge between cars without using the crosswalk. When a cabbie laid on his horn, she laughed out loud. "See what I mean? We could get killed just walking across the street."

The hand still holding hers tightened painfully. "I certainly can't argue that fact." When they reached his pickup in the short-term parking garage, he finally released her.

She kept quiet until they were both seated, then turned to face him in the gloomy interior. "What did I say?"

"Nothing." He gripped the steering wheel but made no move to start the engine. His voice was low when he finally spoke. "That's how Jayne died. Crossing the street. She was a social worker on her way to see a client." His knuckles gleamed white as he let out a long breath. "Granted, the neighborhood wasn't the best, but it was only a half a dozen blocks from our home. She was gunned down in a drive-by shooting."

Nina covered her mouth and pressed hard to hold back a gasp. The pain in his eyes when he met her gaze broke her heart.

"That's horrifying. I don't know what to say except how sorry I am."

"I don't talk about it often. I'm doing my best to let go of all the rage that was tearing me up inside. That's why I made the decision to move to Oregon. I needed some distance, physical and emotional, if I ever hoped to find peace."

"I can certainly understand why you're protective of Keely." She scooted closer and touched his cheek. "Letting her go today took a hell of a lot of strength. You're an amazing man, Teague O'Dell."

"Let's not get carried away." His tone was laced with irony. "I've been a basket case since I agreed to this trip." He kissed her palm. "I'm glad you're here with me. Honestly, it helps."

The warmth of his lips on the sensitive skin of her hand sent a quiver through her. With an effort, she tried to defuse some of the emotional tension. "Do you know what will help even more? Picking out favors for a bachelorette party. I'm thinking decks of cards with hot guys who strip when you fan them out."

He reared back in the seat. "You've got to be kidding."

She didn't even blink. "Not in the least."

"I guess cards that strip are better than actual men who do."

"Oh, we'll have one of those at the party, too. Paige and I plan to send Leah off in style this time. We're doing everything we didn't do for her first wedding."

He started the engine and backed out of the parking slot. "This is your friend's second marriage?"

"Yeah. Her ex-husband is a total idiot currently serving time in jail for . . ." She paused. "Long story. Anyway, we threw a very sedate bridal shower for her first wedding, which is why we're going a little wild this time in an effort to change her luck. Not that she'll need it since Ryan is a wonderful man, but why tempt fate?"

"Why indeed. You're the navigator. Where are we going?"

"The art store first, and then I'll shop for the party. Turn right when you get to the main road, and don't worry about getting lost. I have an excellent sense of direction."

"Good to know."

Two hours later, Nina walked out of the party store carrying a bulging bag. At her side, Teague avoided all eye contact.

"I can't believe you're blushing. That's hilarious."

"Pink balloons shaped like penises? People buy those things?"

"I didn't. The owner of Castaways, the bar where we're holding the party, said we have to be discreet."

He pulled the car keys out of his pocket to click the remote. "I saw you toss that bag of X-rated sour gummies in your cart. Practically everything in that aisle was shaped like male genitalia."

"Men don't think twice about objectifying women, but when the G-string is between the other cheek . . ."

His blush deepened, and her heart warmed.

"Aren't you funny?"

"I have my moments." She opened the passenger door, then tossed her shopping bag in the rear seat with the art supplies. "Are you offended?"

"No, but you don't look like the type to sip your drink through a straw shaped like a . . . I can't even say it." He shook his head as they took their seats. "What the heck do women do at bachelorette parties, anyway?"

"Probably nothing as horrible as you might think. At least not our group of friends. We'll drink margaritas and dance and laugh a lot, maybe tell a few embarrassing stories about Leah and Ryan from their younger days. Oh, and then bring in the stripper." She gave him an assessing look. "I don't suppose you want to show up in your fireman gear, then take it all off?"

"Definitely not."

"Too bad." She fastened her seat belt. "So, are we ready to head home now?"

"It's almost six. Do you want to go get some dinner first? Maybe find someplace decent instead of stopping for fast food along the freeway?"

"Sure. I'd like that." Nina pulled out her phone. "What are you in the mood for?"

"Your mention of margaritas has me craving tacos carnitas."

"I could go for that." She tapped her phone and scrolled through a list of restaurants. "Hmm, here's a place with a four-star rating that isn't super fancy and has decent prices. It's only a couple of miles from here."

"Great. You haven't gotten us lost yet. Lead on."

"Take a left onto the street, then your first right."

Not long afterward, Teague parked in the lot next to a restaurant with a red terra-cotta roof and glanced over. "We make a good team. Competency, trust, and no misdirection."

"Sounds like the slogan for a law firm."

"Good one." He got out and shut his door. As she reached his side, he put a hand at the center of her back to guide her toward the lighted façade.

The warmth of his palm penetrated the thin cotton of her shirt and heated her clear through. When they reached the entrance and he leaned into her to pull open the arched wooden door, she couldn't resist resting her cheek against his shoulder for just a moment. Apparently her hormones hadn't gotten the news flash that their relationship was friends only, because every nerve ending sizzled at the contact.

Nina could only hope the blast of festive music coming from inside covered the little moan that escaped when he finally stepped away. Or maybe it hadn't. When his glittering gaze locked with hers, she was pretty certain she wasn't the only one affected by the contact.

"Two for dinner? Right this way."

She tore her attention away from Teague and released a shaky breath as she followed the hostess dressed in a black skirt and red blouse toward a table in the corner, some distance from the noisy bar area. Taking a seat, she smiled her thanks as the woman laid menus on the table.

"Your server will be right with you." The hostess flashed a bright smile. "Enjoy your evening."

"Thanks. We will." Teague leaned back in his chair after she walked away. "It smells great in here, like roasted peppers. I bet their salsa packs a punch."

"I like spicy, but not too hot."

"Is that why you rejected the bottle coolers with the sequined uh, you know?"

She grinned. "Maybe. It's also possible I'm still hung up on those old adages my mom used to spout when I was in high school, about being a proper lady or the boys would expect things. She never explained exactly what those *things* were, and I'll admit I was tempted to do something a little wild just to find out."

"Did you?"

She waited to respond as a young man delivered chips and salsa and glasses of water to their table. "Can I get you folks something else to drink?"

Nina sipped her water. "Shall we have margaritas?"

"Go ahead. I'll stick with a beer since I'm driving." Teague glanced up at the server. "A Pacifico, please."

"What the heck. I'll have a house margarita on the rocks."

"I'll be right back with your drinks."

Nina picked up a still-warm chip and dipped it into the salsa. "To answer your question, not while I was in high school."

"Huh?" He crunched down on a chip.

"I saved any wild tendencies for college in Paris."

"You studied abroad?" His eyes watered a little. "Careful. That salsa should come with a warning label."

She set down the chip and flipped open the menu. "Hey, it does. Three little red peppers next to it. Maybe we should ask for guacamole instead."

"This stuff is actually really good." He ate another chip then gulped water. "How'd you end up on the Oregon coast if you studied in France?"

"I grew up in Siren Cove before going to art school in

Paris, where I met Keith. He was a few years older than me, a Marine stationed in Germany, on leave at the time."

"I guess dating a Marine could be considered wild."

Nina glanced down at her menu. "Our relationship started out as a fling, but we kept seeing each other whenever we could." She couldn't seem to stop talking as the words spilled out. "After he finished his tour, we got engaged. I'd graduated by then and wanted him to come home with me to go to med school on the GI Bill the way he'd originally planned."

Teague reached across the table and covered her clenched fist. "I take it he didn't."

She shook her head. "He was hooked on the military life and reenlisted despite my protests. We put our wedding on hold." She paused when the server returned with their drinks, and Teague released her hand.

"Are you folks ready to order?"

Nina snapped her menu closed without reading the choices. "I'll have chicken enchiladas with black beans, please."

Teague handed over his menu. "Carnitas tacos."

"Great. Your food shouldn't take too long to arrive." He hurried away, leaving silence in his wake.

Nina swallowed a mouthful of icy-cold margarita before facing her dinner companion. "Why am I telling you all this? I certainly didn't intend to."

"The same reason I explained what happened to Jayne. We're getting to know each other, and these tragedies in our pasts made us who we are now."

"I suppose so." She ate a chip she'd dipped in salsa and coughed. "Wow, that stuff really is hot. Where was I? Oh, Keith wanted me to move to Germany with him, but then he got stationed in Afghanistan instead. I stayed in France until word came he'd been killed." Her voice broke. "I didn't ever find out how it happened since he was on some top-secret mission."

Teague reclaimed her hand. "I'm so sorry, Nina."

"Yeah, it was rough. Anyway, I moved back home to Siren Cove afterward. I needed something familiar to hold on to."

"Having family around helps."

"I had my best friends, Leah and Paige. They were rocks for me. Still are, actually. My mom moved away from Oregon while I was still in college. She married a widowed clergyman from the Midwest and lives in Kansas now." She ate another chip, maybe so she'd have an excuse for her watering eyes. "I see her every couple of years."

He sipped his beer. "What about your dad?"

She was grateful he didn't offer any sympathy that surely would have shaken her composure. "I never knew him. He left my mom when I was just a baby, which was the reason behind all her early warnings to act like a lady. She didn't want me to repeat her mistakes."

"I admire the hell out of you."

"You do?"

"Yeah." He turned her hand over and squeezed her fingers. "You are one tough lady. A survivor who can still face life with grace and kindness."

"Bitterness isn't very productive. I tried that for a while and didn't like the person I'd become."

"I know what you mean, but I had Keely to inspire me to get my shit together in a hurry. I'm not sure I would have managed without her."

She smiled at him. "You definitely would have because you have a solid inner core of strength. You wouldn't be able to run into burning buildings without a strong heart."

He didn't respond, just released her hand when the server returned with their steaming plates.

The man stepped back from the table. "Let me know if you need anything else."

"This looks great. Thank you." After he departed, Nina picked up her fork and glanced across the table at Teague. "No more depressing topics, okay?"

"Deal." He took a swallow of his beer. "Nina?"

She scooped up a bite of black beans. "What?"

"Thanks for sharing so much of yourself with me, but I'm afraid you've shaken my resolve."

She frowned. "What are you talking about?"

"Our plan to be just friends." He set down the bottle with a thump. "We might have to rethink that."

Chapter Nine

Teague pulled into his driveway, turned off the engine, then glanced over at Nina. Not that he could see her in the dark of a moonless night. Maybe that actually made the whole situation easier. During the drive home, he'd had three hours alone with her to decide if he wanted to push their relationship in a new direction, but his head and heart—not to mention other parts of his anatomy— were still at odds.

He settled for the mundane. "We're home."

"Yes, we are." She was quiet for a moment. "Thanks again for driving me to Portland."

He covered the hand resting on her thigh. "Hey, having you along on the trip made dropping off Keely tolerable."

"I'm glad." She let out a breath. "Well, I'd better haul all my stuff across the street."

"I'll help." He released his seat belt and opened the door, then blinked in the glow from the interior light. From the direction of the house, barking erupted. "Just as soon as I free Coco from imprisonment. Stella promised to stop by midafternoon to take her out and feed her, but I'm sure she needs to pee again by now."

"If all that excited yapping is anything to judge by, I'd say you're right."

Coco did sound like she was about to lose it. He pulled the keys out of the ignition, then headed toward his house as the insistent barking grew louder. The second he unlocked the door, the dog shot through. After bounding down the porch steps, she strolled around the yard before squatting to pee. Hurrying back to his truck, Teague lifted the rolled canvases and long strips of framing material out of the cargo area while Nina grabbed the miscellaneous bags from the rear seat.

"Do we have everything?"

"I think so." She slung her purse strap over her shoulder and shut the car door with her hip. "I need to set down this load to get out my keys." Leading the way, she crossed the street and hurried up her dark walkway to the front door. "If I had half a brain, I would have left the porch light on."

"Do you need help?"

"Nope, I've got this." One bag hit the wood planking with a thud before she managed to get the key into the lock. A moment later she pushed open the door, then flipped on the outside light along with the one in the entry. "Now we can see what we're doing. You can bring those inside."

He brushed by her with his armful of canvases. "Where do you want me to put them?"

"If you don't mind carrying them up to my studio . . ."

"I don't." He headed toward the stairs.

She ran ahead, turning on more lights, the heavy bag

filled with the paints she'd purchased bumping against her leg with each step. "Here we go. Just lean them in that corner, please."

He carefully released his load and stepped back.

"Thank you so much for your help."

"You're welcome." He followed her from the studio but slowed to glance into her bedroom. Everything in him wanted to back her toward the shadowy bed and strip off her shirt to cup warm breasts—

Frantic barking from outside disrupted his fantasy. A shudder slid through him as he tamped down feelings that had grown further out of control during the long drive home filled with easy conversation and laughter.

"I wonder what Coco's problem is."

He took a breath before following her down the stairs. "Could be anything from a leaf to a thief to nothing but thin air. Coco isn't very discerning when it comes to barking."

"No more thieves, thank you very much." She glanced back over her shoulder. "I just got my laundry room window fixed."

"I'm glad. Your house wasn't very secure with only cardboard to cover that hole."

"No kidding." She walked out onto the porch and picked up the party store bag she'd dropped, then turned abruptly to lean over the railing. "Hey, the interior light is on in my car. It's pretty dim, which is probably why I didn't notice it earlier. Crap, I hope my battery isn't dead."

He stepped up behind her and rested a hand on her shoulder. "If it is, I can give you a jump start in the morning."

"I might as well find out now." Turning away from him, she set the bag inside the door and pulled the ring of keys from the lock. "I can't believe I left that light on."

As they approached her car, Coco trotted around the bumper and gave one sharp bark.

"What are you doing over here?" Teague stepped across the dog. "It looks like your rear gate wasn't shut properly. That's why the light came on." He pushed against the door until it clicked, and the light went off.

"Except I haven't opened the back in days, and the last time I parked was in the evening. I would have noticed the light." She rubbed her hands up and down her arms. "Do you suppose someone broke into my car while we were gone?"

He walked around to the driver's side. "No broken windows." When he tried the door, it didn't budge. "Locked. Do you have the key?"

She nodded and pushed the remote on her keychain. The locks popped without the accompanying beep.

He pulled open the door. "Don't you keep your car alarmed?"

"It's too old for that, but I do lock it." She hesitated. "Usually. Almost all the time."

"So sometimes you forget?"

"I was carrying my easel the last time I drove anywhere. It's possible I was distracted, had my hands full, and didn't hit the remote."

"But it was locked just now except for the back. Check to see if anything is missing or disturbed."

"I don't keep much in my car except a few CDs." She slid onto the seat, unzipped the case, and flipped through the sleeves. "Nothing's missing, and the player obviously wasn't touched." She opened the glove box and glanced back at him. "That's strange. The owner's manual is on top of my registration and insurance card. I just got that card in the mail last week, and I know I threw it in on top of everything."

He frowned. "That *is* weird. Nothing's missing, but someone might have looked through your glove box and opened the rear hatch, then locked the car when they were finished. Why the hell would anyone do that?"

"I don't have a clue, but I can't help wondering if it was the same creep who broke into my house. He didn't take anything, either."

"Maybe you have an obsessed fan who likes touching your stuff."

She shuddered. "That's sick. Anyway, my work is hardly well known enough for me to have a psycho fan. It's not like I'm a celebrity."

"But you're beautiful and sexy." He issued the compliment in a matter-of-fact tone. "Have you done any interviews for newspapers or magazines in the past?"

"Actually, I did a piece for a regional magazine about the upcoming art fair last month." Nina stuck the key in the ignition and cranked it. Nothing happened. "Well, the battery is certainly dead. *Perfect.*"

"We'll recharge it in the morning." He slid an arm around her when she climbed out of the car. "I don't want to alarm you, but someone a few bricks shy of a load could have seen your photo in the magazine and started fantasizing about you. It's not much of a stretch to assume you have a stalker."

She pressed her face against his shoulder. "I'm definitely freaked out. What if he tries the direct approach next time instead of slinking around when I'm not home?"

Teague tightened his grip on her. "You can talk to the police."

"I already called them about my window." She let out a breath. "For all the good it did. Ugh. This sucks. I'm scared."

Lifting one hand, he stroked her hair. "Hey, I'm not going to let anything happen to you. Do you want to sleep at my place tonight?"

She wrapped her arms around his waist and held on but didn't respond.

His heart thumped painfully beneath her cheek. "Nina?"

"Obviously that's not a long-term solution. I can't live this way indefinitely, too afraid to spend the night in my own home, but I'll take you up on your offer for now."

"Okay. Why don't you go get whatever you need and lock up your house?" Reluctantly, he let her go. "I'll wait right here." He raised his voice. "Coco, get out of there."

The dog left the flower bed where she was digging and trotted to his side, tags jingling.

Nina actually smiled. "And I thought a gopher was digging up my daffodils. I'll be right back."

He leaned against the Mini and stared up into the star-filled sky. Maybe getting involved with Nina wasn't the wisest move, but the choice to complicate their friendship had been taken out of his hands. For tonight, at least, he was going to do everything in his power to erase the shadow of fear from her eyes.

Anything else they might do was up to her.

Nina followed Coco through the front door, then jumped when Teague shut it behind them with a thump. Her nerves were shot, and she needed to settle down. If she were home alone, she'd go lie in a hot bath with a cup of chamomile tea to relax. Or maybe a double vodka cranberry. Of course if she were home alone, she'd be a complete basket case by morning.

When Teague settled his hands on her shoulders and kneaded tense muscles with his thumbs, she nearly moaned.

His breath stirred the hair above her ear. "You're perfectly safe, so relax."

"I know, but I can't stay here every night any more than I can move in with Paige or Leah." Her blood pressure spiked just thinking about the creep slinking back to search through her car. "What the hell am I supposed to do?"

"You're going to report what we suspect to the cops in the morning. Unless you want to call them now?"

"Why bother? The person responsible is obviously long gone."

"Fine. Then you'll call a home protection company and have their technician come out to secure your house. Until a system is installed, you'll bunk here or with one of your friends."

His voice was so calm she could almost believe the solution was as simple as he made it sound. "You think that'll eliminate my problem?"

He delved a hand into the hair at the back of her neck to massage away the tension. "I do. And if the cops are put on notice, maybe they can catch this guy if he does come snooping around again."

"That would be ideal." She hung her head and let her overnight bag drop to the floor with a thud. "God, that feels good."

"I'm a whiz at back rubs." His voice was a deep rumble as he found pressure points she hadn't known existed. "It's nearly eleven. Why don't you go get ready for bed, and then I'll put you to sleep with a knockout massage."

"Even better than a hot bath. Thanks, Teague. I owe you."

"No, you don't." He stepped back and bent to pick up her bag. "Come on upstairs. I'm afraid I don't have a bed set up in the spare room yet, but you can sleep in Keely's room."

Obviously, he wasn't making any assumptions. She followed him up the staircase and down the hall, their footsteps muffled by a runner with big pink cabbage roses.

He glanced over his shoulder. "Don't judge. I'll rip that thing out when I refinish all the floors. But the kitchen is my first big project."

She couldn't hold back a grin. "I'm not judging, although, as your neighbor who has to look at this place, my hope is you'll repaint the exterior of the house sometime soon."

"You have something against cotton candy pink?" He paused outside the door to a room furnished in white furniture with a purple canopy over the single bed. "Keely's décor might make you a little nauseous if you aren't fond of pastels."

"No, I like lavender. I actually like pink, too, but for a whole house . . ."

He patted her shoulder. "My eventual plan is blue-gray with a dark cream trim. Does that meet with your approval?"

"Definitely." She also appreciated his effort to normalize the situation and make her feel less awkward.

"The bathroom is just across the hall. Make yourself at home."

"Thanks." Taking her bag from him, she entered a room outfitted with a pedestal sink and a toilet with an overhead tank. "Hey, cool."

"Yeah, the fixtures are so old they're back in style." He backed away. "Yell if you need anything."

With a nod, Nina shut the door and leaned against it. Teague was being a complete gentleman. She wasn't sure if she was happy about that or not since she'd kind of hoped he'd make a move. A sigh slipped out. She was a woman with a mind of her own. If she wanted to start something, all she had to do was say so. She was pretty certain he wasn't going to turn her down.

Nina washed her face and brushed her teeth, then changed into a sleepshirt with Eeyore on the front. Nothing sexy about that. She regarded herself in the mirror and bit her lip. Still, she was glad she'd shaved her legs that morning . . . Flipping off the light, she left the room and only hesitated a moment before letting her feet guide her toward the drone of a voice at the end of the hall. Teague's bedroom door stood open, and the TV above the dresser was turned to a news station.

He glanced over and stared at her for a long moment. Heat flared in his eyes before he pressed the remote to turn off the TV. "Are you ready for that back rub?"

She smiled. "Is that what we're going to call it?"

Wearing nothing but a pair of athletic shorts, he levered off the navy comforter covering the bed. His chest was bare, the muscles clearly defined in the lamplight. The man was beautiful. More importantly, he was kind and sensitive to her feelings. The total package was impossible to resist.

"I don't expect anything from you, Nina. That's not why I offered you a place to crash for the night."

"I know. It's because you haven't pushed that I'm willing to take a risk. Unless you aren't interested." She winced at the vulnerability in her voice. Talk about putting herself out there.

"Jesus, of course I'm interested. You take my breath away." He touched her cheek before dropping his hand to the curve of her neck. "I realize things between us could get a little complicated, but—"

"We'll take it one day at a time. I don't expect a commitment to anything more than tonight." She stepped even closer, ran her fingers across the warm, taut skin of his chest, and smiled when he sucked in a ragged breath. "We've both experienced pain and loss and have every reason to be cautious. But there's nothing wrong with taking comfort and pleasure from each other, is there? Not when respect and genuine liking goes along with it."

"Not in the least." He cupped her chin and bent to kiss her, slowly. Thoroughly. "And I do like you. A lot. Besides finding you incredibly hot, I appreciate your subtle wit. Basically, you're one terrific lady."

"Even if what I'm willing to do isn't the least bit lady-like?"

"That kind of comment is exactly what I'm talking about." He kissed her again, his teeth nipping at her lower lip in a way that turned her bones to liquid. "So much hotter than a blatant come-on."

She clung to his forearms to stay upright. "In that case, I'm glad I didn't wear a lace teddy. Nothing says subtle like a sad donkey."

"See, you make me laugh. Now, about that back rub . . ."

She pressed her face against the pulse beating in his neck. "As long as you don't put me to sleep."

"I won't." Pulling away, he flipped back the comforter, then scooped her up in his arms to lay her on the cool sheets. "Roll over onto your stomach."

Nina didn't have to be told twice. Burrowing her cheek into the pillow, she breathed in the scent of Teague. The man smelled almost as sexy as he looked, something earthy, like a walk in the woods. When he straddled her hips, she melted completely.

Hands kneaded the muscles along her spine through soft cotton while something hard pressed against her behind. When he tugged the T-shirt upward, she let out a low moan as those strong fingers touched bare skin.

He drew in a sharp breath. "No underwear?"

"Not subtle enough?" Her voice was muffled as he maneuvered the shirt over her head.

"I'm not complaining, although this massage might not last as long as I'd planned."

She didn't answer, just lay against the sheet in a limp sprawl as he worked all the tension out of her. Eyes closed, she was lost in a world of pleasure unlike anything she'd ever experienced. When he moved off her for a moment, she mumbled a protest, but when he returned there was nothing at all between them. Covering her completely with his naked, warm body, he braced his weight on his elbows and kissed the back of her neck while he settled intimately against her.

"Are you sure?" His voice was hoarse when he spoke.

"Yes." With the insistent prodding at her moist center, she was anything but sleepy. Her insides clenched in anticipation.

"Protection?"

"I've got it covered already, since I assume we're both healthy?" She squirmed to roll over beneath him and wrapped her arms around his neck when he nodded. "Then we're good. So good, I just might die."

He kissed her and kept kissing her as he sank inside her and held her close. She kissed him back, crazy with need to take everything he had to offer and give more in return. They moved together, skin slick with moisture as their breathing increased in tempo.

Nina was lost in a world of pleasure so profound she couldn't hold on. With a cry, she let herself fly.

Chapter Ten

A jarring noise intruded on his consciousness, shatter-ing a dream he struggled to hold on to. Losing the battle, Teague woke slowly, cocooned in warmth and wrapped up in a woman. Her smooth knee rested on his thigh, while a soft arm was draped across his chest, and one bare breast pressed into his side. He was afraid to move, afraid to open his eyes, certain he was still lost in a fantasy. It wasn't until the cell on the bedside table rang again that he came fully to his senses.

Not a dream. Nina. When the phone rang a third time, he reached across her to grab it. He couldn't ignore a po-tential work emergency, even if it was his day off. Glanc-ing at the display, he frowned. Not the fire captain. Doreen.

Had something happened to Keely? His heart skipped a beat as he answered. "Hello."

"Hi, Daddy. Guess where I am?"

Nothing wrong. Just his daughter calling to check in. He slumped against the pillows as a roar sounded in the background.

He smiled. "Hi, Keels. Where are you? In an erupting

volcano? Being eaten alive by a dinosaur? I think I heard the ground shake."

"No, silly. That was a jet taking off. They're really loud. We're waiting to get on our plane, and it's taking forever."

Nina lifted her head off his shoulder, blinked, and smiled.

He tightened his arm around her. "That's probably because your grandparents made sure you got to the airport early. Are you having fun with your cousin?"

"Yes. Hallie got her ears pierced. Can I get mine done? Pretty please?"

"We'll talk about it after you get home."

A loudspeaker blared, cutting off Keely's response. "I have to go now. They just told us to line up. I can't wait to get on the plane."

He smiled at her excitement as he stroked Nina's back. "Have fun on your flight and mind your grandma and grandpa. Okay, Keely?"

"I will. Bye, Daddy. I love you."

"I love you, too." When the phone went dead, he closed his eyes.

"I take it your daughter is about to board her plane."

He nodded and opened his eyes to stare into bright green ones. Nina propped her chin on the hand resting atop his chest and met his gaze as her knee burrowed farther between his thighs. His whole body tightened as the blood left his head to rush south.

"Yes. They have an early flight this morning." He cleared the roughness from his throat.

"Not so early. It's nearly eight now. We should probably get up."

"Or we could . . ." When she brought her knee slowly upward, his eyes crossed, and he forgot what he was saying.

She gave him a teasing smile. "Go take a shower?"

An image of Nina naked beneath a spray of water, soap bubbles sliding down her skin, filled his mind. "Yeah, we could do that." He sat up, then gathered her into his arms and stood. Carrying her high against his chest, he strode across the floor to the connecting bathroom.

She clung to his neck and laughed out loud. "Seriously?"

"You bet." He opened the shower door. "Want to turn on the water? It takes a while to warm up."

With a nod, she twisted the knob. "What shall we do while we wait?"

"I have a few ideas." He shifted her until she could wrap her legs around his waist, then kissed her, taking his time and enjoying the fact that she was as breathless as he was when he finally released her. He rested his forehead against hers. "This is the best morning I've had in a long, long time."

"Yeah, but I think we can make it even better. Is that water hot?"

He leaned sideways and stuck a hand under the spray to check the temperature. "Yep."

She slid down him and landed on her toes, then took his hand. "Let's go clean up."

Steam filled the room as he ran a bar of soap across her curves and worked up a lather. She returned the favor, soaping his chest and letting her fingers trail lower . . . By the time he finally pressed her back against the tile and slipped inside her, his legs were so shaky he could barely stand upright. Holding tight to each other, they shuddered and shook and clung beneath the torrent until the water grew tepid.

"We need to get out of here." His lips brushed her ear.

"I don't think I can move." She pressed her face to the pulse beating at his neck. "You sapped all my energy."

"Try, because I'm too weak to carry you."

"Wimp."

They stumbled out of the shower and wrapped up in towels. After they'd dried off and dressed, Teague was faint with hunger.

"I need food. How does bacon and eggs sound?"

"Greasy." Nina leaned against the counter with her mascara brush poised an inch from her nose. "I'll go home and make a smoothie. I'm not a big breakfast eater."

He paused with a hand on the doorframe. "Serious? You should always eat a solid morning meal."

"Thanks, Mom."

"Funny. I'll go make coffee while you finish up in here."

"Coffee I can get behind. I'll be down in a minute."

He couldn't quit smiling as he filled the pot with water and ground coffee beans to dump in the filter. Maybe getting involved with Nina wasn't such a bad idea after all. They seemed to be getting along pretty damn well.

When Coco strolled into the room and barked sharply, he followed the dog to the laundry room to feed her. As he scooped kibble into the plastic bowl, his practical side protested. *Of course you're getting along, idiot. You've spent over half your alone time in bed.*

He ignored the voice of reason as he headed back to the kitchen, determined to enjoy a morning spent drinking coffee with a beautiful woman who was also funny and smart and kind. They had a full week to test their relationship without worrying about how it might affect Keely. By the time his daughter returned, maybe he and Nina would both know if what they'd started stood a chance outside the bedroom.

"Why the pensive face? Worried about what bacon and eggs might do to your cholesterol levels?"

Glancing up, he smiled as Nina walked straight to the coffeepot and stared at it, obviously willing the machine to spit out the last of the fragrant brew perfuming the air. Her long legs clad in her customary shorts weakened his knees. He gripped the counter for support, just thinking about how she'd wrapped them around his waist.

"Bacon won't kill me. A few more nights like the last one might give me a heart attack, though."

She pulled two mugs from the glass-fronted cupboard before turning to face him. "Oh, I think your heart can handle it. I can vouch for your amazing stamina."

He grinned as she filled the cups. "I was just trying to keep up with you." After adding milk to the mug she offered him, he took a sip. "So, what're your plans for the day?"

She stirred honey into her coffee. "First, I'll talk to the police and a security company, and then I need to spend some time working. What about you?"

"The kitchen remodel begins today. Since the cabinets are solid wood under all that battered paint, I'm going to refinish them to save some money. I'm afraid I blew my budget ordering granite countertops to replace the discolored Formica."

She eyed him over the top of her cup. "A day spent sanding cabinets. Sounds fun."

"You aren't tempted to hang around and help me?"

"Not in the least." She took another swallow. "In fact, I should take off. I've got a lot to . . . damn."

"What?"

"My battery is dead. I can't go anywhere."

"Right. I have jumper cables in the shed. Let's go get

your car started. You can let it run in the driveway until you're ready to leave."

She took a step closer and stood on her toes to drop a quick kiss on his lips. "Thanks. You're a lifesaver."

Teague put a hand on her back to guide her toward the entry as Coco's nails clicked across the wooden floor ahead of them. "The dog can run around outside while we're taking care of your car problem. She's going to be lost without Keely here for company."

Nina picked up the overnight bag she'd left by the door. "I don't doubt it. They seem to be inseparable."

He held the screen open and shivered as he crossed the porch behind her. Fog hung in the trees, casting the yard in gloom as they walked side by side toward the shed. "I hope this burns off."

She rubbed her arms as goose bumps pebbled her skin. "Yeah, it's damp and chilly. Not a great combo. I was hoping to paint down at the beach today."

"You don't want to paint fog?" He pulled open the door and lifted the cables off a shelf.

"I might have to if I don't want to fall behind schedule. I was hoping to wrap up one of my projects today, but starting a new one isn't out of the question. I guess I'd better change into something warmer first."

"If you want to go get your car keys, I'll drive my truck over."

"Thanks."

Fifteen minutes later Nina's engine was running as he stood beside her in the driveway. Reaching out, he stroked a wisp of hair off her cheek. "So, is this going to be awkward, living so close to each other? Should I formally call to ask you out in a couple of days, or can I just drop by when I'm sick of sanding?"

"I'm not big on playing games. If you want to do something this evening, I'm free."

"I'd like that. I guess I'll see you later, then."

She reached up to kiss him, and her lips clung just long enough to make him want a whole lot more. Before he could deepen the contact, she slipped away.

"Have a great day, Teague."

As she walked across the yard, hips swaying in a way that made his heart beat a little faster, he couldn't help thinking his day would be a whole lot better if they were spending it together.

Nina tried to ignore the chill creeping down her spine and failed. For late May, it was damn cold out. The fog hadn't cleared and didn't look like it would break up anytime soon. Wrapped in an old wool jacket as gray as the day, she huddled in front of her easel in the shelter of some rocks near the base of the cliff. The tide had just turned, and she worked hard to capture the rush of the water as it was sucked out to sea. In the distance, the three Sirens were shrouded in mist, and an eerie atmosphere pervaded the deserted beach.

Not so deserted after all. Two figures appeared out of the fog, walking along the damp sand. One was bundled in a padded jacket with a scarf draped over her head and wrapped around her shoulders. Judging by the slow deliberateness of her stride, an older woman. Head down, she left her companion, the young blond girl Nina had seen on the beach twice before, to drop heavily onto a large chunk of driftwood a little farther down the beach. The girl stood nearby at the water's edge, hair flying in the breeze off the ocean. Every now and then she turned to glance toward the woman, who sat with her back to the cliffs. A mixture of angst, sadness, and uncertainty was reflected in the child's eyes.

Drawing in a breath, Nina chose a different brush and squeezed new paints onto her palette. Following an urgent need to capture all that raw emotion, she painted quickly with deft strokes. If she could duplicate the dejection on the girl's face before the child left the beach, she could fill in other details later. The lone figure was what the picture had been missing, a symbol of melancholy in the fog-shrouded landscape that added a human touch and encapsulated the mood of the piece.

By the time the woman stood and called to the girl, Nina had what she needed. All the despondency disappeared from her subject's eyes in a flash to be replaced by a hint of defiant spirit as the girl waited until the last second to run away from an incoming rogue wave.

Laying down her brush, Nina shivered as the two walked away. She'd been tempted to make her presence known, to ask if the child was all right. The spark of mettle she'd shown when confronted by the wave reassured her. The girl was a fighter and wouldn't let whatever was bothering her keep her down.

Still, she'd perfectly portrayed that moment of vulnerability. Nina wasn't certain when she'd ever been so pleased with her work. Ignoring the cold chilling her to the bone, she painted the thin figure from memory, adding a pair of too-short jeans and a blue windbreaker. Her fingers were nearly too stiff to move before she stopped, satisfied with every detail of the painting.

Pulling back her coat sleeve to glance at her watch, she let out a yelp. No wonder she was practically frozen to her stool. She hadn't moved in hours. After packing up her paints, she made two trips down the beach, then up steep steps cut into the cliff to haul all her gear to the car. By the time she'd carefully placed the still-wet painting safely in the back, she was considerably warmer.

After sliding onto the driver's seat, she paused with the key in the ignition to stare out over the endless sea. The fog was beginning to clear, only to be replaced by storm clouds hanging low in the turbulent sky. A crack of lightning slashed through the darkness, and thunder echoed. A not-so-subtle reminder that everything could change in an instant.

For once, she wasn't going home to an empty house. Teague would be—if not exactly waiting for her to walk through the door—only a few yards away. This morning, she'd tried to play it cool, tried not to pressure him with assumptions, and had given him plenty of space. Her only major fights with Keith had been over what he termed her tendency to make unreasonable demands on his time. Her lips firmed as she started the engine and pulled out onto the road. She wouldn't make the same mistake twice.

But Teague had indicated he wanted to see her tonight. Humming to an old Billy Joel hit on the radio, she cruised toward town as a few raindrops spattered against the windshield. She'd cook dinner for him, and afterward— well, afterward could take care of itself. Flipping on her blinker, she turned into the lot in front of the grocery store and parked. After grabbing her cloth tote bags off the passenger seat floor, she stepped out and slammed the door.

"Nina."

Turning, she smiled and waved as Paige hurried in her direction. "What are you doing home? I thought you were at an out-of-town auction."

Her friend shifted the bag of groceries she carried and tucked a strand of blond hair that had escaped from beneath the hood of her jacket behind one ear. "I was, but they canceled the second event I planned to attend. If you still want to go to Portland, we can do it tomorrow. I called your cell earlier, but you didn't answer."

"I was working and forgot to check my messages. Anyway, I went shopping yesterday, so we're all good for the bachelorette party. I know we talked about going with a sixties theme, so I bought everything in psychedelic colors."

"Cool. We need to let everyone know so they can dress appropriately. Were you able to fit all the art supplies in your car?"

"Actually, I went with Teague. He had to take his daughter to the airport, so we drove his truck."

"Oh, really?" Paige's brows shot up. "How'd his wife feel about your road trip with her husband?"

Leaning back against the car door, Nina crossed her arms over her chest as a misty rain fell. "Didn't I tell you? Turns out I was mistaken, and he's a widower. His wife died a couple of years ago in a drive-by shooting."

"Oh, my God. How horrible."

"Yeah. It sucks that we have tragedy in common, but it sort of drew us together. That and the fact he's extremely hot."

"So, are you dating him?"

"Sort of." Nina stared at the ground. "We're sleeping together, if that counts."

Paige gripped her arm. "That's great. At least it is as long as he's treating you right. When do Leah and I get to meet him? I assume if she had already, I would have heard about it by now."

Nina smiled. "This is pretty new, as in our friendship escalated quickly into something more last night after we got home. And since he has a young daughter to consider, it may get a little complicated. Right now, we're just getting to know each other better."

"You said his daughter—"

"Keely. She's six."

Paige didn't even pause to take a breath. "Is out of town. I hope he's not just having a fling while—"

"No, of course not. Teague's a really nice guy. Honestly. We weren't planning to start anything, but after my stalker struck again—"

"Stalker! What the heck are you talking about?" She set down the bag of groceries. "What stalker?"

"Those are going to get wet. It's starting to drizzle."

"I don't care. Tell me what happened."

"Some creep broke into my house and pawed through my clothes last week. Nothing was stolen, and I got my window fixed afterward."

"Did you report it?"

Nina nodded. "Yeah, I talked to Chris Long. He thought it was a random act, maybe someone looking for cash or drugs. Then, after Teague and I got back last night, I discovered someone had searched my car. No damage other than a dead battery since the rear door wasn't shut properly."

"That's seriously scary. Jesus, Nina."

"Yeah, it is." She clenched and unclenched her fists at her sides. "I was freaked out, so I spent the night at Teague's. At first, he was a perfect gentleman, but I sort of instigated a little more."

A half-smile curved Paige's lips. "Don't distract me from the main point. How do you know this vandal is a stalker?"

"Just a guess. I did a magazine interview that published a couple of weeks ago. Teague came up with the idea some psycho saw it and became obsessed with me, since all he's actually done is touch my things."

"And what do the police think?"

"Chris agreed it's a possibility. They're going to schedule frequent drive-bys in my neighborhood. I also called a security company. After I told them about the break-ins, they promised to have a system installed and functional by tomorrow."

"That's good, at least. Why didn't you call me? You could have stayed at my place."

"It was late, and Teague volunteered to keep me safe. I was good with having a big strong man around. Does that make me sound pathetic?"

Paige grinned. "No, since I would have done exactly what you did. But if you need a place to sleep tonight, you're welcome to stay with me. I don't want you alone in your house until they install that security system."

"I'm too big a chicken to stay home by myself, but I suspect I'll have company."

"Good for you." Paige stepped over her bag of groceries and gave her a quick hug. "If Teague makes you happy, then I'm a fan."

Nina couldn't hold back a smile. "He does, but it's early days yet. We'll see if what we have is more than just chemistry."

"There's certainly nothing wrong with hot sex."

"No, there isn't."

"Then you go, girl." Paige patted her arm. "If anyone deserves happiness, it's you."

Nina squared her shoulders and nodded. "I guess we'll see what happens, but for now, I plan to enjoy myself."

Chapter Eleven

Frustration simmered as Teague used the chamois to polish every water spot off the bright red finish of the fire truck. Nina was making him crazy. And not in a good way. He couldn't decide if she was only interested in sex, or if she—

"Are you trying to scrub the paint off, O'Dell?"

"Huh?" Teague glanced over at his coworker, who stood with his arms crossed over his chest.

Mateo Torres was probably his closest friend at the firehouse. Also in his mid-thirties, the man had made him feel immediately welcome in the tight-knit group of firefighters.

"If you rub any harder, you'll be down to the undercoat. What's with the scowl?"

"I was thinking about something."

"Nothing pleasant, obviously." Mateo flashed a grin. "I have a proposition for you that might just change your mood. My girlfriend has an old roommate in town. Want to go out with us tonight? Your daughter isn't back from her trip yet, is she?"

"No, Keely doesn't get home from Hawaii for a few more days, but I think I'll have to pass on tonight."

"Dude, I promise Sabrina's friend is a looker, and she's funny. I wouldn't set you up with a dud."

"It isn't that. I'm seeing someone."

"Oh, yeah?" Mateo rocked back on the heels of his boots. "Anyone I know?"

"Maybe. Nina Hutton. We're neighbors."

His jaw dropped open. "Nina? Seriously? Half the men in Siren Cove have tried to date her and been shut down. I'm impressed."

Teague shrugged, feeling like an idiot. "Don't be. Anyway, I'm not sure what we have is going anywhere. She's keeping her distance." *Except in bed.*

"Sabrina and Nina are friends. The woman is . . . I don't know . . . cautious. She's friendly enough, but she doesn't exactly exude warmth."

Teague gripped the chamois a little harder. "Yet every single guy in the vicinity wants to date her, despite the lack of encouragement?"

"Some of the married ones, too." His buddy gave a low laugh. "Christ, I don't have to tell you how gorgeous the woman is."

"No, you don't. Anyway, I'll pass on the double date tonight."

"Not a problem. Sabrina wanted me to ask." He glanced at the big, black watch strapped to his wrist. "Hey, our shift is about over. I'll catch you later."

"Sure." Teague finished drying the truck before heading inside to his locker. He nodded at a couple of the guys coming on duty, but he wasn't in the mood to talk to anyone. Once he'd changed into jeans and a T-shirt, he hurried out to his pickup, determination firming his lips into a tight line. He and Nina needed to have a talk about what exactly she expected from him. Keely would be home in four days, and he wanted to be clear on where they stood.

When he pulled into the driveway a few minutes later, Nina's car wasn't parked in its usual spot. True, they hadn't technically made plans for the evening. But since they'd spent the last five nights together, he'd just assumed . . .

As he stepped out of his truck, a movement in the trees edging the street caught his attention. When a figure clad in a dark jacket turned and hurried away, he ran a few yards in pursuit but stopped when Nina's Mini rounded the bend. He waited while she parked and got out.

"Hey, you beat me home. How was your day?"

"Okay." He frowned. "Did you see that guy bolting out of here when you drove up?"

"What guy?" She reached into the car to pull out her box of paints.

Teague's frown deepened. "You must have seen him. He had on a dark jacket with a hood. I didn't have a clear view."

"That was a woman, not a man. She had on a long denim skirt."

"Oh. That's a relief. I only caught a glimpse of the person from behind." He walked around to the other side of the car to maneuver her easel out of the passenger seat. "Since we don't get much foot traffic down at our end of the street, I thought it might have been your stalker retuning to, well, stalk."

"Not unless a woman is creeping on me instead of a man. I didn't see her face since her head was turned, but she seemed vaguely familiar."

"Probably just someone from the neighborhood out for a stroll. Toss me your keys and I'll take this upstairs for you while you get the rest of your stuff."

She reached in her pocket and threw him the key ring.

"Thanks. Don't forget to punch in the security code after you unlock the door."

"I won't." A few minutes later, he made a return trip to carry in the canvas she'd been working on, which was stretched across a four-foot frame. He studied the bursts of greens and blues in the seascape before following her up the steps to the porch. "This is really beautiful. Are you finished with it?"

"Yes. I finally had a sunny day to work, which is what I needed to get the colors just right. That one's been an ongoing project for a while now."

"Worth the effort. It would look perfect hanging over my couch." He turned sideways to ease through the door. "How much?"

"Since I like you just a little, I'll cut you a deal and let it go for five grand."

He nearly choked. "Apparently original art isn't in my budget."

"I'm kidding, Teague." Her tone grew serious. "If you like it, it's yours. But I'll frame it for you first."

"I can't let you give me something that valuable. I had no idea . . ." He stopped speaking as he reached her studio. "Where do you want me to put this?"

"On the long table in the back. What, you thought I was just a hack?"

"No, of course not, but . . ." He set down the canvas and turned. "I guess I didn't realize how in demand your work is."

Nina set the stool she carried next to the easel. "I'll paint more than a dozen pictures for the art fair in July so I have a decent selection, but I'll be lucky to sell two or three of them. Yes, I make good money off each purchase, but to say my paintings are in high demand is a stretch." She shrugged. "Maybe one of these days. I used to be thrilled when I sold a single painting at one of these events."

"Well, I'm impressed."

She headed toward the door. "And I'm in awe, knowing you risk your life to pull people from burning buildings. Admiring each other's strengths is a good thing, right?"

"I suppose so." He followed her down the stairs and into the kitchen.

She paused with her hand on the refrigerator door. "What do you want to do for dinner? Unless you have something else going on? If so, I can—"

"I don't have plans. If a work commitment had come up, I would have let you know." He took her by the arm and led her to one of the barstools at the counter. "Can we talk? Something has been bothering me."

"I've been trying not to pressure you. I know our relationship is new, and we're both figuring out how it'll work. Maybe we've been spending too much time together. I understand if you need more space."

His heart sank as she pulled away from him. "Is that how you feel? You want space?" He leaned back against the counter. "I'm beginning to think the only time you expect to spend with me is in bed. I'm not sure I like that a whole lot."

"What?" She practically toppled off the stool in her haste to get to her feet. "What the hell are you talking about?"

"We don't go out together, not since our trip to Portland, though I've suggested it a couple of times. We eat, maybe make out on the couch, and then head upstairs. You take off in the morning like you can't wait to escape. It's starting to bug me."

"Oh. My. God!" She clenched her fists at her sides. "You're kidding, right?"

With an effort, he managed to keep his cool. "Maybe some guys would be thrilled, but sex isn't the only thing I want from a woman."

She closed her eyes, and he was pretty sure she was counting beneath her breath. Finally she opened them again. Anger simmered in their depths.

"I was trying to be considerate of your time. We live next door to each other. I didn't want you to feel trapped."

"I like hanging out with you, Nina. If I wasn't comfortable with how often we're together, I would have said something."

"I was hoping to avoid that by not pressuring you to begin with."

The hint of pain in her voice tore down all his defenses. Stepping closer, he slid an arm around her waist and left it there even when she stiffened. "Let's go sit down and discuss this. I feel like we've been at cross purposes, and I'd like to know why."

After a brief moment, she nodded and let him guide her into the living room. He pulled her down with him onto the couch and turned to face her.

"Let's be clear about this. I want to spend time with you. I haven't been looking for an out, and I don't need you to run off every morning. The fact that you think I'm an asshole who expects so little from you is fairly insulting."

"I don't think that at all." She leaned back against the cushions, her thigh pressed against his, and cleared her throat. "Keith used to complain about me clinging. I didn't want to get off on the wrong foot with you."

His mouth fell open. After a second, he closed it. "You

don't cling. I don't know if I've *ever* met a more independent woman who totally has her life together."

"Maybe I've changed. Toughened up. I certainly didn't intend to make you feel like a prime piece of meat."

He snorted and choked on a laugh. "I wouldn't go that far." Taking her hand, he squeezed her fingers. "I don't want you to think I'm bitching about spending time in bed with you because I'm not. But once Keely gets home, we're going to have to back off a little on that front. I guess I was worried we wouldn't have anything in common left between us."

"My feelings are engaged and have been from the start. I'm not used to caring so much, which is probably why I went overboard in an effort not to screw things up. Because you matter to me."

Relief dispelled the knot of anxiety that had tightened in his chest. "I can't imagine not spending time with you. I know this is still new, but I want to give what we have together a real chance to grow."

Nina slid her hand behind his neck and leaned over to kiss him. "I'd like that, too." She pulled back a few inches. "Since I'm totally not in the mood to cook, do you want to go out tonight? Oh, and for the record, the only reason I preferred to stay in when you asked is because I've been beat. Expending so much creative energy drains a person."

"I get that, but I still owe you a real date. I'll go take a shower and . . . crap!"

She reared back. "What?"

"I forgot about Coco. Damn." He levered off the couch. "I'd better go check on her. Thank God I put in that new doggy door or I'd have a real mess to deal with. I'm just surprised she didn't bark when I came home."

"Probably busy digging another hole in your backyard. I'll change and be ready to go whenever you are. Stop by after you've dealt with the dog and taken a shower."

"Right." He tugged her to her feet and dropped a kiss on her lips. "I'm glad we cleared up any misunderstanding. Communication is always key."

"You're right about that. I shouldn't have made assumptions. You're not like . . ." She pressed her lips together. "Never mind. Go take care of Coco."

"Okay, I'll see you in a half hour or so." As Teague headed across the street, he wondered about what she hadn't said. *I'm not like her dead fiancé? Is that a positive or a negative?* Time would tell.

He unlocked the door and walked inside. "Coco, where the heck are you?" When there wasn't so much as a yip in response, worry shot through him. Long strides took him straight past the kitchen to the door at the end of the hallway leading to the backyard. When he gave the newly installed doggy door a push, it swung freely.

He released the dead bolt to open the door and stepped out into the fenced yard. The dog was nowhere in sight.

"Coco." He yelled a little louder. "Coco!"

A breeze stirred the branches of the big pine standing in the back corner of the lot. Nothing else moved.

"Well, shit. How the hell did she get out?" He circled the fence line, searching for a hole beneath it. When he reached the gate that opened to the forest behind his property, he paused. "Damn it."

The gate was pushed shut, but the latch wasn't fastened. When he gave the wood panel a shove, the gate swung open. Coco could be anywhere in the woods, completely lost. If he didn't find the dog, he wouldn't be able to face his daughter.

"Coco, here, girl. Coco. Want a treat?"

"Teague?"

"I'm in the back. Follow the fence," he shouted.

A few seconds later, Nina rounded the northeast corner and waved. "I forgot something in my car and heard you yelling. What's wrong?"

"Coco got out somehow. I don't have a clue where she went."

"That's not good. Did you leave the gate open?"

"I don't think so. The latch is a little stiff, so maybe it didn't shut all the way. If Coco pushed on the gate, it might have swung open."

"She's so little. You think she has the strength?"

"I don't know how else she would have gotten out. I can't imagine anyone came back here and took her. She's not show dog quality, by any means."

Nina turned to scan the thick forest, dense with fir trees, huckleberry bushes, manzanita, and ferns. "She might not have gone too far. Let's start looking."

They split up and pushed through the woods, shouting and calling with no luck. When his phone rang twenty minutes later, Teague pulled it out of his pocket and frowned at the unfamiliar number before answering.

"Hello."

"Do you own a little cream and tan dog named Coco?" A woman's voice spoke in a distracted tone before growing muffled. "Kids, leave her alone." A moment later, the connection sharpened. "I called the number on her tag."

"You found her?" Relief nearly weakened his knees. "That's great. I've been looking for her."

"She showed up in my yard a while ago and started digging in my flowers. When I tried to grab her, she took off but came back later. This time I got a hold of her. She's muddy but seems fine."

"Thank you so much. I'll come get her if you'll give me your address."

"I'm at 320 Spruce Lane."

"I'll be right over." He hung up, stuffed the phone in his pocket, and cupped his hands around his mouth. "Nina, I found her!" His shout echoed through the woods and was followed by a faint reply. By the time he reached the back fence, Nina was waiting for him.

"Where's Coco?"

"Someone over on Spruce found her and called the number on her ID tag."

"That's great." She wrapped an arm around his waist and hugged him as he pushed the gate open. "What a relief."

"Yeah. I was worried. I guess I'd better fix that latch to make sure it hooks properly."

"I still can't believe Coco pushed open such a heavy gate. She can't weigh ten pounds."

"Eight, but nothing else makes any sense."

Nina smiled up at him. "I guess how she got out doesn't matter as long as it doesn't happen again. She's safe."

"Thank God. Keely would have been devastated." He hugged her a little tighter to his side. "Who am I kidding? I love that little fur ball, too."

"You have a kind heart." She pressed a kiss to his cheek. "I like that about you. Among other things. Go get your dog."

Relief lightened his mood as he hurried out to his truck, but the weight lifted from his spirits wasn't all about finding Coco. Nina's feelings toward him mattered.

Maybe more than they should.

Chapter Twelve

Nina stood beside Paige in front of the trifold mirror in All Dressed Up, wearing her bridesmaid dress. The shimmering aqua material seemed to float above her knees. "Wow. We look amazing."

"I know, right? The fact that I can breathe makes giving up ice cream for the last two weeks totally worthwhile."

"Absolutely stunning." Leah circled them slowly before glancing over at the woman who'd done the alterations. "They're perfect, Marge. You did a wonderful job."

The older woman nodded and smiled. "Thank you. Those dresses are so beautiful, working with them was a pleasure." She glanced toward the shop owner. "If you don't need anything else this afternoon, I have an appointment to go to."

"If Leah's happy, then we're all set." Regan Patterson stepped out from behind the counter to face the three women. "Thanks, Marge. Oh, don't forget those two skirts you need to hem. They're in the back."

"I won't."

Confidence and style oozed from the tall brunette. "You two rock those dresses. I'm sorry I wasn't here the first time you tried them on."

"We didn't look this spectacular before the alterations." Paige twirled in a circle. "I feel like a princess."

Leah grinned. "As long as you don't outshine me at the wedding, we're all good."

Nina squeezed her friend's arm. "There's not a chance of that happening. I've seen you in your wedding dress. Ryan may never recover from your gorgeousness."

"Let's hope not. Why don't you two go change while I settle up with Regan."

Paige frowned. "No way. We can pay for our own dresses."

"Nope. Not happening. We've already had this conversation. Anyway, she's giving me the friends-and-family deal."

Regan straightened the skirt on a nearby manikin. "Of course I am, since we've known each other practically forever."

"See?" Leah gave both her bridesmaids a push. "Go get dressed."

"Arguing with her is pointless." Nina headed toward the rear of the shop and smiled as the seamstress passed them on her way out. "We'll find another way to chip in our share."

"Fine. Hey, Quentin is in town for the weekend. We're having dinner at the Poseidon Grill tonight if you want to join us. Leah and Ryan are coming."

Nina entered the curtained cubicle and lowered the zipper on her dress to step out of it. "Sure. Can I bring a date?"

"I assume you're talking about Teague?" Paige popped

her head around the divider. "I wish you would. I'm dying to meet him."

"We were just going to hang out tonight, but this will be fun. His daughter flies home from her vacation with her grandparents tomorrow."

"Is that going to put a crimp in your relationship?"

"I don't think so." Nina pulled on her T-shirt, then reached for her shorts. "We still intend to see each other on a regular basis."

"I'm glad." Paige disappeared into her own dressing room. "You sound happy."

"I am." Nina couldn't remember the last time she'd felt so . . . appreciated. The word *loved* hovered at the edge of her thoughts, but she pushed it away. *Too soon.* She wasn't ready to let herself be that vulnerable. Not yet.

"Hello." Paige pushed back the curtain and snapped her fingers.

"Huh?"

"I asked if you're ready to go. What were you thinking about?"

"Nothing. Yeah, I'm ready. Wait, where's my purse?"

"Here." Paige bent to pick it up off the floor and handed it to her. "I guess we should bag up these dresses."

"I'll take care of it." Regan hurried toward them with Leah following. "By the way, I got the bachelorette party invitation in the mail. Sounds like fun."

"Oh, it will be." After the shop owner slipped her dress into its bag, Nina took the hanger from her. "I sure hope you can come."

"I wouldn't miss it." Regan handed the second dress to Paige. "There, all set." She reached over to give Leah a hug. "I'll see you at the party next week."

"Thanks for everything, Regan."

"You bet."

Nina followed her friends out of the shop with the dress bag carefully draped over her arm and stopped beside her car. "Do either of you need a lift?"

Leah pointed to her old pink cruiser. "I rode my bike."

"I'm good, too. It's only a short walk back to my store." Paige gave Leah a pointed look. "I'll see you both tonight. Seven o'clock sharp."

"I'll try not to be late." Leah laid a hand on Nina's arm as Paige hurried away, her heels clicking on the sidewalk. "Are you going to bring Teague to dinner tonight?"

"Yep. I figured it's about time I introduced him to the most important people in my life."

"Great. We can grill him like the fish special to make sure he's good enough for you."

"Aren't you hilarious? Don't even think about it."

"I'll try to control myself." Leah gave her a quick hug. "I'll see you tonight."

After her friend bunched up her long skirt, slung her leg over the bar of her bike, and pedaled away, Nina unlocked her car and laid her dress across the passenger seat, then walked around to the driver's side. A glance at her watch told her she still had plenty of time for a run before Teague got home from work.

"Damn. I forgot to tell—" Turning abruptly, she slammed into a solid figure.

A shrill squeal echoed as the woman went down with a hard thump, and Nina landed on top of her.

"Oh, my goodness. Miss Lola, are you hurt?" Nina untangled herself from the older woman and scrambled to her feet. "Let me help you up."

"Oooh, I'm going to be black and blue all over." Taking Nina's extended hand, she struggled up off the pavement with a grunt. "Look what I did. I dropped all my bags."

"I'll get them for you."

"Thank you. This was completely my fault. I came hurrying over to speak to you before you drove away and wasn't expecting you to do an about-face and slam into me."

"Sorry. I'd just remembered something I forgot to tell Regan." After scooping up the three shopping bags, she held them while Lola brushed dirt off her backside.

"Ouch! Can bruises form this fast? I guess it's a good thing I have plenty of padding." She broke off and glanced over when a motorcycle slowed to stop beside them. "Well, hello, Stella. I haven't seen you at our book club lately."

Keely's sitter cut the engine and lifted the visor on her helmet. "I was down the street when I saw you two collide. Is everyone okay?"

"I'm fine. Lola took the brunt of the fall," Nina answered.

"I'm a tough old broad. I'll survive."

"I certainly hope so." Nina turned to smile at Stella. "Keely gets home from her trip tomorrow, so I expect I'll see you around the neighborhood a lot more often."

"I imagine so, although her father signed her up for a few summer camps to keep her busy. Not a bad thing since my time is stretched pretty thin right now."

"He did mention something about an outdoor adventure camp." Nina laid a hand on Lola's arm. "If you're certain you're not injured, I need to go talk to Regan for a minute."

"Don't worry about me. Oh, I wanted to tell you how much my granddaughter loves that painting of the robins I hung in her room. She's just tickled with it. Once I get my finances straightened out, I'll be ordering another picture."

"I'm happy to hear that." Nina held out the shopping bags. "If you'd like a ride back to your car, I'll only be in the dress shop for a few minutes."

"No need. I'm parked just up the block."

"Okay then." Nina edged away. "Good to see you again, Stella."

"You, too."

Nina left the two women and hurried back to the shop. The bells over the door jingled as she crossed the threshold.

Regan glanced up from her computer. "Did you forget something?"

"Just to give you an update on the bachelorette party. After we sent out the invitations, Paige and I decided on a sixties theme. I planned to call everyone to give them a heads-up but haven't gotten around to it yet. Since Leah dresses like the original flower child most of the time, we thought it would be fun to harness our inner hippies for the party."

"I like it! What a great idea."

"I'm glad you think so. We can raid thrift stores to find appropriate clothes." When Stella's motorcycle fired up outside, Nina glanced toward the front window. "Geez, I hope Miss Lola isn't too banged up after our collision."

"Lola Copeland?" Regan's eyes narrowed. "That woman is always in here buying clothes for her granddaughter, and between you and me, she's behind on her bill. What happened?"

"We literally ran into each other outside and both landed on the pavement."

"Ouch."

"Yeah. Thankfully, she didn't break anything. Anyway, I just wanted to pass along the party update. One less call to make."

"Sabrina, Kim, and I are going to see that new chick flick tonight. I can let them both know." When the phone on the counter rang, she laid a hand on the receiver. "Unless you'd like to join us?"

"I have plans this evening, but I'd appreciate it if you could pass the word. Thanks."

"No problem." She lifted the receiver. "All Dressed Up, this is Regan."

There was no sign of either Stella or Lola near her car when she left the shop. Pulling the keys from her pocket, she tugged open the door of the Mini.

"My purse!"

Surely she'd had it with her when she left the store the first time. She remembered looking for it in the dressing room . . . which meant she must have dropped it when she fell.

"Crap!" Crouching down, Nina braced a hand to peer beneath her car. Nothing but a soggy piece of newspaper and a grease spot. She pushed to her feet and brushed off her palms.

"If someone stole it, I'm going to scream." Just thinking about the hassle of getting a new driver's license and canceling her credit cards *again* sent her blood pressure soaring. Not to mention her phone was in her purse. "Damn. Damn. Damn."

Sliding into the car, she slammed the door and thumped her fist on the steering wheel. At least no one had taken her dress. When a bulge beneath the bag caught her attention, she lifted the edge. "Oh, my God. I'm such an idiot. Crisis averted."

With a relieved smile, she started the engine. She could still squeeze in a quick run before Teague got home from work. For the first time in years, she was looking forward to sharing a man she cared about with her friends.

It was about damn time.

Teague backed out of the driveway, then glanced over at Nina. "So, Leah is the bride-to-be, and the guy she's marrying is Ryan?"

"That's right, Ryan Alexander. He's the founder of Crossroads. We all went to school together."

He stepped on the brake and turned to stare. "Crossroads, the social media site? Are you kidding?"

"Nope. Ryan is a tech genius, but he's a super nice guy. You'd never know he's filthy rich from the way he acts. You'll like him."

"If you say so." He took his foot off the brake and hit the gas. "And Paige is your other friend who lives here in town?"

Nina nodded. "Paige owns Old Things, the antique shop on the main drag. She lives in the apartment above the store."

"I think I've seen her once or twice in front of the building. Petite blonde?"

Nina grinned. "She's tiny but fierce."

Teague laughed as he turned out of the neighborhood onto the highway. "Kind of like Coco. What did you say her boyfriend's name is?"

"Quentin Radcliff, but he isn't her boyfriend. They've been best friends since our grammar school days. He moved away after fifth grade, but they stayed in touch."

"Sounds like their friendship has lasted longer than

most marriages." Teague gave her a skeptical glance.
"But they aren't sleeping together?"

"If they are, it's the best kept secret in the history of
the world. I'm pretty sure Paige couldn't pull that off, at
least not with me and Leah."

"Maybe he's gay."

Nina laughed out loud. "Definitely not. Quentin dates
a *lot* of women."

Teague turned into the lot next to the Poseidon Grill.
They jolted through a pothole before he parked near a
black Jaguar in the nearly empty lot. "Doesn't look like
the place is very busy."

Nina pointed at the Jag. "That's Quentin's car. I don't
see Leah's or Ryan's, so they must be late." She opened
the car door. "Typical Leah."

Teague joined her near the front bumper and took her
elbow. "Careful of the hole. Are you sure this restaurant
is any good?"

"It used to be, but the owner was arrested last fall along
with a few other upstanding citizens. Long, ugly story.
Anyway, the place has been going downhill ever since.
I'm not sure why Paige chose to come here tonight."

He shrugged. "I can handle one bad dinner as long as it
doesn't make us all sick. Let's go meet your friends."

A girl who looked like she was still in high school
greeted them with a smile as they entered the restaurant.

Nina smiled back. "We're here to meet friends."

"Miss Shephard asked me to be on the lookout for
you." She rounded the edge of the hostess stand. "Right
this way."

They followed the young woman through a spacious
area where only a few other patrons dined to a table near
the bank of windows overlooking the ocean. Nina's
friend Paige and a blond man wearing a sports jacket over

a pair of jeans both stood. Nina hugged each of them before gripping Teague's arm.

"Paige, Quentin, I'd like you to meet Teague O'Dell."

After Teague shook Quentin's hand, Paige gave him a quick hug. "It's about time we met. I was beginning to think you were a figment of Nina's imagination."

He grinned. "No, I'm solid enough."

"So I see." She glanced past him. "Oh, look, Leah and Ryan just arrived."

They all turned at her words. After Teague had been introduced to the newcomers, everyone took their seats and ordered a round of drinks when the cocktail server stopped beside their table. Almost immediately, the three women plunged into a conversation about flower arrangements.

Quentin leaned back in his chair and crossed his arms over his chest. "All those wedding details are enough to drive a person crazy and may possibly be the reason I'm not married."

Ryan laughed. "That's no excuse. All I do is sit back and let Leah take charge. If she needs something, I do it." He nodded toward Nina and Paige as the debate between bowls and vases heated up. "Believe me, she'd rather have their opinions than mine."

"As it should be." Teague tried to wrap his mind around the reality of the clean-cut man with intelligent blue eyes sitting opposite him wearing a pair of khaki pants and running shoes as the billionaire genius who'd created Crossroads.

"Exactly." Ryan watched him steadily. "Leah mentioned you're new to Siren Cove."

Teague nodded. "I moved up here from Southern California with my daughter. I want her to grow up in a small-town environment."

"Siren Cove is a great place to be a kid. I missed it a lot after my family moved away." Quentin paused as their cocktail waitress delivered a tray of drinks, thanked her, then lifted his highball glass. "What do you do for a living?"

"I'm a firefighter." Teague took a swallow of his beer. "When I was offered a position at the station here, I felt like this town would be the right fit for us."

"Well, I hope the move works out for you," Ryan said before glancing over at Quentin. "What brings you to town this time?"

"I'm thinking about—" He broke off as their waiter approached and pulled out a notepad.

"Are you folks ready to order?"

"Are we?" Leah glanced around the table. "I know what I want."

After they ordered, Quentin picked up the conversation where he'd left off but lowered his voice. "I heard a rumor this place would be going up for sale at auction shortly."

Paige whipped around in her chair. "No joke? Are you going to bid on it?"

He nodded. "I wanted to scope out the place, see how much business has fallen off since the owner was arrested."

"A lot." Nina frowned. "This restaurant used to be packed on weekends, but now . . ." She shrugged. "Well, you can see for yourself. The previous chef left, and the guy who replaced him isn't in the same class. The food will speak for itself when it arrives."

Quentin winced. "Sorry to subject you all to a crappy meal, but I wanted to check the place out firsthand."

Teague smiled. "We'll survive."

"Do you intend to move back here if you do buy the property?" Ryan asked.

"For a while, at least. Once I get a new restaurant up and running smoothly, I usually hire a full-time manager to operate it. But this isn't a done deal by any means. Just a scouting mission."

"Interesting." Paige scowled. "Why am I just now hearing about your plans?"

Quentin patted her hand. "Don't get your feathers ruffled. The rumor only crossed my desk a couple of days ago, and I made checking it out a top priority. I'd like the opportunity to spend more time in Siren Cove, and the Poseidon Grill could be a terrific business venture."

"At least we can all be confident you'd turn the restaurant into a success." Leah smiled at him. "Keep us posted on any news."

"Oh, I definitely will."

The conversation became more general, and as their food arrived, Teague realized he was thoroughly enjoying himself. Nina's friends were smart and entertaining, and despite the fact they'd all known each other forever, they made him feel like he belonged. When Nina reached beneath the table to squeeze his hand, his heart swelled. It had been a while since he was part of a group. After Jayne's death, spending time with their mutual friends had been painful, and hanging out with other singles felt awkward. He squeezed back, grateful to her for including him.

Quentin glanced around the table as they finished their meals. "So, now that we've eaten this less-than-inspired cuisine, what do you want to do this evening?"

"Ryan and I are heading home. Since school is finally out for the summer, we plan to spend a few days at his house in Sisters," Leah answered. "Sorry to be so boring."

Ryan reached for his wallet as their waiter dropped off the check and cleared their plates. "We want to leave early in the morning so I can get in some rock climbing tomorrow."

"Sounds fun." Nina released Teague's hand to pick up her purse off the floor and glanced over at her friend. "Just make sure you're here for your bachelorette party next week."

"Don't worry. The party takes priority over dangling from cliffs, but we needed a break before the wedding."

"As long as it isn't a literal break. No falling off those rocks." Paige pushed back her chair. "I'm going to go use the ladies' room."

"I'll join you just as soon as we settle up."

When Nina opened her purse, Teague laid a hand on her arm and spoke quietly but firmly. "I've got this."

She didn't argue. "Thank you." Her smile turned to a frown as she glanced down. "Oh, my God!"

Leah paused halfway out of her chair. "What's wrong?"

"My purse is a huge mess. What the heck?"

Her friend held up an oversized bag. "Mine's always a train wreck. I thought you were the organized one of the group."

"I am." Nina's hand shook a little as she tucked a short strand of hair behind her ear. "My purse was perfectly neat the last time I opened it."

Teague frowned. "Then how did it get messed up?"

"I don't know." She turned to meet his gaze. Her eyes were wide with uncertainty and a hint of anger. "Unless someone, somehow, went through my things. For the third damn time!"

Chapter Thirteen

The opportunity to search Nina's purse had presented itself like a gift from the gods. Not that she'd had a lot of time at her disposal, and fear of getting caught red-handed had made her sweat. She'd dumped out everything in the bag, then searched each zippered compartment in addition to the wallet. The lottery ticket was nowhere to be found, and she'd had no time to be neat in returning the contents to the purse. Not that she cared a whole hell of a lot at this point.

Her scouting mission to the fireman's home had been slightly more productive. She'd discovered if she lay flat on the back stoop and stretched her arm up through the doggie door, she could just reach the dead bolt. Too bad the fur ball had started barking like a lunatic, discouraging any temptation to go inside.

Frustration sizzled along her nerve endings. When Lynette threw the book she'd been looking at down on the coffee table, her anger erupted.

"If you can't treat your belongings with more respect,

I'll take them away until you can." Her voice slashed through the quiet room.

"These are baby books. If I could have new ones, I'd be more careful."

Tension sparked between them, and her head pounded. "They're perfectly suitable for a girl your age. I took great care in choosing each one."

"They're old and falling apart."

She clenched and unclenched her fists at her sides. "If you took better care of them—"

Lynette scurried to the other side of the couch. "I will. I promise."

Some of her rage faded away, and she smiled. "That's a good girl. It's getting late. Go brush your teeth and get ready for bed. I'll come tuck you in in a few minutes."

Without a word, Lynette nodded and left the room.

After stacking the picture books neatly on the table, she rubbed her temples and considered her options. Her special numbers taunted her, dancing through her mind. She wasn't ready to give up on them yet, not by a long shot. Maybe Nina had taken the ticket out of her purse and put it somewhere in the house for safekeeping. The woman hadn't cashed in her windfall yet, of that she was certain. In a town the size of Siren Cove, news would have spread.

Breaking into the artist's home with the new security system in place would be impossible without setting off the alarm, which meant she'd need to search for her missing ticket while Nina was at home. A risky proposition that might end in someone's luck running out. A tight smile curved her lips. It wouldn't be hers.

* * *

Nina lay in bed next to Teague, but sleep was as far away as the moon visible through his bedroom window. A glance at the digital clock on the nightstand told her it was well past midnight, and all she wanted was to close her eyes and drift into oblivion. But she couldn't turn off her brain. When she rolled from her side to her back, his arm tightened around her.

"Are you still worried about your purse?" His voice rumbled close to her ear.

"Yes. I'm sorry I woke you."

"I'm not." His hand slid down to rest on her hip. "Why waste time sleeping when we could be doing other things?"

"Aren't you tired from the last two times you tried to make me forget about my stalker?"

He slumped back against the pillows without letting go of her. "I'm afraid you're right. I'm completely drained. Doesn't mean we can't cuddle."

She pressed her face to his warm chest and grinned at his choice of words. "I like that idea, but you need your sleep. You have to drive to Portland tomorrow to pick up Keely."

"I can function just fine without a lot of rest. Tell me what you're thinking."

"My purse was in my car this afternoon while I ran back into the dress shop. I didn't notice anyone lingering on the street, but if I have a stalker, I assume he wouldn't have wanted to be seen."

"True." He brushed a strand of hair off her cheek. "Nothing was missing from your bag? You're certain?"

"Absolutely."

"And that's the only time your purse was out of your sight all day?"

"I went for a run on the beach after we tried on our

dresses. I'm almost one hundred percent certain I locked my car, but I was thinking about introducing you to my friends when I came back, and I opened the door by rote. I can't recall if I unlocked it or not, but I think I did."

"Which means there's a slim chance your purse was accessible while you ran."

Nina nodded, her cheek sliding against his skin. She drew in a breath, enjoying the scent of him. "I'm just not sure."

"Either way, someone pawed through your stuff again but didn't take anything."

"Yes." She shuddered. "It's beyond creepy."

"I agree, and I don't like that this freak is keeping such a close watch on you. If he's hiding out in our neighborhood . . ."

She raised her head to glance up at him. "What?"

"Keely plays in the yard. She likes to come visit you and doesn't always ask permission first. I moved here so I wouldn't have to worry every time she walks out the door."

"The cops are still driving down our street on a regular basis. I saw a patrol car shortly before we left for dinner."

"I know that, and I appreciate their efforts. But . . ."

Nina's stomach knotted. "I certainly understand your concern, but it's not like I asked to have a stalker."

"I'm not blaming you, for Christ's sake." He held her a little tighter.

"Kind of sounded like you were."

His chest rose and fell. "No, but having Keely home will add another dimension to my worry."

"I don't know what to say."

"I don't expect you to say anything. I just want both you and my daughter to be safe."

Guilt weighed on her like a lead shroud. After what

Teague had gone through with his wife, she appreciated his fear of collateral damage. "So far, this guy's been passive-aggressive. I'm not too worried he'll physically harm me. The man seems more like the type to be a Peeping Tom than an abuser."

"You're probably right, but what if he escalates? Have the cops made any progress on your broken window case?"

"If they have, no one's told me, so I assume the answer is no."

He rested his chin on her head. "The whole situation sucks."

She didn't answer. Wishing wouldn't make the problem go away, and she certainly didn't have any useful insights. Except . . .

"Maybe I should keep my distance."

He jerked back against the pillows. "What?"

"If I stay away from you and Keely, hopefully I won't draw this freak into her vicinity."

"You live next door. That's hardly a solution."

Irritation simmered as she pulled away from him. "So you want me to steer clear of Keely, but you don't want to give up . . . *cuddling*, is that it?"

He was silent for a long moment before he moved to his side of the bed and curled an arm beneath his head. "Wow, you really don't have a great opinion of me, do you?"

Tears smarted in her eyes and slid down her cheeks. "I'm sorry." She tried to clear the thickness from her voice. "I'm upset and worried, and I don't know how to fix the problem. I've been known to use sarcasm as a weapon, and you don't deserve that."

When Teague rolled over and touched her damp face, she jerked back.

"Hey, I didn't mean to make you cry. I'm sorry, too."

His soft tone soothed some of her raw nerves. "I can stay with Paige. She has a futon bed in her office, and I'm sure she wouldn't mind a houseguest."

"For how long?"

"I don't know. Until my stalker gets bored and goes away? I can stop showering, wear baggy sweatpants, and eat candy until my face breaks out. Maybe that would disgust him, and he'll quit sooner."

"Or just wear longer shorts." His voice was colored with a hint of amusement. "That might do the trick."

A grim smile curved her lips. "I don't own any, but I can buy some."

He slid closer and pulled her into his arms. "Look, I don't expect you to move out of your home. I'll just make it clear to Keely she's not allowed to wander over to your house by herself until this situation is resolved. I can keep a tighter rein on my daughter, but I'm still concerned about your safety."

She rested her cheek on his bicep. "There's a reason I got that expensive alarm system. I'm not stupid or careless. I won't take any chances."

"You run alone on the beach all the time."

"You're right. I guess I should find a running buddy. I don't like the idea of curtailing my freedom, but I'm less excited about confronting some psycho who has a creepy infatuation with me."

"Carry pepper spray."

"I already do."

He stroked the hair off her cheek. "Are we good now? I feel a little sick when we're arguing. I care about you, Nina, and the last thing I want is to make you feel worse."

"We're fine. I expect you to say what you're thinking

without pulling any punches. I'm just sorry I jabbed back."

"Don't be. I'm glad you aren't afraid to defend yourself." He shifted slightly to surround her with his warmth. "Let's give this discussion a rest and get some sleep. Okay?"

She nodded, thankful for Teague. Grateful for his willingness to forgive and sort out misunderstandings instead of letting arguments escalate. Still, she couldn't help thinking he was almost too good to be true.

Nina slept late and woke to an empty bed. Blinking in the stream of sunlight pouring through the open blinds, she yawned and glanced at the clock. "Good grief. It's after eight."

"Hey, you're finally awake." Teague stood in the bedroom doorway dressed in jeans and a T-shirt. He smiled as he crossed the room to the side of the bed.

Tugging the sheet up over her breasts, she scooted back against the pillows. "I would hope so. I'm usually up by six. Why didn't you wake me?"

"You were sleeping pretty soundly, so I figured you needed the rest." Sitting on the edge of the mattress, he bent down to kiss her. "I have to head out. I don't want to be late to the airport."

"Of course not. I know you're dying to see Keely."

"These last nine days would have been unbearable if not for you." The gray of his eyes darkened to pewter. "You look incredibly tempting, all warm and inviting."

She responded with a teasing smile. "I guess you should have woken me up earlier, then."

"My mistake." Cupping her face in his hands, he kissed her slowly and thoroughly.

When he finally let go, she was breathless and flushed. "Next time, definitely wake me."

He drew a finger across the tops of her breasts. "I'll make a note." With a sigh, he rose to his feet. "You don't have to rush off. Just make sure Coco doesn't sneak out, and lock up when you leave."

"I will. Drive safely."

"I always do. See you later."

After he left the room, Nina slumped back down into the nest of covers that smelled like Teague and closed her eyes. Moments later, toenails clicked against the hardwood floor before something light landed on the bed. She cracked an eyelid when stinky breath fanned her face.

"I hate to break the news to you, but you're no substitute for your dad."

Coco let out a shrill yap.

"Yeah, yeah, I'm getting up."

An hour later she'd showered, dressed, taken the dog for a quick walk around the neighborhood, checked the back gate to make sure it was firmly latched, and left a forlorn Coco to fend for herself. After she unlocked her front door and punched in the alarm code, she made herself a berry smoothie and then called Chris Long's direct line at the police station.

"Officer Long here. May I help you?"

"Hi, Chris. It's Nina Hutton."

"Hey, Nina. What can I do for you? I'm afraid we've had no luck identifying the person who broke into your house, if that's why you're calling."

"Yes, but I also wanted to let you know someone searched my purse yesterday while it was in my unlocked car. Before you say anything, I know. Careless and stupid. Anyway, my stalker—or whatever you want to call him—is apparently still watching me."

"Was anything stolen?"

"No. Even the cash was still in my wallet. But my bag was a jumbled mess, and that's not how I keep it."

He was silent for a moment. "I don't doubt you know how you left your purse, and I'm definitely concerned. The perp's actions are beginning to feel more like those of someone looking for a particular item than of a man obsessed with a woman."

She set down her glass and dropped onto a bar stool at the counter. "You think? Is that better or worse for me?"

"I guess it would depend on how desperate this person is to get whatever he's after. Any idea what that might be?"

"Not a clue. The most valuable belongings I own are my paintings, and he didn't take any of those when he searched my house. If he expected to find this *thing* in my purse, it must be small."

"I don't suppose you recently found a piece of jewelry or a wad of cash or a bag of cocaine when you were out for a run or strolling through town?"

"I'm afraid not."

"Then our original assumption is probably correct. This is just some repressed jerk who gets off on touching your stuff. I'll see if I can get the okay to increase patrols in your neighborhood. In the meantime, don't leave your home or car unlocked, and be vigilant when you're out in public. Avoid areas where someone might find you alone."

"I'll be careful. Thanks, Chris."

"I wish I could be more help. Call me if anything else unusual happens."

"Oh, I will. I'm not feeling terribly brave at the moment."

"That's good. Caution will keep you safe. Bye, Nina."

"Bye." She set down her cell. "Well, this sucks. Right back to square one." Levering off the stool, she headed to the front door to make sure it was locked, then went up-stairs to her studio. She had half a dozen frames to build, and they weren't going to construct themselves.

It was after two before she clamped the last glued frame together and came downstairs to find something to eat. When an engine rumbled outside, she dropped the ham on rye on a napkin and sprinted to the window. Not Teague back from the airport. Just the mailman. She had it bad, acting like a besotted teenage girl in love for the first time.

"Pull it together, Nina," she muttered. After unlocking the door, she went out to collect her mail and stood for a moment to sort through the envelopes. "Bills, junk mail, and more bills." She shuffled through the envelopes. "Exciting."

What she needed was a little exercise to clear her head. Her flip-flops slapped sharply along the walkway as she headed toward the house. Of course that meant finding someone to go running with her. Anger simmered, and she gave the door a shove. Talk about inconvenient. What she really wanted was to confront her stalker—preferably with a baseball bat—and end the whole damn drama once and for all.

When a shoe scuffed against the brick walkway behind her, the hair on the back of her neck prickled. Before she could turn, pain exploded in her head. She lurched forward as her world went black.

Chapter Fourteen

"Can I go say hi to Nina?" Keely bounced on the seat as Teague pulled into the driveway.

Since her Mini Cooper was parked where she usually left it, Nina was probably at home.

He glanced in the rearview mirror as he turned off the engine. "Didn't we just have an important conversation about you not walking over to Nina's house anytime you feel like it?"

"That's why I'm asking. Duh, Dad." His daughter unfastened her seat belt and pulled a puka shell necklace out of the backpack sitting beside her booster seat. "I want to give Nina the present I bought her."

Dad, not *Daddy*. Gone nine days, and he was already noticing the not-so-subtle differences. Her cousin was only ten months older than Keely, but after listening to her chatter on the long drive home from the airport, he got the feeling Hallie had a wealth of life experience far beyond her years.

"Fine, we'll let Coco out and then go visit Nina."

Keely pushed open the car door and dropped to the

ground. "I can live with that. Hurry, Dad. Coco's barking. She probably knows I'm home."

I can live with that? When had his six-year-old turned sixteen? After grabbing her suitcase out of the back of the pickup, he followed her to the house and unlocked the door. Coco exploded through the opening, dancing in an insane frenzy around her small mistress. Shrieking in laughter, Keely dropped down on the patchy lawn and rolled in the grass with the dog.

Teague leaned against the porch railing and smiled at the two. God, he'd missed his daughter.

Once her shorts and T-shirt were thoroughly covered in grass stains, Keely pushed to her feet. "Okay, I'm ready to give Nina her necklace now. Can Coco come, too?"

"Hold on just a minute." Picking up her suitcase, he took it inside and looked through the downstairs. Thankfully, Coco seemed to have left the place intact while he was gone.

"Hurry, Dad!"

"I'm coming." A minute later, Teague rapped a couple of times on the door and waited.

His daughter shifted from one foot to the other and frowned. "Maybe she's not home."

"I guess she could have gone for a run." When muffled thumping echoed from somewhere inside the house, unease slithered through him. He pushed Keely behind him and turned the knob. The door swung open and hit the wall with a bang.

"Nina."

Another thump sounded from deep in the house.

Grabbing Keely by the shoulders, he backed her across the porch. "I want you to take Coco and go home. Lock the door and wait for me."

Her smile dissolved. "What's wrong, Daddy?"

"Maybe nothing, but do as I told you. Go. Now."

Without another word, she raced across the lawn with Coco running at her heels. He waited until the two disappeared inside the house before entering Nina's home.

"Nina." His shout echoed in the stillness followed by more thuds.

"Shit!" Glancing around, he grabbed an umbrella out of the stand beside the coat tree and hurried through the kitchen, following the thumps. Cupboard doors had been left open, and food packages were scattered across the countertops. What looked like a typical junk drawer had been upended on the floor. Beyond the refrigerator, the door to the laundry room was shut.

Cautiously, he pushed it open.

Nina sat on the floor in front of the dryer with her hands and feet bound by duct tape. A towel was tied over her face. As Teague stared in horror, her heels came down against the tile floor in a thump, along with a muffled cry.

"Shit. Bloody hell. Hold on, babe." Dropping the umbrella, he knelt beside her and unfastened the towel. She blinked back tears as he carefully peeled a strip of tape off her mouth and cupped her chin in his hand. "Are you hurt?"

She cleared her throat as more tears fell. "My head aches where he hit me. I was praying you'd come looking for me."

"I'd like to kill whoever did this." Teague tried to loosen the tape binding her hands.

"There are cooking scissors in the knife rack."

"Good idea." He glanced over his shoulder. "Did the psycho leave?"

"I think so. All the noise stopped about twenty minutes ago."

His legs shook as he pushed upright. "Let's get you free, and then I'll call the cops."

"I think I left my phone on the counter." She sniffed hard as her nose ran. "I'll call them while you free me."

"Okay." Gently he wiped her face with the towel. "I'll be right back."

His hands trembled as he sorted through the mess on the counter in search of the scissors. When he finally found the knife rack, minus the scissors, he chose a carving knife and took a deep breath to steady his soaring temper. Spotting Nina's phone next to an uneaten sandwich, he grabbed it and hurried back to her side.

"Let me free your wrists." With care, he slipped the sharp blade between her skin and the adhesive and sliced through the tape.

As soon as her wrists were loose, she jerked the tape off and took her cell from him while he worked on her ankles.

"Jesus, your heels are all bruised."

"I pounded them on the floor, hoping someone would hear me." She scrolled through her contacts and tapped the phone, then waited. "Chris, this is Nina Hutton again." Her voice broke. "Someone hit me over the head, then tied me up and searched my house." She was silent for a moment. "My neighbor is here with me now, and whoever it was is gone. Yeah, I'll be waiting."

He removed the last of the tape and helped her to her feet. "Are the police coming?"

"Yes." She clung to him as she limped out of the laundry room into the kitchen. "Oh, my God. What a freaking mess."

When she let out a whimper, he scooped her up in his arms.

"What about the rest of the house?"

"I haven't looked yet. I heard your thumps when I opened the door. I sent Keely straight home before searching for you." He set her on the couch. "Seeing you all bound up like that . . ."

"I'm fine. The creep didn't hurt me much, except what I expect is a sizable lump on my head."

He threaded his fingers through her hair but stopped when she winced. "Yeah, there's a knot. Did he knock you out?"

"Only for a few seconds. I remember a sharp pain in my head, then coming to and feeling dizzy for a minute. My face was covered, and someone was taping my hands." She broke off. "Is that a car? The police must be here."

He bent and dropped a kiss on her forehead. "I'll let them in. Right now I need to go check on Keely, and then I'll take you to the ER."

"The ER isn't necessary. Honestly, I'm okay. Go to your daughter, Teague."

When he reached the front door, two officers were halfway up the walk. He waited while they approached. "I'm Teague O'Dell, Nina's . . . neighbor."

A man around his age with a serious expression studied him for a moment. "I'm Officer Long, and this is Officer Cantrell. You're the one who found Miss Hutton?"

"Yes." He glanced from the younger cop to Cantrell, an older man who had walked with a slight limp. "My daughter is home alone. I need to go."

"That'll be fine." The officer spoke in a gravelly tone. "We'll get a statement from Miss Hutton first."

"She's waiting for you inside." Teague stepped out of the way. "I won't be gone long."

"May I ask what your relationship is to Nina?" the younger cop asked.

He turned to face Chris Long. "We're dating."

When the other man only responded with another narrow-eyed stare, Teague stepped past him and ran across the yard. When he reached his own front porch, the bolt slid back with a click as Keely opened the door.

"Where's Nina? Why is there a police car outside?" She sniffed loudly. "How come you were gone so long?"

"I'm sorry, Keels." Reaching down, he hoisted her onto his hip and held her tight. "Nina is fine. Someone broke into her house, so we had to call the police."

She clung to his neck. "Did they take away her pretty pictures?"

"I'm not sure yet. I hope not." He carried her into the living room and set her down on the couch, much as he'd done for Nina. Once he'd settled beside Keely, Coco jumped up and crawled onto her lap, obviously sensing she was upset.

"If I give Nina the necklace, maybe that'll make her feel better."

He smiled and stroked her hair. "I'm sure it will, but first she has to talk to the police officers. I need to talk to them, too. Do you think you can stay here with Coco and watch cartoons while I do that? I'll be just across the street."

"I'm not a baby." A bit of her bravado returned.

"That's my brave girl." After dropping a kiss on her head, he stood, picked up the remote, and handed it to her. "Here you go. I won't be gone long."

She glanced up at him. "Are you going to take care of Nina now?"

He let out a slow breath. "Yes, I definitely am."

*   *   *

Nina gave Teague a tired smile as he entered his living room and dropped down next to her on the couch. "Is Keely asleep?"

"Yes, and Coco is curled up by her feet, just to make sure she doesn't leave again. Between exhaustion from her trip and the drama that played out at your house earlier, Keely was asleep before I finished reading her favorite story."

"I bet. She was a trouper, helping clean up the mess with the adults."

He took her hand and threaded his fingers through hers. "It was nice of Paige and Quentin to spend their evening restoring order and dining on takeout pizza with us."

"We help each other out. That's what we've always done. If Leah and Ryan weren't out of town, they would have joined us." She leaned her head back against the cushions, wincing when she bumped the tender spot. "As it is, Leah was a little freaked out when I talked to her on the phone. The similarities to what happened to her last fall hit a little too close to home."

"What are you talking about?"

"We dug up a time capsule our fifth-grade class had buried twenty years before. Unfortunately, someone had hidden a roll of film in it that exposed a really twisted local group. Leah had the film, and they nearly killed her trying to get it back."

"Jesus."

"Yeah, it was damn scary, but the cult members are all in jail now."

"I'm glad to hear it." He frowned. "Who would have thought a town like this would harbor a bunch of freaks."

"I know, right?"

"So, the fact that your house was searched brought back a few awful memories for your friend?"

Nina nodded. "For me, too, if we're being honest. I'm starting to believe I have something in my possession someone wants, and I don't have a clue what it is."

Teague released her hand to slide his arm around her and pull her close. "Is that the official police theory?"

"Chris is leaning in that direction. He thinks if this psycho simply had a thing for me, he would have . . . done something about it while I was helpless."

Teague tightened his grip. "I can't begin to describe how angry that idea makes me."

"I had a few uncomfortable moments while I was trussed up like a Thanksgiving turkey, wondering if he'd come back for me."

"This little shit deserves a slow, painful death, just for scaring you." His voice grew tight. "So much for the alarm system providing protection."

"I went out to get my mail." She rested her cheek against his shoulder. "I guess being on alert twenty-four seven isn't practical, but maybe the creep found whatever it was he's after. Maybe he won't come back."

"I'd certainly like to believe that's true. You don't remember finding anything unusual?"

"No. Chris questioned me about that, but I can't think of anything."

"He doesn't like me much."

"Huh?" Nina turned to stare up at him. "Who doesn't like you?"

"Officer Long. I've been on the receiving end of a few cool stares. I'm not sure if he thinks I'm the one who trashed your house, or if he's jealous of my relationship with you. I told him we're dating."

"Oh." She rubbed her thumb over the faded denim covering his knee. "He asked me out, sort of casually, after the trouble Leah went through."

"Did you say yes?"

"Not exactly. We ended up on one awkward group date together a few months ago, but I wasn't interested in pursuing anything more personal."

Teague covered her hand with his warm palm. "Well, that would explain his attitude."

"His sister is a friend of mine. He's actually a really nice guy. Just not my type."

"What is your type?"

"You."

He pressed her back against the couch, then lay down beside her and cupped her chin in his hand. "Yeah?"

"Yeah. Smart. Caring. Hardworking. Hot."

He ran his lips up the side of her neck, sending heat rushing straight to her core.

"Especially hot."

He raised up on one elbow. "Stop. You'll give me a swelled head."

She wiggled against him. "Too late. I think I already have."

"You're right about that." He kissed her, taking his time to thoroughly explore her mouth before he pulled back. "Want to go upstairs?"

"Keely—"

"Isn't going to wake up. Anyway, I'm not letting you go home alone after what happened."

"I won't say no to that. My nerves are shot."

He stood and pulled her to her feet. "You'd be inhuman if they weren't. Honestly, I feel a little more confident under the assumption this asshole wants something other than you. Since he went out of his way to search your house without harming you more than necessary, maybe he isn't inherently violent."

She grimaced when her heel bumped against the coffee table. "Ouch. He's determined, that's for sure."

"Careful." When Teague flipped off the lamp beside the couch, darkness enveloped them. "Do your feet hurt? Want me to carry you?"

"I can walk."

He tucked her close to his side as they climbed the stairs together. Pausing in the hallway, he peeked into Keely's room, which was illuminated by the dim glow of a Cinderella night-light. "She's sound asleep."

Nina waited in the doorway while he pulled up the covers that were bunched down around the dog. Once he returned to her side, she pressed her face against his shoulder. "I'm sorry Keely's first night home was such a disaster."

"Not your fault. Anyway, she was thoroughly entertained by Quentin and his jokes. The guy is good with kids."

"He has a laid-back, teasing attitude they can relate to. I expect when he has a couple of his own, he'll be the fun parent."

"That was Jayne's role. I've always been the serious one. The cautious dad. The disciplinarian."

She wound her arms around his waist after he turned on the bedside lamp in his room. "Your daughter will grow up knowing she has boundaries. But her independent spirit probably means she'll test them."

"I wouldn't have it any other way." He bent to kiss her. "I should take a quick shower. If you need anything . . ."

"I have a toothbrush, so I'm good."

While the shower ran and steam filled the room, Nina washed her face and brushed her teeth. Eyeing the shadowy figure behind the opaque glass, she was tempted to

join him but resisted. If Keely woke up . . . She touched
the puka shells around her neck and smiled. After rinsing
her mouth, she headed back into the bedroom, stripped
off her clothes, then slid into bed.

The water shut off a minute later, and she turned on
her side to face the bathroom door. Teague came out
wearing nothing but a towel wrapped around his waist.
The man was incredibly gorgeous, all hard muscle and
damp skin. But it was the wealth of emotion in his eyes
that melted her heart.

The towel fell to the floor with a soft plop. When her
breath hissed out, his lips curled in a smile before he
reached over to turn off the light and climb into bed beside her.

She cuddled close. "I thought we weren't going to
make a habit of this after Keely got home from her trip."

His chin came to rest on top of her head. "We aren't,
but tonight I need to hold you and know you're safe."

"I can't tell you how much I appreciate everything
you've done for me, the moral support you've provided."
She pressed a kiss to the tough skin of his chest, still
moist and smelling like soap. "That means a lot."

When her hand drifted lower, the muscles of his ab-
domen contracted, and his breath rushed out. "I care about
you, Nina." He rolled her onto her back and pressed her
into the mattress. "Maybe more than I've been able to put
into words. I—"

She touched a finger to his lips. "You don't have to say
anything more. Your actions tell me everything I need to
know."

He kissed her finger, then her lips, building her need to
a fever pitch. As he slid inside her, she quit wondering
why she'd stopped him from speaking his mind. Words

she wasn't sure she was ready to hear, or maybe fear that he wouldn't truly mean them. It was easier to simply enjoy.

Their breathing came in harsh gasps as they pushed together toward release. Wrapped up in Teague, all she wanted was to forget her problems—not create new ones. When she came apart in his arms with a soft cry, all she cared about was the here and now. Better than anything she could have imagined.

Chapter Fifteen

Nina adjusted the neckline of her off-the-shoulder white peasant blouse and sipped her margarita through a penis-shaped straw. The bachelorette party was in full swing. They'd taken over all the window tables at Castaways and kept the cocktail waitress assigned to them hopping as the live band warmed up in the far corner.

Leah's grandma jiggled her arm, then leaned in close to be heard over multiple shouted conversations. "When's the stripper coming? I may have to pace myself so I don't fall asleep before he gets here."

Nina grinned in response. Evie Grayson was past eighty and could probably drink them all under the table if the way she'd been belting back cocktails was any indication. She twirled a strand of beads hanging from the macramé headband around her fluffy purple hair.

"Not until later. The owner of the bar agreed only on the condition the stripper didn't show up until midnight. He didn't want a bunch of rowdy women hooting and hollering and scaring away the tourists too early in the evening."

"Probably smart." She pushed away her half-empty glass. "I'd better slow down since I might just ask him for a lap dance. At my age, it may be my last chance."

Nina sputtered and choked on her drink. "Seriously? What would your gentleman friend have to say about that?"

"Oh, Magnus would cheer me on." She winked. "When I left this evening, he told me he wouldn't complain if I came home in the mood."

Leah broke off a conversation with Regan to frown at her grandmother. "Gram, quit embarrassing Nina." She helped Evie down from her stool. "Go talk to Ryan's mom and let me chat with my BFF for a minute."

"Fine, but she doesn't look embarrassed to me."

Nina couldn't wipe the grin from her face. "Not in the least. You're my hero, Evie. I want to be just like you when I'm your age."

"An admirable goal." Leaving her cocktail, the older woman departed.

Leah plopped down on the vacated stool and hooked her pink patent leather go-go boots over the rail. "Thanks for the party. You and Paige outdid yourselves, and everyone is having a wonderful time."

"Good. As long as you're happy, I'm happy."

"Oh, I am. I can't wait to be Ryan's wife, but one last girls' night out as a single woman is a terrific send-off." She leaned her elbow on the table. "I haven't talked to you since we got back from Sisters. Has the creep who hit you and tied you up been caught yet?"

Nina took another sip of her margarita. "I'm afraid not. But on a positive note, there haven't been any more attacks, either. My hope is he found whatever he was after and will leave me alone from now on."

"God, I hope so. Are you and Teague still . . ."

Nina nodded. "We are, though not as often since his daughter returned from seeing her grandparents."

Leah scrunched up her nose. "Wow, you and my grandma are quite the pair this evening. I meant are you still dating, not are you sleeping with him."

"So did I. Who has sex on the brain now?" Nina raised a brow as she twirled the straw between her fingers. "He's busy with work and Keely, and I've been painting like a fiend to prepare for the Summer Art Fair."

"You really seem to like this man. Are you two serious?"

Nina nodded. "I care about him more than anyone I've dated since Keith, but I'm just not sure . . ." She bit her lip.

Leah touched her arm. "What's the problem?"

"I don't know if I'm ready to risk my heart to a committed relationship."

"It's been over five years. I don't mean to sound insensitive, but Keith died, not you."

"My concerns aren't what you're thinking. I loved Keith and intended to marry him, but we were struggling with priorities. Work always came first for him, and our engagement changed my expectations. Honestly, it's a whole lot easier to simply keep things on the lighter side."

"That's true, but casual doesn't fill your soul with joy the way being in love does. What does Teague want?"

"I'm not sure since we haven't discussed it yet. He's packing a lot of emotional baggage, too."

Leah eyed her steadily. "Are you hesitant to commit because he has a daughter?"

"No. Keely and I get along very well. She's a terrific little girl." Nina fiddled with the straw again. "Making

their life here in Siren Cove work for his daughter is
Teague's top priority. She matters more to him than anything."

"As it should be."

"I know, and that's why I'm not ready to push too hard
or too fast. I'm fine with what we have . . . at least for
now."

Leah's brow wrinkled. "If you're sure?"

"I am." Her tone reflected none of the doubt niggling
at the back of her mind. Maybe because she was determined to ignore it. When a hand touched her shoulder,
she jumped.

"Would you like to dance?"

The man standing behind her, probably in his mid-
twenties, had anxious brown eyes and a sweet smile. He
was good looking in a boy-next-door sort of way, and
Nina suspected half the women in the bar would be happy
to dance with him. Despite the speech she'd just given
Leah about not wanting a committed relationship, the
only man she was interested in dancing with was Teague.
Maybe she needed to broaden her horizons.

Straightening her shoulders, she slid off the barstool
and smiled. "Sure."

"Really?"

"Why not? I like this song."

He took her hand and led her onto the dance floor as
the local band covered a classic Beach Boys tune. "My
buddies said you'd turn me down." He glanced toward a
corner table where two young men laid bills on the surface, then gave him a thumbs-up.

Definitely not locals.

She put a little distance between them when he pulled
her in close. "They bet on it?"

His cheeks colored. "Seemed like a sure thing from their perspective since you're the hottest woman in the bar."

"Thanks, I think. Just so you know, uh . . ."

"Weston. And you are?"

"Nina. Just so you know, Weston, this isn't going further than a dance. If you bet money on anything else, you're going to have to pay up."

"Wow, I'm not that stupid. Class practically oozes from you, not to mention you have an aura of untouchableness surrounding you. Is that even a word?"

"I don't think so." She swayed to the chorus of "Good Vibrations." "Then why did you ask me to dance?"

He smiled. "I like a challenge. Plus, women at bachelorette parties tend to forgo some of their natural inhibitions. I thought I might get lucky."

Nina glanced toward their tables where Janice had just delivered a tray of shots. When Paige waved a hand and gave the cocktail server a questioning look, the woman pointed toward Weston's two friends.

Nina laughed out loud. "Your buddies are trying to loosen us up, I see. You never know. You might still get lucky." She stepped back as the song ended. "Just not with me."

The hint of regret in his eyes turned to alarm. "Please tell me I didn't just hit on the bride-to-be?"

"Nope, the bride is the woman with the long brown hair I was talking to earlier. You might try asking the petite blonde or the tall brunette to dance. Both ladies are single."

He released her hand. "But you're not?"

"No, I'm definitely taken." Apparently it didn't matter if she was reluctant to venture into a committed relationship. Teague already had her heart—whether she liked the idea or not.

"Can't blame a guy for trying. Have a nice evening, Nina."

"You, too." After he walked away, she approached Paige and pointed at the row of shot glasses lined up on the table. "You planning on drinking one of those?"

"What?" She spun around then laughed. "Maybe. Those guys in the corner bought them for us."

"I was dancing with one of them. Tourists hoping to end their night with a little action."

"I saw." Paige gazed across the room. "He's actually pretty cute."

"His name's Weston. I told him to ask you or Regan to dance since I'm not interested."

"I wouldn't be, either, if I had a guy like Teague to go home to. Are you still staying with him?"

Nina shook her head. "No, there's Keely to consider. I'm diligently alarming my house and sleeping with a canister of pepper spray beside my bed." Her voice hardened. "I refuse to be frightened out of my own home. Anyway, nothing's happened since that creep tied me up last Saturday. I'm beginning to think I can finally relax."

"But you still don't know what he was after?"

"I've racked my brain trying figure out what it could possibly be, but I'm at a loss."

"The whole situation is scary weird." Paige rubbed her hands up and down her arms. "I hope you're right and he's gone for good."

Nina picked up her drink and sipped. "Enough depressing talk. Hey, is Quentin going to put in an offer on the Poseidon Grill?"

"He isn't sure yet. He's waiting for reports from various inspectors, and there's some problem with a lien. Before he left town, Quentin had a chat with the current manager, and the guy thinks they're going to close the place down for good soon."

"That's too bad. The Poseidon Grill is a real landmark in town."

"I'm hoping Quentin will make an offer. I—oh, my." Paige grabbed Nina's arm and turned her to face the door. "Do you think that's our stripper? If so, he's early."

A man in a white suit with subtle sequin accents strolled into the bar. He took off a pair of dark glasses and surveyed the room.

Paige scowled. "I don't recall requesting an Elvis impersonator. Not to mention he looks old enough to be Leah's father."

"If nothing else, Evie should like him." Nina eyed Leah's grandma, who was in an animated conversation with Ryan's mother near the windows. "She mentioned something about a lap dance."

When the man waved and veered off toward a group sitting near the band, Paige let out a breath. "Oh, thank God. He's just a guy with tacky taste. We dodged a bullet there."

"After that scare, the real stripper has got to be an improvement."

"We can only hope."

Teague grabbed one end of the stretcher as the winch hoisted the accident victim to the top of the cliff. "One, two, three lift," he shouted over the beeping of the wrecker as the truck backed into position. He and Mateo carried the injured man to the waiting ambulance and relinquished him to the paramedics.

"Damn idiots." Mateo nodded toward the second passenger, who'd been able to walk away from the mangled vehicle. Currently, he was bent double, heaving his guts out on the side of the road. "Drinking and driving. What a bunch of morons."

"Not to mention we got called in after our shift was over to rescue their asses. Between this wreck and the out-of-control backyard bonfire occupying the regular night crew, this has been one hell of an evening."

At the edge of the highway, Officer Long loaded the third member of the trio into the back of his patrol car. The driver had taken the corner too wide and sent his sports car sailing off the side of the cliff. Flashing lights on top of the police vehicle reflected off the fire truck and wrecker, creating an eerie glow in the night sky. Teague glanced over the drop-off as he and Mateo gathered up their equipment. The Porsche had crunched like an aluminum can on the rocks below. The drunken tourists had been damn lucky no one had died, though one member of the group had sustained a compound fracture and the other two were covered in abrasions.

Mateo slammed the compartment door on the side of the truck. "I had nothing better to do tonight since Sabrina is at a bachelorette party. But I'd rather be at home in my recliner watching Netflix than here."

"I had to call for a babysitter. Thank God Stella was available since Nina's the one who organized Leah's party." Teague shut the second compartment before heading toward the driver's side of the truck. "She's been pretty great about helping me out with Keely when I need someone to watch her in an emergency."

Mateo climbed into the truck and glanced over at him. "I'm tempted to stop by Castaways just to make sure all those women have a ride home. After what we just witnessed, I don't want any of them driving tonight."

"Surely they have designated drivers or will take cabs." Teague started the engine and pulled around the police cruiser onto the highway.

"I think I'll drop by, just the same." Mateo glanced at his watch. "It's after midnight. They should be wrapping up the party by now. If you want to go straight home, that's understandable since you're paying for a sitter."

The idea of seeing firsthand what was going on at the party was tempting. Memories of the decorations Nina had purchased taunted him, and he couldn't help wondering . . . "I can afford an extra half hour. In the name of community safety, of course. I'll follow you over there."

Mateo grinned. "Sure, that's what we'll call it. Community safety. We'd never dream of checking up on our women."

Twenty minutes later, Teague ignored the guilt nagging at him, knowing Stella probably wanted to go home to bed. He parked on the mostly deserted street near Castaways and climbed out of his pickup. When Mateo joined him a few seconds later, they approached the bar. The grinding beat of a bass drum reverberated from inside.

"Sounds like the band is still playing. Maybe the party isn't over yet," Mateo said. "I guess we'll just have to join the fun."

"I really can't hang out for long. When you have a kid waiting at home, your priorities change."

"Just another reason for me to put off popping the question. Lately, Sabrina's been hinting I need to fish or cut bait. She says her biological clock is ticking."

"Don't mess up a good thing, dude." Teague pulled open the door to a blast of music accompanied by raucous cheering. "Becoming a father was the best moment of my life." Two steps into the room, he stopped and stared. "Serious? They hired a fireman stripper?"

Mateo snorted. "Damn, maybe I'm not putting on enough of a show in the bedroom. I should start bringing my gear home with me."

In the center of the room, a blond guy with impressive abs wore nothing but a fireman's helmet, a red G-string, and a smile. A yellow flame-retardant suit lay on the floor, and he had a hose wrapped around the bride-to-be. Her face was nearly as red as the material barely covering his package as he did some serious gyrating.

"Jesus. Maybe we should take off." Teague's gaze zeroed in on Nina, laughing and cheering and waving dollar bills with the rest of them. "None of these women look like they're ready to leave."

"Oh, my God! Was that a twenty Leah's grandma just shoved in that guy's crotch? I swear she copped a feel."

Teague stared as an elderly woman with purple hair did a bump and grind with the stripper. "He's probably just a college kid."

"Not a bad way to cover the cost of tuition." Mateo straightened as the song concluded in a clash of cymbals. "Hey, it looks like the band is wrapping up for the evening. We caught the big finale."

"I think Leah is forcibly restraining her grandma. That guy better get his clothes on in a hurry."

"At least he isn't doing solo performances in a back room. Let's go see if anyone needs a ride."

Teague threaded his way through the tables to the group of women near the windows. Nina stood with her back to him and her phone out. When he rested a hand on her shoulder, she spun around.

"Teague! What are you doing here?"

"Mateo and I were called out on an accident. After we

hauled three drunks up the cliff out of their totaled car, we thought we'd stop by to see if anyone wanted a ride home."

"Were they hurt?"

"One guy was, but no one died. I don't mean to imply you and your friends aren't responsible, but—"

"No problem. I'd planned to call for a couple of cabs. Kim hasn't been drinking, and Ryan's mom is fine to drive, but I think Sabrina and Regan could use rides."

Teague nodded toward Leah's grandma, still swaying to music that had stopped several minutes before. "I hope she isn't driving."

"Evie? Heavens no. I'm taking her home. Paige just has to walk a couple of blocks, but Leah rode her bike here. I don't want her riding along the highway this late at night."

"I can put her bike in the bed of my truck and drive her." He let his fingers drift up to stroke the back of Nina's neck. "You're okay?"

"Sure. I nursed a single margarita for most of the evening and avoided the shots some guys bought us. I'm fine." She stood on her toes and wound her arms around his neck to kiss him. "Thanks for stopping by."

He lingered over a second kiss. "You're welcome." As he stepped back, Mateo approached with his arms around Sabrina and another pretty brunette.

"I'm giving these two lovely ladies a ride home. Everything under control?"

Teague nodded. "Yep, we've got it covered."

"Great. I'll see you next shift."

After his buddy walked away with the two women, Nina pressed a hand to his chest. "I should get Evie back to her apartment."

"Okay, but if you get home before me, I want you to be careful. It's late, and that asshole—"

"I'll keep my pepper spray handy."

Reluctantly, he released her. "Okay."

He didn't move while Nina spoke briefly with the cocktail waitress and handed the older woman a roll of cash. She paused to chat with Leah and Paige, gave them each a hug, and then slipped an arm around Evie to lead her from the room. Nina gave him one backward glance filled with promise before disappearing through the door.

He started when Leah touched his arm. "I hear you're giving me a ride."

"I am. Your grandma is quite a character."

"Isn't that the truth? I'm just glad my mother and sister left before Gram felt up the stripper. Mom would have had a stroke."

Paige pressed a hand to her lips but couldn't suppress a grin. "I nearly peed, I laughed so hard. I'm pretty sure the guy wished it was . . . er, never mind." She gave Leah a hug. "Go home to Ryan. I'm out of here."

Teague willed himself to keep a straight face. "I can drop you off, if you'd like."

She glanced up at him. "No, thanks. It's a short walk, and I could use the fresh air. Good night, Teague."

"Night, Paige." He waited while Leah picked up a giant tote bag filled with what he assumed were gifts and thanked the bartender, then walked beside her to the door. "Seems like you ladies had a good time."

"It was a fun evening." She stood beside his truck and shivered while he lifted her pink cruiser into the back. After he unlocked the door, she slid onto the seat.

Hurrying around to his side, he climbed in and started the engine. "Which way are we headed?"

"Go north out of town." They were quiet for a minute before Leah spoke again. "If you want a relationship with Nina to work, you're going to have to push her a little."

"Huh?" He turned to stare.

"She'll act like she doesn't want anything serious. Heck, maybe she's convinced herself that's true. But I know her well enough to understand what she really needs."

He faced forward and focused on the road. "What does Nina need? Exactly?"

"She needs to know she's someone's priority. I don't want to speak out of turn, but I also don't want to see my best friend get hurt. Turn left just up ahead at the mailbox."

It took him a moment to realize what she was talking about. Teague slowed, then turned onto a long, rutted driveway that led to an older home on a bluff overlooking the ocean. He stopped and put on the parking brake. "Please, I'd like to understand her better."

Leah lifted the tote bag onto her lap and played with the strap. "I only met Keith a couple of times." She gave him a sharp glance in the glow of the outdoor light. "Nina's told you about her fiancé who died?"

"Yes."

"He was a good guy, a Marine who served his country with honor. I don't doubt he loved her, but he made it clear his career came first. I think it was eating her up inside, even though she never complained."

"Maybe he couldn't put her needs first. Military families have to make sacrifices all the time."

"That's true." Leah's voice was calm but held an underlying tension. "Except his tour was up. Nina wanted to move back to the States. Keith agreed, then signed on for four more years without talking it over with her first."

"Wow."

"Yeah, wow. She never got a chance to shout and yell and work out her feelings because Keith was killed. I think it's the reason she won't commit to another relationship. She has some issues, but she also has a beautiful heart and deserves to find someone to love who loves her in return. If you have any interest in being that man, you're going to have to put in some work and make sure she knows her needs matter."

He gripped the steering wheel a little tighter. "We haven't gone past the getting to know each other stage yet, but I do care about Nina. A lot."

"Good."

"I also have a daughter."

Leah touched his arm. "I know that, and she shouldn't be a problem unless you make her one. I'm just looking out for my friend because I know she cares about you, too, maybe more than any man she's dated in a long, long time."

He stared out into the night. "Thanks for talking to me. I appreciate it."

"I'm not trying to scare you off."

"I know, and the last thing I want is to hurt Nina."

Leah's eyes were thoughtful as she met his gaze. "That's all I ask." She opened the car door and stepped out onto the driveway. "Thanks for the ride."

"I'll get your bike."

"Thanks."

A minute later, she pushed the cruiser into the carport, and the outdoor light went out. Teague stood without moving as the breeze off the ocean sent a shiver through him. He definitely had a lot to think about.

Chapter Sixteen

She stabbed the tip of the shovel into the earth with a grunt, then heaped the loosened dirt on the ground near the hole. Her arms ached, as did her back and every other part of her body. In the past, digging the burial chamber hadn't taken so much effort. As it was, she'd have to work for the better part of a week to dig the hole deep enough. Some days more than others, getting old was a trial. As she leaned on the shovel and gasped for breath, her mind fogged with visions of all the other pits she'd dug over the years.

Regret ate at her. Each and every time she'd been certain the girl in question was Lynette come back to her. Watching the pretender morph into someone unrecognizable as her darling child was horrifying and painful. Unfortunately, with each passing day she was more certain the current inhabitant of her home was an impostor. The time to bury her mistake was drawing near.

Groaning, she straightened and kept digging, despite her exhaustion. With each downward slash of the shovel, fear that she wouldn't have the wherewithal to pack up and leave with her precious girl after the inevitable was over gnawed at her stomach. She bent double in pain, needing to stop the ache. If only she'd found that damn winning lottery ticket, her worries would be a thing of the past. But she'd failed, and she was beginning to fear the key to her financial security was lost forever.

She'd conquered hardships in the past. Granted, the times she'd been flush with cash had always proved easier, but she would overcome any and all obstacles ahead of her. Because this time would be the last. The sweet child with the missing tooth and sunny smile was her very own Lynette returned to be with her like a gift from above. She'd been watching her more and more often to make certain she was right. The next step would be a few questions to case any final concerns. This time, there would be no mistake to bury on a late June day sometime in the future. She'd never been more certain of anything. Never.

Nina tried to ignore her growling stomach . . . and failed. "Well, I totally blew it. I should have planned ahead."

At her feet, Coco opened one eye before closing it again to stretch out in the bright patch of sunlight and groan.

"I brought treats for you, so of course you don't care." The dog chews looked like beef jerky, maybe if . . . Nina shook her head. She wasn't that hungry. With renewed determination, she worked to add finishing touches to her drawing of the patch of pink and white phlox growing around the base of a western red cedar. The tree stood in a shaft of sunlight, and the contrasting colors and textures were so spectacular she hadn't been able to resist pulling out her sketch box filled with colored pencils.

A half hour later she surveyed the finished drawing with satisfaction before returning the box and artist pad to her pack. Rising up from the flat rock where she'd sat cross-legged to work, she winced and stretched to ease away the stiffness.

"I would have chosen something more comfortable to sit on if I'd known I was going to be here so long."

Coco stood and shook before giving her an enquiring look. The fur hanging from her ears fluttered in the breeze.

"Yes, we're going home. I've had enough adventure for one day."

If she could figure out exactly where home was. They'd left the trail some distance back when Coco had taken off in fearless pursuit of a rabbit. Of course if Coco hadn't chased the bunny, she would never have found the cedar tree and phlox. She shrugged the daypack onto her shoulders. One thing was certain, if she and Coco headed straight downhill, they would eventually come out somewhere in the vicinity of their neighborhood.

Pushing through the dense forest was hard work, and Nina was sweating and scratched after hiking for three-quarters of an hour. She'd given up trying to find the trail some time back and simply focused on getting down the hillside. When the trees thinned ahead, relief flooded through her. "Oh, thank God. We must be almost home."

Coco's tail dragged, and she gave what Nina swore was a discouraged woof.

"Not much farther now. You know this is all your fault, right?" When the dog cocked her head to one side, Nina grimaced. "You're the one who had to chase the damn rabbit."

But the small clearing didn't back up to any of the neighborhood houses. The trees closed in on all sides. Perched on the branch of a Douglas fir, a blue jay squawked raucously in the stillness. Coco left Nina's side to sniff branches scattered over the ground next to a fresh pile of dirt.

The hair on the back of her neck lifted. "Get away from there, Coco."

The dog ignored her. When the branches gave way, she plunged downward with a yelp.

Nina ran forward and stopped at the edge of a hole about four feet deep and maybe a yard in diameter. Coco scrambled to climb up the side, but the dirt slid down around her. Kneeling on the branches, Nina reached down to grab the dog and haul her up.

"Why the heck would someone dig a pit out here?" Hands on her hips, she turned in a slow circle before spying a break in the barrier of trees. "Looks like that's the direction they came from. Let's go, Coco."

The trail was rough at best, and Nina stopped a few times, fearing she'd lost the path altogether. About fifteen minutes later, she and the dog emerged through the trees at the end of a cul-de-sac much like her own.

"About damn time. I know where we are now." Picking up her pace, she hurried down the street past the burned-out shell of a house before reaching the corner. "Only a few more blocks to go."

Coco flopped down on the pavement and wouldn't budge even when Nina prodded her with the toe of her hiking shoe.

"Fine, I'll carry you, but I'm going to be covered in dirt." Picking up the filthy dog, she headed for home. She'd just turned down her street when Teague's pickup slowed to a stop, and both passenger side windows lowered.

Keely hung out the back one. "Hi, Nina. How come you're carrying Coco?"

At the sound of the girl's voice, the dog yipped and squirmed until Nina set her down. Dashing across the pavement, Coco put her paws up on the running board and barked.

Teague eyed her steadily from the far side of the cab. "She looks a little dirty."

"A lot dirty. A minute ago, she was pretending she didn't have the energy to walk home." Nina pointed at the bouncing, yapping dog. "Obviously a complete lie."

He leaned forward to push open the front passenger door. "Hop in."

After lifting Coco onto the seat and waiting for her to scramble into the back with Keely, Nina climbed in and shut the door. She set her daypack at her feet and turned to face him. "By the way, I took your dog for a walk. I didn't want to bother you at work, and I didn't think you'd mind."

"Not in the least." He shifted into gear. "From the state both of you are in, I'd say you had quite a time."

Nina glanced down at the dirt stains on the front of her T-shirt and the faint scratches on her arms. "We got a little lost, then Coco fell into a hole someone dug out in the woods. The good news is I spent a couple of hours drawing a sketch in a lovely spot I never would have found if your dog hadn't chased a rabbit."

"Coco loves chasing bunnies." Keely giggled. "And squirrels and cats. Anything that runs away from her."

"I figured that out about a quarter mile into the pursuit."

Teague parked in his driveway and turned off the engine. "What prompted you to take her with you to begin with?"

"I couldn't find anyone to go running with me. I was tempted to go alone, but then a car I didn't recognize turned around in our cul-de-sac, and I started wondering . . ." Nina climbed out and waited for Keely and Coco to jump down.

Teague slammed his door and walked around to stand at her side. "Did you see the person driving?"

"No. The windows were tinted, and whoever it was left right away. We get tourists just cruising around sometimes, but I was still a little nervous."

He laid a warm hand on her arm and squeezed. "I don't blame you."

"Anyway, I decided to go for a hike instead of a run."

"And you took Coco for protection?"

"More like an early warning system. I figured she'd bark if someone followed us, and I had my trusty can of pepper spray in my pack."

His gaze drifted to his daughter and the dog as they ran in circles on the lawn. "So, you both got lost chasing a rabbit?"

"Coco chased. I followed, and I wasn't lost, exactly. I knew the general direction we needed to go to get home, but I wasn't on the trail."

"Keely's going to have to give the mutt a bath. That should be fun."

Nina couldn't hold back a smile. "Do I detect a note of sarcasm? Hey, I didn't ask your dog to fall in a hole. It was the weirdest thing, not terribly big around but about four feet deep out in the middle of nowhere."

"It's summer, so kids are getting bored. A few from the neighborhood probably decided to build a trap and didn't want their parents to find it."

"Well, the trap worked, because they captured Coco. When I first saw the mound of dirt, I was afraid someone had buried a pet out there. It gave me the creeps. Then

Coco fell through the branches covering the hole, and I was relieved I wasn't standing in some sort of pet cemetery."

He laughed. "Shades of Stephen King."

"Stop. That book traumatized me." She nudged his arm. "What's new with you? I've barely seen you in the last couple of days."

"Just work. Keely seems to like her outdoor adventure camp. Oh, I asked for Saturday off so I can go to Leah and Ryan's wedding with you."

"Thank you." She leaned her head against his shoulder when he slid his arm around her waist. "Having you there is important to me."

"The captain okayed it, so we're good. Keely's spending the night with a new friend from camp, which means I won't have to worry about a sitter and getting home early."

"You're the best."

He pressed a quick kiss to the top of her head before releasing her, then stepped away when Keely and Coco scrambled up off the grass to head in their direction. "I want to make you happy, Nina."

"You do."

His daughter stopped in front of them, and a little frown creased her brow as she glanced from Nina to her dad. "What's for dinner?"

"Enchiladas."

"Yum. Can I give Coco a bath in the tub?"

"I'd rather you used the hose outside."

"I can help." Nina laid a hand on Keely's shoulder. "Since it's my fault she's such a mess. Anyway, I can't get any dirtier than I already am."

"Good idea. I'll make dinner while you're torturing Coco. She's not a huge fan of baths."

"I figured as much." Nina glanced at Keely and smiled. "Let's go do this."

After Teague unlocked the front door, Keely led the way through the house and out into the backyard. Nina stopped in the laundry room to take the dog shampoo and old towel he handed her.

"Thanks for helping out."

She leaned against the doorframe. "I *did* take Coco hiking with me, so I'll shoulder the extra work . . . if I get enchiladas in exchange."

"Seems like a fair deal. Good luck out there."

"I have a feeling I'll need it."

Nina let the back door swing shut behind her as she walked down the steps to where Keely was unwinding the hose. Coco's leash was attached to the girl's wrist, and the dog strained against her hold, eyeing the back fence.

"That's weird. Did you open the gate just now?"

Keely glanced up and frowned. "No, it was already like that."

"I'm positive I shut it after I let Coco out earlier." Nina crossed the yard and pulled it closed. It stuck briefly before the latch fell into place.

"It's hard to shut. Daddy told me not to mess with it."

"I guess I didn't click it firmly. Well, it's closed now. I don't want Coco to try to escape during her bath."

"She's pulling my arm off."

"Here, I'll take her." Nina set the shampoo and towel on the picnic table and reached for the leash. Fifteen minutes later, she was almost as wet as the dog as she held her while Keely hosed off the soap. "I think that's good enough."

"I hope so. Coco looks like she might bite you."

Nina studied the dog warily. "I got that feeling, too, but I think she's over it now."

Coco shook, sending water flying.

"I can dry her." Keely dropped the hose to pick up the towel. "She likes being rubbed."

"Good to know." Nina relinquished the dog into the girl's care. "I need to go shower. I'm soaked."

Keely glanced up from where she kneeled beside Coco. "If you're already wet, why do you need to shower?"

"I may be wet, but I'm far from clean."

"Are you having dinner with us?"

Something in her tone made Nina pause. "I was planning to if that's okay with you."

"Sure, but . . ." Keely kept her head down and patted the dog's fur.

A sinking feeling swept through Nina's stomach as she crouched down beside the two. "But what? Is something wrong?"

Keely regarded her coolly, hair straggling around her face. "Are you sleeping in my dad's bed? Traci at camp said that's what grown-ups do, even when they're not married. She said sometimes a mistake happens. That's how she got her little brother. Having a brother sounds horrfying."

Nina forced herself to breathe. "You mean horrifying."

"Yeah, that. A baby sister wouldn't be so bad."

She wondered what to say. Discussing sex with a six-year-old wasn't an option. "You should probably talk to your dad about this, but I can assure you, you won't be getting a baby brother or sister by mistake."

"That's good." Her hands stilled on Coco's back. "Does that mean you don't sleep in bed with my dad? I've seen him kiss you."

"Sometimes adults kiss when they like each other a

lot." She floundered for something else to add, knowing exactly what she'd like to say to the precocious Traci's parents. "Uh, we're just . . . dating."

"As long as I won't have to deal with a stupid boy. Today, this kid at camp tripped me, so I put a worm in his lunch."

"I'm not so sure the worm was a great idea, but you don't have to worry about a boy invading your life anytime soon."

"Traci said grown-ups do stuff in bed, but she didn't know what."

Thank God for small favors.

Nina changed the subject. "Is Coco dry?"

"Pretty much."

"Then you can let her go. The poor thing looks uncomfortable." Nina could relate.

Keely released the dog and scrambled to her feet. "Do you think dinner is ready yet?"

"Probably not. I'm going to go home to shower, but if you still have concerns, you can talk to your dad about them."

The girl skipped toward the door. "Nope, I'm good. I'll watch cartoons until it's time to eat. I'm allowed an hour a day, but sometimes Daddy lets me cheat and watch more."

"Bending the rules a little isn't always a bad thing when no one gets hurt."

"That's what Daddy says. Sometimes you sound like my mom." She wrinkled her forehead in a frown. "I don't remember her very well anymore." Her shoulders drooped. "I forgot what I was saying. Oh, yeah. If you want to be a mom, don't have boys. They're nasty."

"I'll keep that in mind."

After she disappeared down the hall into the living

room, Nina took a few steps and slumped in the kitchen doorway. Teague worked efficiently on the black granite countertop of the center island he'd recently installed. He finished rolling a tortilla filled with something that smelled amazing, then glanced up and smiled before turning back to the stove.

"You look beat. Was washing the dog that much of a challenge?"

"No, but afterward your daughter asked me if we're sleeping together."

He dropped the tongs, and the tortilla fell into the hot grease with a splat. "What?"

"Some girl at camp told her grown-ups who kiss sleep in the same bed, and then they have baby boy mistakes. Apparently Keely's not down with a little brother."

"Good God."

"Yeah, I told her she wouldn't be getting a sibling in the near future."

"Is that how you left the discussion?"

"Yep, and by the way, since we now have Keely's blessing, I won't have to sneak out at the stroke of dawn again."

Teague winced. "I'm sorry about that."

"It only happened once, but I'll admit it didn't make me feel great."

Teague wiped his hands down a towel before walking over to slide his fingers behind her neck. "I'm sorry. I didn't like it either."

"I understand why it's easier. Since neither of us is ready for a commitment, why confuse Keely?"

"About that. Maybe I am—"

"Teague, the pan!"

He spun around as grease crackled, and smoke billowed up from the frying pan. A second later, the smoke detector went off with a piercing shriek.

"Shit."

Nina grabbed a towel off the counter to fan the air. "Why am I not surprised? It's been that kind of day."

Chapter Seventeen

Teague sat next to Quentin Radcliff and his date, facing the flower-covered arch where Ryan and his two groomsmen waited beside the minister for the women to appear. Behind them, the ocean stretched to the horizon on a picture-perfect afternoon. Teague wondered what they would have done if it had rained.

"Here comes Paige." Quentin spoke quietly. "That woman is extremely fine. I don't know what's wrong with the men around here. She should be involved with someone."

Paige was gorgeous in a dress the color of the sea that swirled around her knees as she exited the clubhouse to walk down the path covered with rose petals. Her blond hair was swept up in a mass of curls wound with flowers. Her eyes sparkled as she glanced their way before a hint of shadow dimmed the light shining through them. Teague couldn't help thinking it had something to do with the pretty redhead sitting on the other side of Quentin.

When Nina stepped out onto the patio, all speculation about anyone else died. Spectacular didn't begin to describe her. She wore the same dress as her friend, but the two women were as different as night and day. Nina was simple, elegant perfection on a pair of cream-colored heels that somehow made her legs look even better than they did in shorts. Her short dark hair was in its usual carefree style, but a strand of flowers was threaded through it. As she drew even with him, a smile curved her pink lips.

When Quentin nudged him, he tore his gaze away from her retreating back.

"Dude, stand up. Here comes the bride."

Teague surged to his feet as the music changed and Leah appeared. She'd left her hair long and straight, shimmering like a waterfall past her waist with a wreath of lilies and roses settled over the crown of her head in place of a veil. Her dress was strapless, similar to Nina's and Paige's, but the gown flowed to her feet before flaring out in a short train that brushed the ground with each step. Her true beauty, however, was reflected in the sheer joy glowing in her warm brown eyes as she gripped her father's arm.

"Ryan is a lucky man."

Quentin nodded. "Without a doubt."

Teague's attention returned to Nina as the ceremony commenced. He wondered if she was thinking about her fiancé who'd died, and the wedding that had never happened for her. An image of Jayne standing opposite him, young and lovely and full of dreams, grabbed him by the throat when the minister spoke clearly and solemnly.

"Do you promise to love, honor, and cherish her until death do you part?"

"I do," Ryan responded in a reverent tone.

Words Teague had never expected would have such a fatal impact on his life five short years after he'd spoken them. No one as vital and dynamic as his wife should have been denied a future.

"Are you okay?" Quentin spoke in a low voice.

Teague relaxed his white-knuckled grip on the chair in front of him and wiped the sleeve of his suit jacket across his damp brow before glancing toward the other man. "Yeah. The memories are a little rough, but I'm going to be okay."

He focused on Nina, who was the singular reason for the truth of his statement. Without a doubt, she was the most beautiful woman he'd ever dated, but she had so much more to offer than physical appeal. Wit, humor, and intelligence. A kind heart. He didn't just want to spend time with her. She filled an empty place deep inside him, and he knew he'd be a fool not to tell her how he felt. Uncertainty nagged at him, a fear that she wasn't ready to hear it.

The ceremony finished in a blur, and before he knew it, the happy couple walked down the aisle to the clapping and cheering of the crowd. Nina met his gaze as she passed him on the arm of the best man, but he was forced to wait until the rows in front of him emptied before he could search for her. When he entered the clubhouse, she broke off a conversation with Leah's grandmother to hurry toward him.

Nina reached for his hand. "Wasn't the ceremony beautiful?" She blinked back tears, and her smile wobbled. "I'm so happy for Leah and Ryan."

Teague slid an arm around her waist and glanced toward the bride and groom, who were both beaming as they chatted with guests. "They do look pretty darn thrilled to be hitched."

"High school sweethearts who found their way back to each other. It doesn't get much more romantic than that."

She was quiet for a moment before seeming to shake her reflective mood. "I saw you sitting by Quentin. Who's his date?"

"Uh, her name is Blaze something. Is Paige okay with her being here?"

"I don't know why not." Nina nodded toward her friend, who was standing near the wedding cake with one of the groomsmen. "She was pretty chummy with Tom, Ryan's rock climbing buddy, at the rehearsal dinner last night."

"I'm sorry I couldn't go with you, but since Stella already had another commitment . . ."

"It wasn't a problem, honestly. I'm used to attending events like that alone."

But she shouldn't have to. "Maybe it's time I found a few backup babysitters."

Guilt ate at him as they stopped at the bar to order drinks before they mingled with the other guests, slowly threading their way through the crowd as Nina paused to introduce him to friends and acquaintances every few feet. When dinner was finally served, they filled their plates at the buffet and sat at the table reserved for the wedding party. Teague was happy to drop onto a chair and let the pleasant smile he'd been cultivating fall away as he dug into an excellent meal of chicken breast stuffed with wild rice.

"Is everything okay?"

He glanced up from his plate to meet her gaze. "Sure. The food is terrific."

"I meant with you." Nina's brows pinched. "You've been pretty quiet."

"Just trying to process and remember everyone you introduced me to. Is there a single person in this room you don't know?"

"Maybe a few of Ryan's business colleagues. Is that a problem?"

"No, but I have some work to do in order to fit into this community." He sipped his beer. "Socializing hasn't been a priority for me when simply managing my job and Keely takes up most of my time."

"I don't go out a lot, either." She laid a hand on his arm. "I don't expect you to be available on command for random social events. I know you have your priorities, and that's fine. Really."

He covered her hand with his. "You're a priority. I hope you know that."

"I do." She smiled. "Why so serious when this is a happy occasion?"

"Maybe because I noticed a few men eyeing me the way a stray checks out a dog with a particularly juicy bone. I have a feeling any of those guys would be happy to take what I'm lucky enough to have."

Her grin broadened. "Most of them have probably already tried." She bent closer. "And failed."

He cupped the back of her head to pull her in for a kiss. "Good to know."

"So relax and enjoy yourself." She retreated a few inches. "Besides, you know people. Mateo is over there with Sabrina at a table near the bar. You two can talk about work or whatever while I perform maid of honor duties later."

"Sounds good since I'd make one awkward-looking wallflower."

"You know what, Teague?"

He picked up his fork again as he met her amused gaze. "What?"

"You entertain me."

He answered with a smile, then focused on his meal while she leaned across the best man on the other side of her to talk to Paige. He couldn't be a carefree bachelor like the men she was probably used to dating, but maybe she really didn't mind. He sure as hell hoped not, because committing to their relationship was what he wanted, what he needed. And he intended to tell her how he felt the minute they had some time alone.

Which didn't seem likely anytime soon. Not unless he wanted to shout to be heard.

After the caterers cleared the food, the band began playing in earnest as the dancing got under way. The lights dimmed, and myriad stars were projected across the ceiling in a dizzying array. Surrounded by other couples on the parquet floor, Teague took Nina in his arms and held her close as they swayed to an old Frank Sinatra classic. Her bare back was warm and smooth beneath his palm. She looked as happy in the moment as he felt.

Snuggling close, she pressed her face to his neck. "I'm so glad you're here. Are you enjoying yourself?"

"I have the most beautiful woman in the room in my arms." He slid the hand on her back downward as his body tightened. "What's not to love about being with you?"

"It goes both ways. Usually, I'm perfectly content on my own, but being half of a couple can be a whole lot better." She pulled back to smile up at him. "I'd forgotten— or simply convinced myself I didn't need anyone. Maybe I was wrong about that."

When the song ended, Teague guided her toward the French doors leading outside. Twilight had descended over the beach, and the patio was deserted. There was nothing to disturb them but the crash of waves on the shore.

"About the couple thing. I know I said—" When his phone vibrated in his jacket pocket, he hesitated. "I can let it go to voice mail. This conversation is important."

She let go of his hand. "True, but it could be work."

Reluctantly, he pulled out his cell and frowned. "That's weird. Sorry, I need to . . ." He swiped the screen to connect the call and raised the phone to his ear. "Hello."

"Teague, this is Bobbi Sandburg, Alexis's mom. I hate to bother you when you're at a wedding, but I thought you'd want to know Keely fell roller-skating out on the street. She skinned her knees and elbows and is a little upset, but I've cleaned the abrasions and bandaged them. She'll be fine. However, I didn't want to give her ibuprofen or acetaminophen for the pain without making sure she isn't allergic to either of them first."

"No, either one is fine." He glanced at Nina, and his chest ached. "I should probably come pick her up, though."

"She really is okay now. She cried a little but stopped once I got the bandages on. I'm so sorry it happened at all. I told those girls not to skate down the hill, and they promised to stay in front of the house where I could see them. I went inside to take a phone call, and—"

"It wouldn't be the first time Keely did something a little reckless." He couldn't tear his gaze away from Nina as the words tumbled out. "I really think I should bring her home. I'll be by to pick her up shortly."

As he thanked the woman for calling and hung up, Nina's eyes darkened. "Is Keely okay?"

"Bobbi Sandburg says she's fine. Keely crashed roller-skating and apparently lost some skin. I need to go check on her. She was upset."

"I'd be upset, too, if I skinned myself. Road rash is never fun, even when it's mild."

"I'm glad you can sympathize." Conflicting feelings—a primal need to go to his daughter along with the fear of disappointing Nina—rose in his chest and made drawing breath an effort. "I don't want to leave you without a ride home."

She retreated a step. "I can get a lift from someone. As you pointed out, I know everyone here. Anyway, I'm used to being on my own at parties."

"Nina—"

"I understand Keely comes first. You should go."

He wanted to protest that her needs mattered, that he hadn't asked for this situation. But the reality was, despite his misgivings, he fully intended to leave. "I'm sorry." Stepping forward, he tugged her close and kissed her. The sweet scent of her along with the softness of her lips nearly weakened his resolve. "Really, really sorry. I'll talk to you tomorrow. Okay?"

"Sure."

Not knowing what else to say, he backed away from the disappointment in her eyes, then took off at a run across the sand toward the parking lot. As he climbed into his truck and jammed the keys into the ignition, helplessness ate at him. "Shit!" The word echoed back in the moment of silence before he revved the engine and roared out of the lot.

At a speed that should have earned him a ticket, Teague drove back toward town. Except the cop Nina was so chummy with had been at the wedding instead of patrolling the streets of Siren Cove. Maybe Chris Long would give her a ride home. He slammed his fist down on the steering wheel.

Slowing when he reached the neighborhood where Keely's friend lived, he pulled into their driveway and turned off the engine. The outdoor flood lights were on, illuminating the walkway in apparent anticipation of his arrival. He got out of the truck and pushed the door shut. By the time he reached the porch steps, the front door swung open.

"Hi, Daddy." Keely skipped through the opening and leaned on the railing. "I crashed hard. There was blood."

His foot hovered above the final step as he locked gazes with his daughter. Her gap-toothed smile appeared.

Is she bragging about hurting herself?

"I heard you skinned yourself up pretty good. How do you feel?"

"Not too bad." She held up her forearms. "Alexis's mom put stinky stuff on the scrapes and princess bandages. We used the whole box."

He surveyed the first aid job. "Impressive."

"I used gauze pads on her knees, but she liked the princess bandages better."

Teague glanced toward the doorway where Bobbi Sandburg stood, wearing a pair of gray sweatpants with a bloodstain across one thigh. His daughter's blood, he assumed.

"It looks like you did an excellent job. Thanks for taking such good care of Keely."

"I'm just sorry it happened. Alexis won't be available to play for a week. She's grounded for disobeying direct orders."

"Alexis said a bad word." Keely's whisper could probably have been heard out in the yard.

Teague pressed his lips together in a tight line. "Don't think there won't be consequences for you, too."

"Huh?" Her eyes widened. "I was the one who got hurt. Isn't that enough consquence?"

"Consequence, and no, it isn't. I had to leave Nina at the wedding because you misbehaved."

"You didn't have to come get me. It's not like I'm dying or anything."

He gritted his teeth, wondering if all six-year-olds talked back to their dads, or if his was just special. With an effort, he kept his voice mild. "So I see. Get your bag and tell Mrs. Sandburg thank you."

Keely's feet scraped the decking as she walked slowly back to the door to take the flowered overnight bag the woman handed her. "Thank you. I had fun before the crash."

"You're welcome, hon. Maybe we'll see you once Alexis can have friends over again."

His daughter nodded, then trudged down the steps.

Teague glanced back. "I do appreciate you calling me. Even if she isn't on death's doorstep."

Bobbi responded with an amused grin. "No problem. Good night, Teague."

"Good night." He put a hand on Keely's shoulder to usher her down the walkway to his pickup. "Climb in."

She obeyed without comment and was silent for the first half of the drive. Figuring out her best line of defense, he assumed.

"It wasn't my fault."

He glanced up at the review mirror and noted his daughter's mutinous pout as they passed under a streetlight before turning off the main road into their neighborhood. "What, Alexis forced you to skate down that hill?"

"No, but some lady wanted to talk to us. She waved at me to come down to her."

Teague frowned. "Did Alexis know her?"

"I don't think so. It was starting to get dark, so we

couldn't see her very well. We skated down the hill, and then I crashed. It hurt a lot. I cried even though I tried hard not to."

He wasn't falling for her *poor me* tone. "Did the woman come help you?"

"No, but other neighbors came running outside. Then Alexis's dad carried me back to their house, and her mom fixed me up."

"I owe them for their stellar first aid efforts." He pulled into the driveway and sat for a moment before turning in his seat to face her. "I still don't understand why you would skate down a hill you were told to avoid in order to talk to a stranger. That's reckless and dangerous."

"Don't you think I've been punished enough already?" Her voice escalated. "I bled all over the place."

"We'll discuss your punishment tomorrow." He opened the car door. "Right now, I want you to go to bed. It's late, and I'm sure you're tired after your traumatic experience."

"I'm a little tired. I bet Coco will be happy to see me."

"I'm sure she will." As he stepped out of the truck, he glanced over at Nina's house. This certainly wasn't how he'd envisioned the evening ending. She'd said she understood why he had to leave, but he wasn't sure she did. He rubbed the back of his neck where tension grabbed hold.

"Does your head hurt?"

"Huh?" he glanced down at Keely. "No, I'm just . . . never mind. Let's go take a look at your knees."

"They're going to be all scabbed up." His daughter took his hand and skipped beside him toward the house. "Alexis's brother said they'll look gross." Her trusting gaze met his with a questioning look. "Will the kids at camp make fun of me?"

Apparently I've been forgiven . . . or she's trying to make me feel sorry for her.

"No. With all those wounds, I imagine they'll treat you like a war hero."

"Cool." She leaned against him as he unlocked the front door. "I'm sorry."

He glanced toward Nina's dark house once more before entering his own. "Yeah, I'm sorry, too."

Chapter Eighteen

The bouquet came at her with the accuracy of a sinker hurled by a major league pitcher, sailing through the crowd of women and girls to nearly smack her in the face. Nina raised her hands in self-defense . . . and caught it. The crowd clapped and cheered. Feeling a little self-conscious, she waved the flowers over her head and executed a curtsey.

"Nice snag."

Turning, she smiled at Paige. "I wasn't trying to catch it."

"Why not? Maybe flutter it in Teague's face to give the man a few ideas." A frown wrinkled her brow. "Speaking of Teague, I haven't seen him in a while. Where—"

"He left during the dancing."

Paige's jaw hung open. "What? Why?"

"His daughter fell and hurt herself, so he rushed off to pick her up."

"Oh, no. I hope she didn't need to go to the ER."

"Nothing like that."

Paige touched her arm. "You were pretty quiet during the cake cutting. You aren't upset, are you?"

"No. Well, maybe a little. Teague and I were talking about our relationship and what we need from each other, so the timing of the call kind of sucked."

"I'm sure you'll finish your conversation later."

"I guess so. I was just feeling so . . ." Nina waved one hand. "I don't know . . . complete, having him here with me. No guy I've dated since Keith has broken through my protective barriers. But Teague's daughter will always be his top priority, and I understand that."

Sympathy registered in Paige's eyes. "But?"

"No buts. His integrity is part of why I lo . . . like him so much. Keith had it, as well. I took a back seat to his career. Always." She pressed a hand to her chest to rub the ache. "I feel like I'm facing the same obstacles all over again. Just in a slightly different form."

When Paige reached out to hug her, holding back tears became an effort.

"A child isn't the same as a job, no matter how important." She pulled back to look at Nina. "Do you love him?"

"I . . . probably." Her shoulders slumped. "We've avoided using the L-word so far. Not to mention we haven't been together all that long."

"What does time have to do with your emotions? You either feel something or you don't."

"I guess so, but love won't solve all our problems. Sometimes love can make you feel worse rather than better."

"Yeah, it certainly can." Paige's gaze drifted across the room to where Quentin and his date stood, apparently deep in conversation. She turned back. "Look how long it took Leah and Ryan to make their love work. But they were able to get past her failed marriage and his feelings of betrayal. Seems like you and Teague need to talk about your concerns and address them. Communication is key."

"True." Nina smiled. "You know, you really should have taken your psych degree and gone into therapy instead of opening an antique store."

"What can I say? I'm a woman of many talents." Paige grinned as the band broke into a striptease number. "Hey, check out Ryan. He's pulling off Leah's garter with his teeth. My guess is that man still has a few surprises in store for our lucky friend."

"I hope so."

Nina clapped along with everyone else until the garter was removed. When Ryan turned his back and tossed it over his head, the scrap of satin and lace slipped through Quentin's fingers to be scooped up by Chris Long.

"Dodged a bullet there."

"Huh?" Nina glanced over at Paige. "What do you mean?"

"Never mind. Hey, Chris is trying to get your attention. The photographer probably wants a shot of you two together with the bouquet and garter."

"He's waving me over. I'll talk to you later, Paige."

"Okay. I think I'll go find Tom. Ryan's rock climbing buddy is a hottie, and right now I don't care much that we don't have a whole lot in common." She gripped her arm before Nina could walk away. "Talk to Teague. You two have a good thing going, and I don't want to see you let it slip past you."

"You're right, but I need to figure out a few things first. Thanks for listening to me whine."

Paige smiled. "Anytime."

Nina was still thinking about her friend's advice when she joined Chris Long and the photographer for a couple of quick pictures before the man hustled off to shoot a few final photos of the bride and groom as they prepared to depart.

"I guess the party's over."

Nina gave Chris a brief smile. "Yep. I need to tell Leah goodbye before she and Ryan take off."

"I couldn't help noticing your date disappeared. If you need a ride home . . ."

"Actually, I do. I was going to ask Paige, but she may have other plans for the end of the evening. If it isn't any bother, I'll take you up on that offer."

"Of course not." His steady gaze held hers. "Go talk to Leah. I'm ready to leave whenever you want, but no rush."

"Thanks, Chris."

The police officer really was a nice guy. As Nina waited for Leah to finish her conversation with a pair of older relatives, she glanced back over her shoulder and discovered him still watching her. With Teague, a tingle would have shot straight through her the minute they made eye contact. As it was, she didn't feel even a hint of a spark. After a moment, she turned away.

When the elderly couple moved on, Leah reached out to snag Nina's wrist. "I've been trying to get two minutes alone with you for a while now. Being the bride is busy work."

Pulling Leah in close, Nina hugged her. "You've made a spectacular job of it. I'm so happy for you."

"I'm happy for me, too. Ryan's chomping at the bit to get out of here, and honestly, I'm ready for some alone time with my husband."

Nina smiled. "Does saying that feel awkward?"

"Maybe a little new still, but exactly right." Leah pulled back to regard her closely. "Where did Teague disappear to?"

"His daughter had an issue, so he had to leave." Nina

rushed on, "Nothing major, so don't worry. I want you to have the best honeymoon ever."

"I intend to." Leah glanced over Nina's shoulder. "Looks like Ryan needs me. I'll call you from Austria in a few days, maybe text you some pictures."

"You do that. Safe travels."

With a wave and a swirl of her skirt, Leah ran to meet her man. When he greeted her with a quick kiss and a hand at her waist, Nina's heart ached.

"Ready to go?" Chris stopped beside her and gave her an enquiring look.

"Sure. Let's get out of here."

Nina shivered a little as they hurried through the chilly night air to his car and waited while he unlocked the classic Mustang. Once she was seated inside, he shut the door before running around the front to slide onto the driver's seat.

"Thanks for offering me a ride."

He started the engine and let it idle for a minute. "No problem. Kind of shitty of O'Dell to ditch you at a wedding. Did you two have a fight?"

Nina gritted her teeth, sick to death of explaining Teague's absence. "No. His daughter hurt herself, so he went to pick her up."

"Oh." He was quiet for a moment. "I just assumed . . . Guess I was wrong." He shifted into gear. "I'll take you home."

Nina leaned against the seat back. "I don't suppose you've had any luck tracking down the person who broke into my house."

"I'm afraid not. Since you haven't been bothered . . ." He raised a brow. "At least I assume you haven't?"

She shook her head. "Not since he tied me up."

"Maybe the perp found whatever he was after. I hope he won't return again."

"While it would be nice to see the creep arrested, at this point I'll take simply being safe."

Chris glanced over as he slowed to turn up the street leading to her neighborhood. "Exactly, but don't let down your guard."

"Oh, I won't. Still, it's damn inconvenient trying to find someone to run with me."

"Give me a call. If I'm not on duty, I'd be happy to go."

When he stopped in front of her house, she turned on the seat. "I'll keep that in mind. Thanks again for the lift home. I appreciate it."

"No problem." He turned off the engine. "I'll walk you to your door."

"You don't have—"

"Yes, I do. It's late, and you forgot to turn on your porch light." He opened the door and stepped outside. "Safety first."

"I'm not going to argue with that."

She stumbled on the brick walkway, and he took her arm. "Careful."

"I really should have remembered that light." When they reached the porch, she turned to face him. "That's what happens when you're in a rush."

"Which is why I don't want you to become inattentive. Being a little late never killed anyone. Being careless has."

A shiver that had nothing to do with the chill in the air slid through her. "Good point." After she unlocked the door, flipped on the light, and turned off the alarm, she leaned against the wall and smiled. "Safe and sound. Thank you."

"You're welcome." He hesitated for a moment then stepped backward. "Good night, Nina."

"Night, Chris." Shutting the door behind him, she pressed her fingers to her eyes as exhaustion weighed on the lids. It had been a long evening, emotionally draining and filled with highs and lows.

When a knock sounded on the door, she frowned as she reached for the knob to swing it open. "Did you for-get—Teague."

"Expecting Officer Long to return?"

She eyed him steadily. "You would rather I had hitch-hiked home?"

"Sorry." Teague stuck his hands in the back pockets of his jeans. "I shouldn't be sarcastic since it's my fault you needed a ride."

"Are you coming inside?"

"Keely is home asleep, so I—"

"How is she?"

"Fine. She'll have a few scabs, but she doesn't seem terribly traumatized."

"Well, that's good."

"Yeah, it is." He reached out to touch her cheek. "I just wanted to make sure you were okay and say I'm sorry for leaving you at the wedding."

"I'm fine. Why wouldn't I be?"

He shifted from one foot to the other. "I was out on the porch when Long drove up, and I couldn't help noticing you stumbled up the walk."

Her lips tightened. "I tripped. I didn't spend the rest of my evening drowning my sorrows, if that's what you're implying."

"Sorry. Sorry. Sorry." He moved in closer until his breath brushed her face. "I blew it tonight. I hope you aren't angry."

"You did what you needed to do." When he threaded his fingers through her hair and tipped her head back, a tremor shot through her. "I don't think I'm ready for a serious conversation right now. I just want to go to bed."

"With Keely home, I can't stay here, but you could—"

"I'm tired. Can we put this on hold until tomorrow?"

He let his hand fall back to his side. "Sure." He gave her a half-smile. "Go get some sleep."

"Thanks for understanding. I'll stop by in the morning."

"I'm working tomorrow." His voice held an edge.

"Okay, later in the day, then. Good night, Teague."

With a nod, he stepped back. "Good night."

Nina slowly shut the door behind him, but not before a quiet expletive echoed in the stillness. She winced. Obviously, he wasn't happy.

She straightened her shoulders as she locked the door and set the alarm. She needed some time to think, and she certainly couldn't be objective about the situation snuggled up with Teague. If he didn't like going home by himself, too bad.

Her steps were heavy as she climbed the stairs to her room. After taking off her dress and hanging it in the closet, she pulled a long T-shirt over her head and shrugged on her fleece robe, feeling the need for warmth. *Or maybe I just want familiar comfort I can count on.* She stuck her feet into her slippers, then made her way to the bathroom to wash her face and brush her teeth. After removing the strand of flowers from her hair, she flipped off the light. Standing at the window overlooking the street, she gazed toward the light still shining in Teague's bedroom window.

Did I make a mistake, pushing him away? She bit

down on her bottom lip as she searched conflicting feelings swirling inside her for an answer.

"What the hell?"

Leaning on the sill, she peered through the darkness illuminated only by intermittent moonlight as clouds shifted across the sky. A shadow moved near Teague's shed. After a moment, a muted glow appeared.

Someone checking a cell? The same person who tied me up?

Grabbing her purse off the dresser, she pulled out her phone and tapped the screen to call Teague. While it rang, she ran down the stairs.

"Nina?" His voice was hesitant.

"Someone's outside. I'm going to find out who the hell has been stalking me once and for all."

"Jesus. Hold on while I put on some pants. Don't you dare confront him on your own!"

"Then hurry, because I don't want him to take off." She hit the foot of the stairs and skidded on the soles of her slippers, then raced across the entry.

"Stay where you are, Nina. I'm on my way."

When the connection went dead, she stuffed her phone in her robe pocket, threw the dead bolt, and unlocked the door. She would just check to make sure the creep was still there then wait for Teague. She eased the door open and stepped outside. Staying in the shadows, she peered through the darkness. Surely the shifting movement near the trees edging the road was the pervert.

When the alarm went off behind her with a shrill peal, she nearly jumped out of her skin.

"No!" She ran across the porch and down the walkway.

Out on the street, footsteps slapped against pavement and faded in the distance before she could cross her yard.

"Go turn off the alarm. I'll go after him." Teague's shout stopped her cold.

As he sprinted down his driveway and took off after the stalker, she turned back.

"Damn it! How could I have forgotten to turn off the stinking alarm?"

Reaching the house, she punched in the code, and blessed silence ensued. When her landline rang, she hurried to the kitchen to answer it.

"Hello."

"This is Ted at Armor Security Company. Our remote data shows you've had a break-in at your residence."

"I forgot to turn off the alarm."

"I'll need your name and password to cancel a response."

Nina provided the information and apologized. As she hung up, she wondered if she should have let the service call nine-one-one for help. If Teague caught the person who'd tied her up—

"He got away."

"What?" She spun around.

"He disappeared, probably through someone's back-yard into the woods. A couple of dogs were barking up the street, but I couldn't see worth shit. All I had for a light was my phone."

"Oh, no. I can't believe this!" She slumped against the counter.

"I could have kept looking, but the chances of finding him weren't great, and I was worried he might circle back around while I was searching and grab you. The front door was still wide open, and I walked right in."

"Not very smart of me, but then I didn't exactly use my best judgment tonight." She let out a frustrated breath.

"Should we call the cops? I had the alarm company cancel the emergency response."

"What would be the point? I'm sure the guy is long gone by now. What did you actually see before you called me?"

"Just a shadow move near your shed. Then a dim glow. I assume he looked at his phone while he was standing there."

Approaching slowly, Teague slid an arm around her waist and squeezed. "I'm sorry I didn't catch him, but he had a decent head start."

"My fault for setting off the stupid alarm. Thanks for trying." Her hand shook as she pushed a lock of hair behind her ear. "Teague?"

He pulled her in closer and rested his chin on her head. "What?"

"Is your offer still good?"

He pulled back to look down at her. "What offer?"

"To spend the night. I don't think I want to be alone."

He tilted her face and kissed her. "If you hadn't asked, I would have camped out in your yard. I don't have any intention of leaving you alone. Not now or ever."

Breathing hard, she collapsed into a chair in the dark front room. She'd escaped, but only because she'd tripped and fallen into a ditch. Her pursuer had run right past her while she tried to gather her wits. Once he'd turned back, she'd crawled onto the road and limped home.

A stupid, stupid risk to take, but she'd been worried.

With a moan, she pushed to her feet. Climbing the stairs was an effort, but she conquered them. When she reached the door to Lynette's—not Lynette, the impostor's—door, she paused. All was quiet on the other side. She removed the padlock and dropped it in her jacket pocket. The time to bury her mistake was drawing near, but until then, she couldn't take any risks.

Which was why her actions tonight had been so foolish.

After flipping on her bedroom light, she shed her filthy clothes and pulled a flannel nightgown over her head. She needed a shower but was too exhausted. Instead, she entered the bathroom to brush fir needles and twigs out of her gray hair and wipe dirt streaks off her face.

With trembling hands, she fumbled with the cap to her pain meds. After swallowing two, she snapped off the light and headed to bed. The cool sheets soothed her aching limbs as she flopped down with another moan.

She'd been a fool tonight, but having only a few yards of space and thin walls separating her from Lynette had been a comfort. Then Nina had come home, and the car headlights had nearly caught her in the beams. When Teague left his house to rush to her side, she'd been oh so tempted to take what belonged to her then and there.

Too soon.

The day of Lynette's birth was only a couple of weeks away. She could wait until the time was right. In the meantime, Nina was becoming a real problem, an obstacle to her ultimate goal. Not to mention the woman still had the stinking lottery ticket. She'd have to think about the best way to eliminate the threat.

She didn't fight it when her lids slowly closed. For now, she'd sleep on it.

Chapter Nineteen

Teague woke to the blare of the alarm early Sunday morning. Reaching across Nina, he slapped down hard on the clock to stop the noise. Instead of rolling back to his side of the bed, he snuggled in close. He could think of worse ways to begin his day than waking with her in his arms.

"You know that thing has a music setting, right?"

He smiled at her grumpy tone. "Yes, but I sleep right through it." Nuzzling his nose against her neck, he breathed deep. "You smell good."

"Peach-scented lotion." She turned over and blinked in the faint light filtering through the blinds. "Don't you have to get up for work?"

"I have some extra time, and I'd rather eat breakfast on the fly if it means hanging out with you a little longer." He ran the pad of his thumb across her cheek. "Anyway, I think we need to talk."

"About the fact that we didn't make love last night?"

Lying beside her while keeping his hands to himself

hadn't been easy. "I wouldn't take advantage of the situation, and you made your feelings pretty clear earlier in the evening."

"I don't know how I managed that when *I'm* not even sure how I feel." She pressed one warm palm to his chest. "I think that's part of the problem."

Beneath her hand, his heart beat a little faster. "No problem on my end. I know what I want— you."

"We discussed not rushing into anything, taking it slow to see how we do together."

"In theory that sounds smart, but in reality . . ." He gathered her close and kissed her, a long, slow, drugging kiss that left him keyed up and wanting more. "I can't imagine not having you in my life."

"I think I'm in love with you, Teague."

Her words came out of nowhere, and his mouth dropped open. He'd expected to have to push and prod her into a committed relationship. For Nina to lay her heart out in a vulnerable confession changed his whole strategy.

"But—"

Here it comes . . . "Does there have to be a but? I love you, too."

"I know."

His brows lowered. "You do?"

"Your feelings are honest and open. I know you care about me. I expect you'd like to take casual dating to the next level."

"I definitely would."

"But on your terms. You want to insert me into your life without disrupting the balance you've worked so hard to achieve over the last few weeks. Your priorities will still be Keely, work, and then me."

"I can't ignore my daughter when she needs me." Pain flared in his chest, but he couldn't hold back the truth. "I have to make a living."

She touched his cheek. "I know that. I don't expect—or want—you to neglect Keely. Obviously your job makes demands on your time. For you, working late may mean the difference between life and death for someone. But I'm not sure I want to be squeezed in around the edges. I've been there and done that, and honestly, I wasn't very happy making all the compromises."

"I'm not Keith."

"No, you're not, and I'd like to think you'll try harder to understand my needs instead of dismissing them in favor of your own."

"Yet you were still going to marry the guy."

She nodded. "I didn't know then what I know now. I loved him, but we might not have lasted as a couple over the long run."

"That's not what I want to have happen to us." He held her a little tighter and tried not to notice the way her breasts, covered only in thin cotton, pressed against his chest. "I also don't want you to walk away. Can't we work on this?"

"Of course we can, but I wanted to let you know where I stand."

"I appreciate that." He met her troubled gaze. "No relationship comes without its fair share of problems. Compromise by both parties, along with a willingness to keep trying, is always necessary."

"True."

"My marriage wasn't perfect. Jayne and I had different priorities and fought about them."

"Can I ask what they were?" She kept her gaze steady.

"Not to be nosy, but to understand what's important to you."

"Money. Jayne lived in the moment. She thought it was more important to make memories than save for the future. I have a more practical nature. I wanted to start a college fund for Keely. She wanted to take her on an African safari."

Nina nestled her head against his shoulder. "Wasn't your daughter a little young to appreciate a trip like that?"

"My point exactly. I told Jayne there'd be plenty of time for vacations once we were better off financially." His gut tightened. "Turned out, she didn't have all those tomorrows I was counting on."

"You couldn't have anticipated what happened."

"No, but now I wish I'd gone along with what she wanted." He brushed a strand of hair off Nina's cheek, the skin so soft beneath his fingertips. "My point is I'm more than willing to consider your perspective. I know I have a tendency to be overprotective. Last night was a perfect example. Keely really would have been fine staying at her friend's house. I didn't have to leave you at the wedding."

Nina pressed a little tighter, aligning her curves to his angles. "I don't intend to make unreasonable demands on your time. But—"

He touched her lips with his finger. "When something matters to you, I should be there to support you. I get that."

She smiled. "On that note, maybe we should end this conversation." She wiggled against him. "Or don't you have time?"

A soft groan escaped as his body heated. "For this, I can make time."

Cradling her in his arms, he was happy to stop talking and kiss her instead. He couldn't get enough of Nina. From the passion shining in her beautiful eyes as they slowly closed, to the long, shapely legs she wrapped around his waist as he rolled her beneath him, he only wanted more. To give and to take. After tossing her T-shirt to the floor, he cupped her naked breasts in his palms and went in for another kiss before slowly sinking into her.

She ran her hands up and down his back and clutched his ass to hold him closer. When little whimpers of need escaped her throat, he nearly lost it.

"God, I love you. I want you here with me every day."

She nodded in response as she thrust against him. When a soft cry wrenched from her throat, he shuddered against her before collapsing full-length on top of her.

Holding him tight, she strung kisses up the side of his neck. "I love you, too."

"I'm crushing you."

She gripped his shoulders harder. "No, don't move. I want this for just a minute longer."

He was happy to stay . . . until he caught a glimpse of the digital clock on the bedside table. "Crap!" He pressed one more kiss to her lips before levering off her. "I'm going to be late for work." He headed toward the closet. "Stella's due in a few minutes to babysit. I called her last night after I brought Keely home."

"Are you kidding?" Nina scrambled off the bed. "Geez, I don't want to announce to the whole world we're sleeping together."

By the time he grabbed pants and a shirt off the built-in shelves he'd added to the closet, she had her T-shirt and robe on and was looking under the bed for her second slipper.

She glanced up, her hair rumpled. "I'll get out of here and talk to you later."

"Nina, I—" He broke off when his cell rang. Scooping it up off the dresser, he glanced at the display. "Speak of the devil." He raised the phone to his ear. "What's up, Stella?"

"I threw out my back getting out of bed this morning. I thought I could suck it up and make it over there, but that's not happening." Her breath hissed through the receiver. "I'm in some serious pain."

He massaged the back of his neck. "Do you need help getting to the doctor?"

"Don't worry about me. I'll call a neighbor or a friend, but I'm sorry to leave you in the lurch with Keely today."

He glanced over at Nina as she rose to her feet holding the missing slipper. "I'll do the same and call a neighbor. Hopefully Nina can watch her."

"I really am sorry."

"You just take care of yourself, and let me know if you need anything."

"Thanks, Teague. Bye now."

He clicked off his phone, then glanced down and realized he was still naked. Moving quickly, he opened the dresser drawer to pull out briefs and socks.

"Do you need me to babysit?" Nina dropped down onto the edge of the bed.

"If you don't mind. I hate to take advantage of you, but Stella threw out her back."

"Hey, don't worry about it. I was going to paint today, and I still can. I'll just bring Keely with me. She can paint, too. We'll have fun."

He turned to face her. "I'll make a few phone calls when I get to work to see if I can arrange a playdate for her. But until then . . ."

"Don't be silly. Get dressed and take off. I'll hang out with Keely."

All the tension drained out of him. "Thank you."

"It's not that big a deal, but it's terribly distracting talking to you when you're bare-ass naked." Her gaze dropped.

He grinned. "Fine. I'm out of here. Well, after I get dressed."

She smiled back. "That's probably a good idea."

Nina focused on the square of canvas propped on the easel in front of her. Tipping her head, she examined the burst of colors in shades from palest pink to deep fuchsia before studying the climbing roses covering the back fence of the playground. She'd gotten the variations right, and the weathered boards behind the climbing vines made a gorgeous rustic backdrop for the blooms.

"Look, Nina. Isn't my picture pretty?"

She turned to admire Keely's painting of the roses clipped to the chunky plastic easel. "Wow, you did a terrific job. I'm sure your dad will want to put that up on the refrigerator."

The girl stood and dropped her paintbrush into the cup of water. "Maybe we can frame it and hang it on the wall."

Near the base of the easel, Coco rolled over and opened her eyes. After a moment, she scrambled to her feet.

Nina nodded. "I can help you with that, but first the painting needs to dry. I'll tape the edges of the paper down so they don't curl."

"Can I go play on the slides? I don't want to paint anymore."

She glanced toward the playground behind them where several kids were running between the swings and various climbing structures. A few women occupied the benches placed strategically throughout the area, most of them on their phones.

"Do you know anyone here?"

"No, but I can talk to those girls by the drinking fountain."

Nina smiled. "Go ahead. Maybe you'll make some new friends. Keep Coco on her leash, though. I don't think dogs are allowed to run loose."

"Okay." She scooped up the leash and looped it around her wrist. "Come on, Coco."

After Keely and the dog ran off, Nina pulled a roll of masking tape out of her bag and taped the corners of the wet painting to the easel before sitting back down to work on her own project. She needed at least another hour to complete it and hoped Keely could occupy herself for a while. Mixing shades of green to the perfect tint for the leaves, she went back to work.

Every few minutes, Nina glanced over her shoulder to pick Keely out of the thinning crowd of kids. As the sun climbed higher in the sky and the noise behind her decreased, she hurried to finish her painting. Satisfied with the results, she laid down her brush and gave a fist pump. "Yes! Someone out there will want to hang this baby above their living room couch or give their office a splash of color."

Wiping her hands on a rag, she turned to search for Keely. When she didn't immediately see her or the dog, she rose from her stool to better scan the playground. A flash of color in the parking lot caught her attention. Keely's bright pink shirt. She stood between a car and a van with her back to the playground.

The hair on Nina's neck rose. "Keely! Get over here right now!" Dropping the rag, she sprinted toward the parking lot.

When Keely turned to head her way with Coco following, Nina slowed and stopped beside the swings, then pressed a hand to her chest.

"Hey, Nina! Why did you yell like that?"

When the girl reached her side, she controlled the urge to shake her. "You scared me, that's why. You should know better than to wander alone into a parking lot. Anyone in a car could open a door and grab you."

Keely's eyes widened. "I wasn't alone. I'm not stupid."

Out in the parking lot, an engine started, and a white sedan pulled onto the street. At their feet, Coco sat on her butt and scratched furiously behind one ear with her back paw.

Nina stared at the dog. "Coco doesn't count."

"Not Coco, the lady I was talking to. She saw a baby bunny and asked if I wanted to look at it, but Coco must have scared it away."

"You followed a stranger out to her car?" Nina tried hard to keep from shouting.

"She said it was okay because she's your friend."

Nina's frown deepened. "What was this woman's name?"

"I don't know, but she didn't look scary. She looked like a grandma." Keely's lip wobbled. "Are you mad at me?"

Nina slipped her arm around the girl and hugged her close. "I'm not mad, but you never, ever walk off with a stranger. I don't care if the person says they know me or your dad. It isn't safe. I should have been watching you more closely. This was my fault."

"Nothing bad happened."

"I'm very thankful for that. Maybe the woman who talked to you was harmless, but you still can't wander off with a stranger."

Keely scrunched up her forehead. "I thought I might know her, but I couldn't remember for sure."

"If something like that ever happens again, I want you to run back to me. Understand?"

"Okay. Can we go home now? I'm hungry."

"That's because it's past lunchtime. The good news is I finished my painting, so we can definitely leave."

Keely skipped beside her, tugging Coco by the end of the leash. "I want to see your picture. I bet it's pretty."

"Maybe not as pretty as yours, but I'm happy with how it turned out. We'll pack up our gear, load the car, and then go get something to eat."

Keely put both hands over her stomach. "I might starve first."

Somehow, she managed to survive until they got home and made grilled ham and cheese sandwiches. Taking the gooey golden triangles and a bowl of strawberries out to the porch, they sat on the steps to eat while Coco sniffed the grass along the edge of the driveway.

"I like it here." Keely bit into a strawberry. "It's not as hot as where I used to live. My mom said we could get a pool, but then she died." Her voice quavered. "She used to take me to the park, too."

Nina's heart ached for her. "I'm glad you have good memories of your mother."

"Her picture is by my bed. Looking at it helps me remember stuff." She ate another strawberry. "Can I bring my animals downstairs? I think they'd like to come outside."

"Sure. Everyone should take advantage of a fog-free afternoon."

When Keely scrambled to her feet to race into the house, Nina pulled out her phone to check for missed calls. One from Lola Copeland. She wondered if the woman had gotten her finances in order and wanted another painting. Before she could return her call, Keely returned with a bear under one arm and an elephant clutched to her chest. The screen door slammed shut behind her.

"Trudy and Anna-Banana are missing." Her high-pitched voice sounded as if she was on the verge of tears.

Nina patted the step beside her, then slipped her arm around Keely when she sat down and scooted in close. "Who are Trudy and Anna-Banana?"

"My fluffy kitty and my monkey. They weren't in my room."

"Maybe you left them downstairs or in the backyard. Did you look?"

"I tucked them both into bed with me last night. They were still there when I woke up."

"They must be somewhere. I've seen Coco carry around stuffed animals before."

"*Her* animals. She doesn't take mine."

Nina wasn't so certain the dog knew the difference. She stood and pulled Keely to her feet. "Don't worry. We'll find them."

Fifteen minutes later, Nina was beginning to have her doubts. After searching the entire upstairs with no luck, she paused in Keely's bedroom doorway. "What are you doing?"

The girl jumped down from her bed. "Looking on the closet shelf. My Belle dress isn't on the floor anymore."

"I bet your dad put it in the dirty clothes. Let's go downstairs to look for your animals."

"I didn't leave them down there."

After a fruitless search, Nina had to agree. "We'll check outside. Coco might have dragged your animals through the doggy door."

"How could she do that? I think Anna-Banana is bigger than she is."

"We'll still look." Nina reached for the dead bolt and frowned. "Did you unlock the door before we left for the park?"

"No. Why would I do that?"

Nina opened the door and scanned the yard. "I don't see your animals, but let's look around."

Coco shot past her feet and headed straight to the back gate. Giving it a head butt, she pushed it open far enough to squeeze out.

"Hey!" Keely ran after her dog. "Come back here!"

Nina followed and swung the gate wide. Thankfully, Coco hadn't gone far.

"Back inside. Both of you." She herded the dog and Keely into the yard before closing the gate. When she gave it an extra jerk, the latch clicked into place. "Did you notice anything else missing?"

"I don't think so." She turned in a circle as her lip began to quiver. "See? Trudy and Anna-Banana aren't out here."

"I guess not. Hey, no crying." Nina hugged the girl close. "We'll figure out what happened to them. I promise."

If she *had* left the back door unlocked, no one in his or her right mind would have stolen stuffed animals. There definitely had to be another explanation.

Chapter Twenty

Teague gave Keely a huge hug, questioning if spending two days and a night away from her was the right thing to do. She felt so small in his arms. Fragile. All he wanted to do was wrap his daughter up and protect her from the world. But a glance across the street to where Nina loaded her suitcase into her Mini reminded him of all the reasons why they needed some time alone together.

"Dad, you're squeezing me too tight."

"Oh, sorry." He released her. "You mind Stella."

"I will."

He looked toward the porch and smiled. "Thanks for doing this, Stella."

She came down the steps to lay a hand on Keely's shoulder. "Happy to help out. I'm just glad my back is feeling better. I had a rough few days there, but I seem to be as good as new." She snorted. "Well, as good as can be expected of an old broad."

"You aren't old, just well-seasoned."

"Isn't that the truth?" She waved a hand. "Go. Enjoy

your getaway. Keely and I will have a great time together, and I'll make sure she gets to summer camp on time tomorrow."

"I know you will." He retreated across the lawn. "I'll check in tonight and again tomorrow morning. We should be back by early evening at the latest."

"No worries. I don't have any place I have to be." She made another shooing motion. "Go already. Nina's waiting."

"Okay, I'm out of here." Reaching down, he grabbed the handle of the bag he'd dropped on the grass to hug Keely one last time. "Bye, Keels."

"Bye, Daddy."

Turning, he hustled across the road and tossed his case through the open hatch and slammed it shut. He met Nina's gaze. "Ready?"

"Are you sure you want to do this?"

He smiled . . . or at least tried to. "Positive. Who's driving?"

"I am." She gave him a long, contemplative look before opening the driver's door. "You can chill in the passenger seat, maybe figure out why you asked me to go away with you in the first place."

"I know why I asked you." He pushed the seat back to accommodate his long legs and waited while she started the engine. "Letting go is always a little tough, but I've got this."

"Good." She backed out of the driveway and gave a couple of toots on the horn. "I'm looking forward to this trip. A break from painting is mandatory every now and then, but we could have taken Keely with us."

"No, we need some alone time. I've barely seen you all week." He waved a final goodbye, then turned to face forward. "I really want this."

"I bet. A week without sex is pretty hard to take. Which direction?"

He couldn't hold back a grin. "Well, there is that. Head south."

She turned left out onto the coast road. "Are you going to tell me where we're going? Your instructions to bring casual clothes and sturdy shoes didn't give me a whole lot to go on."

"I guess I can let you in on the surprise now. Crater Lake."

"Oh, yeah?" A smile tilted her lips. "The lake is spectacular. I haven't been there since I went with my Girl Scout troop twenty years ago. We camped, and I earned three badges that weekend."

"No camping this time. I booked a room at the Crater Lake Lodge."

"Seriously?" She turned to stare. "I can't believe they weren't sold out."

"I guess we got lucky. They had a single day available between two longer stays, so I took it. We can do some hiking and just hang out."

"Sounds wonderful." She reached over to squeeze his knee. "Thanks for planning this."

"I told you your needs matter to me. This is my way of trying to make up for ditching you at Leah and Ryan's wedding." He grinned. "In addition to getting a little action."

She smiled back, and the heat in her eyes made him wish they didn't have a three-and-a-half-hour drive ahead.

He shifted on the seat to adjust his shorts and cleared his throat. "So, what have you been doing all week?"

"Finishing up a few projects and framing them, including Keely's painting of the roses. She's very proud of that picture."

"We hung it in her room. Thanks for taking the time to help her frame it."

"I enjoyed spending the afternoon with her." She passed a slow-moving camper on a straight stretch. "I think I convinced her less is better when it comes to both paint and glue."

"I'm forever in your debt." He studied her profile and wondered how anyone could be so . . . perfect. With an effort, he focused on their conversation. "That's all you've been doing? Just work?"

"That and sending out follow-up emails to art enthusiasts who've bought paintings from me in the past. Marketing for the Summer Art Fair is fairly time consuming, but having a good turnout is critical. This is my major selling event of the season, actually for the whole year."

"Most of the time you paint on commission?"

She nodded. "I have pieces in a few galleries on the West Coast, but I rely heavily on orders from past customers for income." A frown creased her brow. "I had a call from one of my regular patrons last week. Apparently she made some bad investments and is in financial difficulties. She'll be selling her house and leaving the area."

"That's too bad."

"Yeah, it sucks for Miss Lola, but also for me, since she won't be buying any more of my paintings. She mentioned being closer to her granddaughter, though, which seemed to make her happy."

"You'll make up for the loss by selling a lot of your art next weekend." He reached over to lay a hand on her knee and squeeze. "Have faith."

"One can only hope." She slowed to make the turn onto Route 38.

He settled back in his seat. "I assume you know where you're going?"

"Sure. We follow this road along the Umpqua River, then take Route 138 across to Crater Lake. It's a pretty drive."

"I'll sit back and enjoy the scenery, then."

The drive through heavily forested countryside was certainly beautiful, but he spent more time looking at Nina than out the window. They discussed topics ranging from music to politics, not always agreeing but finding common ground more often than not. They'd definitely needed this quiet stretch of togetherness to get to know each other better. Nina was confident and assertive without being overbearing, and she was willing to listen to his opinions before sharing her own. He found the combination of self-confidence overlaid with respect incredibly attractive. There were layers to this woman that went far deeper than her surface beauty.

"You're awfully quiet."

"Hmm?" He blinked and dragged his gaze away from her to glance out the window as the car slowed. "Are we stopping?"

"Bathroom break. There's a trail to a waterfall that's pretty amazing. I thought we'd take a short hike to stretch our legs. Paige and I stopped here once when I went on an antiquing trip with her."

"I'm all for getting a little exercise." After she pulled into the parking area and turned off the engine, Teague climbed out and worked a few kinks from his back. "Your Mini doesn't give a person a lot of room to stretch out."

"I refuse to apologize for my car." She met him at the front bumper and snuggled in when he slid an arm around her waist.

"No need to. I'm the one who wanted to leave my

truck for Stella. When she suggested letting Keely ride on the back of her motorcycle, I nearly had a heart attack before I realized she was just yanking my chain."

Nina grinned up at him. "I bet." She slid out from beneath his arm. "Let me use the restroom, and then we'll go see the falls."

A few minutes later, they set out through old-growth forest, following the trail toward Toketee Falls. Deep blue water frothing with white foam flowed between moss-covered rock walls below them, and the damp air was redolent with the scent of dense vegetation. Overhead, birds tweeted and chirped in cacophonous chatter.

"This place is primeval." Taking her hand, he swung their clasped fingers. "I feel like I'm in an ancient world where time no longer exists."

"Except for the path, this place probably hasn't changed much in the last millennium." She moved ahead of him as the trail narrowed. "Wait until you see the falls. They're spectacular."

Spectacular was an understatement. The two-tier falls dropped over a hundred feet into a deep pool at their base. Wrapping his arms around Nina from behind, he rested his chin on her head and let the beauty of their surroundings ease away all his stress. After a few minutes of quiet contemplation, he shifted to meet her gaze. "Looks like we could get over the fence and climb down to the pool if we want."

"Probably, but we'd get soaked by the spray. An adventure for another day."

He liked the idea of future trips with Nina. "Next time we'll bring raincoats." When a family group descended onto the viewing platform, he reluctantly released her. "Time to go?"

"Let me take a photo or two first." She snapped a couple

of shots with her phone, then glanced over at a teenage boy who'd distanced himself from his younger siblings. "Would you mind taking our picture?"

"Sure." The kid took her phone and waved them toward the rail.

Teague slid an arm around Nina's waist and smiled.

"Got it." The boy handed her cell back.

"Thank you." She slipped the phone into her pocket.

"Let's go." Teague touched her arm. "My breakfast is wearing thin. Didn't I see a bag of snacks in the back seat?"

"Lucky for you, I planned ahead. Crater Lake is only about forty minutes from here, so I don't think you'll starve."

He bent to drop a kiss on her smiling mouth. "I'd better eat an apple and not risk it."

The look she gave him was long and lingering. "We definitely need you to keep up your strength."

Nina flopped over backward, breathing heavily as the sheen of perspiration on her bare skin dried in the breeze coming through the open window. "Wow. Just wow."

At her side, Teague grunted but didn't bother to open his eyes. "I may never have the energy to move again."

She eyed the man she'd come to love, in all his naked glory stretched out on the pure white sheet, and swallowed. "How lame would we be if we stayed in our hotel room for the next twenty-four hours and didn't go exploring?"

"I don't think I have the stamina." Finally he turned his head to stare at her. "Hiking burns fewer calories than making love with you."

"Are you complaining?"

"Hell no." Moving swiftly, he rolled her beneath him. "I'm bragging."

She wrapped her arms around his back. "I guess we should get up, maybe go for a walk before dinner. Nothing too strenuous that will tax your strength."

He grinned down at her. "Fine. Since we came all this way, we should at least go appreciate the lake." He bent to kiss her and lingered long enough to make her heart beat faster. "Okay, this is me, climbing out of bed."

She held on tighter. "You aren't moving."

"That's because you're clinging like a limpet."

After he kissed his way down the side of her neck, she finally let her arms slip to the mattress. "Okay, you're free."

His gaze sobered. "I don't think I am. At this point, we're bound together, and I don't want to let you go."

"Good, because I'm pretty happy all wrapped up in you." She stroked her thumb across his check. "This is a good thing for us both, right?"

He nodded. "You make me believe in happily ever after again." A rueful smile curved his lips as he sat up. "Before you start thinking I'm a total girl for comments like that, let's go enjoy the outdoors. I love the ocean, but that lake out there is practically a religious experience."

There was nothing feminine about Teague's muscled backside as he bent over his suitcase to dig out a pair of jeans and a button-down shirt. With an effort, she tore her gaze away as he pulled on a pair of briefs and focused on getting herself dressed. She chose a short forest-green skirt and matching sleeveless top she could wear with flats that would be appropriate for dinner in the restaurant downstairs and comfortable for a casual walk beforehand. Ten minutes later, they left the lodge to stroll hand in hand along the path edging Crater Lake.

Beneath the early evening sky, dark indigo water filled the deep caldera far below that formed the pristine volcanic lake. They walked for a half hour, not saying much, just enjoying the natural beauty on display.

"That looks like a good spot to stop." Teague pointed toward a fairly flat boulder a short distance from the trail.

"I agree." Sitting beside Teague, Nina rested her head against his shoulder as the breeze whispered through nearby fir trees. "I know I'm supposed to be on vacation, but my fingers are itching to paint that view."

"I bet. Did you bring a sketch pad?"

"Of course. I don't go anywhere without that."

"Then maybe you can draw tomorrow." He tightened his arm around her. "I wouldn't want you to go through creative withdrawal."

"Always a risk when I attempt to take a break." After a moment, she changed the subject. "I've been meaning to ask if Keely ever found her stuffed animals. I didn't want to question her if she was still upset about losing them."

He shook his head. "No, they flat out disappeared. It's the damnedest thing. One of her princess dresses is also missing, along with a few other clothes. I have a feeling she left those at her friend's house, though she swears she brought everything home. I've been meaning to call Bobbi Sandburg to ask but keep forgetting."

The breeze that had seemed warm enough a few minutes before chilled her. Goose bumps pebbled Nina's arms. "Nothing else is missing? You don't think someone broke into your house, do you?"

"There's no sign to indicate anyone was in our home. Anyway, why would a thief steal a couple of stuffed animals and leave a valuable necklace that belonged to Keely's mother lying on her dresser? I have to think Coco is the guilty party in this mystery. My bet is she hauled the animals out through her doggy door and buried them somewhere."

"She does like to dig. Hopefully they'll turn up eventually, even if they are a little the worse for wear."

"I bought Keely the American Girl doll she's been wanting. It cost me a freaking fortune, but I hated to see her so upset." He grimaced. "And, yes, I know I'm a sucker and that move wasn't exactly stellar parenting."

"Wait until she's older and some boy breaks her heart." Nina tried to keep a straight face and failed. "Are you going to buy her a car to ease her pain?"

"No, I'll probably just kill the kid. Any boy stupid enough to dump my daughter doesn't deserve to live."

"That's pretty darn funny." She waved a hand. "Your protective streak might just span the whole lake."

"I know. I really do need to dial it back. I'm here with you, though, so I really am trying hard not to hover. I read about helicopter parents in a magazine at the dentist's office, and the thought that I might be one is terrifying."

"You have too much common sense." She slid her arm around his waist and squeezed. "I don't see you as a micromanager, and Keely definitely isn't spoiled, as far as I can tell."

"That's a relief." He stood and pulled her up into his arms. "Thanks for making me feel better about how I'm raising her. Sometimes it's rough not having any support and feedback."

"I don't want to ever butt into your business with unwanted advice." She stood on her toes to kiss him. "But I won't shy away from giving my opinion if you ask for it."

He kissed her back, taking the embrace to a much higher level. Nina was dizzy with need and completely breathless when he finally let her go.

She held on to his forearms to steady herself. "If that's

my reward for a few supportive comments, I may never shut up."

"Since we're in full public view of anyone walking by, I figured I'd better quit before we got arrested." His voice was a low rumble that grazed her ear. "Remind me why we left the privacy of our room."

"The view. I know. Stupid, right?"

"Shortsighted for sure, because now I have to return to the lodge with my pants cutting off the blood supply to my—"

"Stop!" She couldn't quit laughing. "It can't be that bad."

Turning his back to the deserted trail, he pressed her hand to the rigid fly of his jeans. "Want to feel for yourself?"

Her body tightened and heated. "You do have a problem."

"Completely your fault, but I'm going to grit my teeth and bear it."

Giggles bubbled up. "I hope not literally or you *will* be arrested."

"Funny. Let's go. If we can't do the deed here and now, I guess we'll have to go eat dinner instead. I need sustenance for the night ahead."

Nina wouldn't have minded in the least leaving her palm right where it had been. Instead, she tucked her hand through his arm as they hiked back to the trail. A flurry of emotions swirled inside her, happiness warring with her innate caution.

"I can't remember the last time I simply let go and laughed. Just so you know, I'm not usually the giggly type."

He smiled down at her. "No, your humor has an ironic twist."

"My first impression of you the day you moved in was to wonder if you were always so serious. I guess we're good for each other."

"I'd sure like the opportunity to put that to the test." He hesitated for a moment. "I want to spend more time with you after we get home. This past week, I didn't much enjoy looking out my bedroom window at night and seeing the light on in yours. I wanted you beside me."

Joy, along with a hint of relief, burst inside her. "What about Keely?"

"I'll always worry my choices might hurt my daughter." Teague stopped and turned to face her. With a gentle hand, he brushed a strand of hair off her cheek. "But I trust you. I believe in what we have, and I'm ready to take a risk."

"Wow."

"Wow? That's all you have to say?"

She swallowed back tears. "Yeah. I haven't been this happy in a long time, maybe ever. Thank you for your faith in me. I don't intend to abuse it."

He pulled her into his arms." Thank you for just being you. I love you, Nina."

"I love you, too."

Chapter Twenty-one

If she could gain the child's confidence, taking Keely—no, not Keely. The beautiful girl was her own Lynette. She would never use that other name, even in her thoughts. If Lynette grew to trust her before the big day, bringing her home where she belonged would be much easier.

With both Teague and Nina gone on their romantic tryst, this morning would be all about laying the groundwork. Anger burned in her chest. No father worthy of the title would desert his child to go off to fornicate with a woman who was no better than a tramp. The fact that the man in charge of Lynette's well-being could be so short-sighted reinforced her certainty that saving her child from this untenable situation was urgent. Vital.

God's will.

In the foggy morning chill, she shivered and hoped she wouldn't have to wait too much longer for her chance. She'd thought about searching Nina's house again for the lottery ticket, but surely she would have set the alarm before leaving town. Not a risk she could take.

When the screen door creaked open, it seemed like a

sign from above. She straightened but kept out of sight behind the shed. If Lynette wasn't alone . . .

Her girl skipped across the porch with the damn dog at her side, but Stella was nowhere in sight. Coco glanced in her direction, growled low in her throat, then barked.

"What's wrong? Hey, a squirrel."

The dog shot down the steps, tearing off in pursuit of a squirrel stupid enough to run headlong toward Nina's yard instead of scampering up the nearest tree. Lynette raced after her pet but lost steam when Coco disappeared into their neighbor's backyard. She paused beside the mailbox and kicked a loose rock.

"Don't worry. Your dog won't catch that squirrel. It's too quick."

"What?" Lynette spun around, her pink princess dress swirling around her ankles. "Hey, you were at the park. What are you doing at my house?" She backed up against the mailbox, eyes wide.

"I don't live very far away, and I was just out for a morning walk." She smiled, unable to contain her joy at being so close to her daughter. Emotion swelled up inside her like a balloon ready to burst.

"Oh."

"Don't you remember me?"

"You said you saw a bunny. Then Nina was mad because I talked to a stranger." Lynette glanced over her shoulder. "I should go inside." Raising her voice, she shouted, "Coco, come here right now."

Why doesn't she know her own mother?

Forcing back a cry of disappointment, she clenched her fists at her sides. They never did in the beginning, but this time should have been different.

"You can't be too careful these days, but I'm not a stranger. I'm Lynette's mother."

Her forehead wrinkled. "The girl I talked to on the beach?"

"My daughter isn't feeling well today, but maybe you'd like to come over to play sometime soon. That would make us both happy since we don't often have company."

"Lynette was nice. I can ask my dad when he gets home."

"No reason to just yet since I'm not sure when she'll be well enough for a playdate, but I'll be in touch." She laid a shaking hand on Lynette's shoulder. "That's a pretty dress."

"Today I'm Aurora." She scowled. "I lost my Belle dress."

"I'm sure you'll find it again soon."

When Coco came running across the lawn, barking to wake the dead, she stepped back.

"Keely, what's all that noise about? Did you get the newspaper?" Stella's booming voice preceded her as the door swung wide.

Turning sharply, she hurried away. Sweat dampened her brow, but she forced herself not to run, which would surely trigger all Stella's protective instincts.

"Who were you talking to?" The question cracked like a shot in the morning air. "Come back inside right now. Coco, stop that racket."

The barking and voices faded. *A close call.*

Still, nothing awful had happened, and she'd had a wonderful conversation with Lynette. She'd gained her trust. Soon they'd be together again. Very soon.

But first she had to get rid of the impostor. The day of reckoning was close. She couldn't wait.

* * *

Teague slowly opened his eyes. Contentment flowed through him like a gentle wave as he tightened his arms around Nina. Warm and naked, she molded to his side. A glance toward the window where bright sunlight streamed through told him they'd slept late. Not a surprise after waking more than once to make love in the dark hours of the night. But that didn't stop him from wanting her again.

He had a feeling he'd never get enough of this woman.

"Teague?"

"You're awake."

She yawned and pressed a hand to her mouth. "Hard to sleep when I'm being prodded in the hip."

"Sorry." He grinned. "Morning boner."

"Then maybe we'd better do something about it." She rolled him onto his back and lay full-length on top of him.

Before he could breathe, let alone think, he was buried deep inside her. He didn't move, just held on tight and savored the connection.

"Do you know how good this feels?" She rested her cheek against his neck. "Remember when you were a kid, snuggled in bed on Christmas morning, knowing it wasn't time to get up yet, but anticipating the excitement of opening your presents? That's what waking up with you is like."

"You're the only gift I want." He ran his hands up and down her back, gliding calloused palms over silken skin. "But you're already unwrapped."

She pressed kisses against his collarbone. "Clothes are overrated. They just hinder the process." Taking her time, she pulled forward, then settled more deeply over him.

He laid his head back and groaned. "Are you ready to find out what's inside that package?"

"I've been holding out for years, waiting for something

this special. I stopped believing I'd ever find a man who could make me happy."

"That's the goal." Cupping her face in his hands, he kissed her deeply as he moved inside her. "This. Just this."

She clung to him as he increased the pace. They moved together, heat flaming between them. When he couldn't hold on for a moment longer, he rolled her beneath him and pushed them both over the edge . . . into heaven.

His ringing cell phone tugged him back to reality. Reaching toward the bedside table, he grabbed it just as the call went to voice mail. With a grunt, he slid off Nina and flopped over.

"Who was it?"

"I don't know. I need a minute to gather my wits. I'm practically brain-dead after that."

"I can relate." When she stretched, the sheet slid down to her waist.

He swallowed hard, his gaze glued to her breasts. Surely he couldn't—

"Maybe you should check."

"Huh?"

"To see if the call was important."

"Oh." Focusing on the phone, he tapped the screen to bring up the voice mail and put it on speaker.

"Teague, this is Stella. Something strange happened this morning. I'm a little concerned. Call me."

He jackknifed upright to return her call. His heart pounded in an erratic rhythm until she answered. "What happened?"

"No need to panic. Keely is fine, but a woman approached her when she ran outside to get the paper this morning. I found it odd but in no way threatening."

He pushed a hand through his hair. "What woman? A neighbor?"

"She said she was on a walk and lived nearby. But she took off pretty quickly when I came outside, so I didn't get a look at her. Keely's only description was that she's old like me."

He met Nina's gaze. "Sorry about that."

"Just telling it like it is." Stella snorted. "Anyway, I wouldn't have thought too much about it until Keely said this same woman approached her at the park last week. She's the mother of some girl your daughter met on the beach, and she asked about a playdate. The whole situation didn't sit right with me, so I called. Sorry to spoil your morning."

"It's not spoiled." He eyed Nina, who scooted back against the pillows and clutched the sheet to her chest. "But I'd appreciate it if you'd mention the incident to the camp counselor. I don't want this woman trying to talk to Keely again when I'm not around until I speak with her first."

"I definitely will. As it is, I'm sorry I let her go outside after the paper by herself. I should have been watching her more closely."

"She likes to run out to get it in the morning. Don't beat yourself up over that." He met Nina's troubled gaze. "We might leave here a little earlier than anticipated. I'll plan to be back in time to pick Keely up from camp this afternoon."

"Are you sure?"

A weight settled on his chest, but he nodded. "Yeah, I am. Thanks for calling me, Stella."

"I felt like you'd want to know."

"You made the right decision. Drop by whenever it's convenient, and I'll have a check ready for you."

"I'll do that. Bye, Teague."

He dropped the phone on the bed, then swung his legs over the side. "What the hell?"

"Keely's fine."

"Yes, but I don't like the idea of someone I don't know approaching my kid."

Nina scooted forward, then reached down to scoop her robe off the rug.

"Stella said this woman is her age, which is probably mid-sixties. Isn't that awfully old to have a young daughter?"

"I figured she was the girl's grandmother when I saw them on the beach the first time."

He turned slowly. "You know this woman?"

"No. I saw her at a distance with a scarf over her head. But she moved like an older person, if you know what I mean. I actually painted the girl . . . her daughter." She stood and tied the belt on her robe. "A quick rendition while she stood at the edge of the water. Keely talked to Lynn—something like that—for a few minutes when we were at the beach on a different occasion."

"I feel better about this woman approaching Keely, then." His frown lifted. "She didn't necessarily seek her out. Just a neighbor being friendly. I still have that city mentality of looking for danger in every random encounter. I'm not used to small towns where people are friendlier."

"We do tend to say hello to perfect strangers." Nina headed toward the bathroom. "I'm going to take a shower. If we're leaving soon . . ."

"About that . . . A knee-jerk reaction to run home to protect my kid before I thought it through." He slowly rose to his feet. "I promised not to do that to you again. I can call Stella back. We don't have to cut our day short."

"Not necessary. I think we both got what we hoped for out of our overnight date."

Guilt ate at him. "But you were going to sketch the lake."

"Really, it's fine."

She disappeared into the bathroom before he could protest further. The door shut behind her with a sharp click.

Something was definitely on her mind. Teague could only hope he hadn't completely blown it. Again.

He ordered a ham and cheese omelet before sitting back in his chair, but the easy companionship of the previous evening was missing. Nina sipped her coffee and stared out the window at the spectacular view of Crater Lake. Other than placing her breakfast order, she hadn't said two words.

Reaching across the table, he touched her hand. "Hey, is everything okay? You're awfully quiet."

The smile she turned in his direction didn't reach her eyes. "Just thinking. Having kids is like putting yourself into a perpetual state of worry. I know Leah and Ryan want to start a family in the near future, but I don't know if I'd make much of a mom."

He frowned. "Why would you say that? You're great with Keely. She adores you."

"Sure, because she has fun when she's with me. But when I'm focused on my art, which is nearly all the time, I can be pretty self-absorbed. I didn't see that woman approach her at the park. It scared the crap out of me when I turned around and couldn't find her immediately."

He set down his coffee mug with a thump that splashed hot liquid onto the tablecloth, leaving a stain. "What are you talking about?"

"You heard Stella. The woman approached Keely at the park last weekend when I was watching her. She took her into the parking lot to see a bunny."

"And you were . . ."

"Painting while she played on the slides and swings. When I turned to check on her and didn't see her, I freaked. As soon as I shouted her name, she ran back between two cars, but my heart stopped for that moment before I knew where she was."

Teague took a couple of deep breaths and held his tongue while the waitress delivered their food. After he thanked her and she left, he stared down at his plate. "So you thought it was okay to let my daughter run wild in a public park without paying attention to where she was at all times?"

Nina's fork clattered against her plate. "I was constantly checking on her. It took me twice as long to finish my painting because of it."

"But she disappeared from sight in only a matter of seconds."

"I guess so."

"And you didn't think to tell me about this before now?" he asked.

"Keely was fine, so I didn't see the need. Anyway, you were tired when you got home from work that night, and I had some phone calls to make. By the next day, I'd forgotten all about it."

He cut into his omelet but left the bite on his plate. "Shit."

"Are you angry with me?" Her voice rose. When the couple at a nearby table glanced over, she lowered her tonc. "If you'll recall, I was doing you a favor that day."

"Yeah, you were." He stuffed eggs in his mouth and

chewed furiously but could barely swallow. "I thought I could trust you with my daughter."

She closed her eyes. When she opened them again, both irritation and hurt were reflected in their green depths. "So now I'm irresponsible and unreliable? Every mother in that park was on her cell phone, not keeping her attention glued to her child each second. You said yourself you let Keely run out to get the paper in the morning."

"Apparently I shouldn't, but I thought I was in a safe neighborhood."

"You are. Siren Cove isn't exactly known for its crime rate." She wadded her napkin in her fist. "You're right, I should have been watching her more closely. I just said I'd make a lousy mother. I'll remember not to babysit Leah's child when she has one."

"I didn't mean—"

"Oh, I think you did. A little food for thought, though. I found your daughter in my backyard, twice, the day you moved in. I guess you let her out of your sight for more than a minute."

"I'm sorry. I overreacted, but the mental image of Keely disappearing between vehicles in a parking lot where some freak could have snatched her and driven off chilled my blood."

"I lectured her about safety at the time. I didn't take it lightly, either, Teague."

"I'm sorry. I mean it. Obviously, I'm far from perfect and have no room to criticize you. Eat your waffle."

"I'm not hungry." She pushed back her chair. "I'll go pack my bag while you finish your breakfast."

"Nina, don't leave."

She was halfway across the restaurant before he could finish his plea.

He pressed fingers to his temples. "Damn, I screwed up." When the waitress approached and gave him a hesitant look, he cleared his throat. "Can I get the check, please?"

"Sure. Would you like me to box up your meals?"

"No, thanks."

She cleared the two nearly full plates. "I'll be right back."

Teague sipped his coffee though it felt like it was burning a hole in his stomach. When the server returned, he paid the bill and headed upstairs to their room. Pausing for just a second, he opened the door.

Nina had her back to him, folding clothes into her suitcase. She didn't bother to turn around. When he stepped closer and touched her shoulder, she flinched.

"On a scale of one to ten, how mad at me are you right now?"

Finally she turned. "About an eight, but that's down from a thirteen."

He jammed his hands into his pockets. "I apologized. I don't know what else to do."

"I don't want you to do anything but pack. I'm ready to leave." She headed into the bathroom.

Gritting his teeth, he shoved what clothes he'd removed back into his bag, then passed her on the way into the bathroom. When she made a point of not brushing against him, his temper flared.

"Are we going to spend the next three and a half hours alone in a car together fighting?"

She gave him a long, thoughtful look. "No. I plan to turn up the music and spend the drive thinking about what a failure I am as a human being."

"Nina, don't."

The hands she fisted on her hips shook. "I made a mistake, and said as much, but your comments hurt. I need some time."

"Okay." His heart ached. "If it helps, I'm a complete ass. I do trust you, and I'm sorry. Take all the time you need."

"I'm sorry, too, but maybe being sorry isn't enough." Her eyes were damp with tears as she met his gaze. "Maybe love isn't enough."

Chapter Twenty-two

Nina straightened the picture of the climbing roses and stepped back to critically study the arrangement of paintings on the back wall of her booth. "Perfect."

"That's quite a display. You don't usually have this many to sell, do you?"

She glanced over at Paige, who was stocking a rack with postcards printed with photographs of her paintings, along with her contact information. "I've been busting my butt to complete them all. Now let's just hope I sell a couple."

"I think you'll do better than that. Did you see the traffic in town? The tourists are thick this weekend." She turned around to lean against the counter and crossed her arms in front of her. "In fact, since you're all set up, I should probably head back to my shop. I hope to make a killing in the next couple of days, too."

"I'm sure you will. Thanks for offering me a hand."

"Why didn't Teague help you? Is he working today?"

Nina swallowed as a burning knot lodged in her throat. "I'm not sure what his schedule is." She stared down at her feet. "We're kind of on a break."

"What? Why?" Stepping forward, Paige laid a hand on her arm. "What happened? I thought the two of you went away together last weekend."

"We did, and it was great." Nina turned to stare out over the ocean, past the other booths set up in a long stretch above the bluffs. "Then Teague found out I let Keely out of my sight long enough for a stranger to approach her, and he went off on me."

"Was she in any danger?"

"I don't think so, but I know she could have been. I apologized, but he made me feel lower than a worm. If he doesn't trust me, then what's the point of being in a relationship?"

"There isn't any, but I'm sure you can work through this. What does he have to say about it?"

"Teague admitted he overreacted."

"Well, there you go."

"Still, I don't know if I want to put myself in the position of being criticized every time I'm around Keely and handle something differently than he would."

"You think he'll micromanage your every move?"

"Maybe. I'm really not sure." Nina gazed out over the ocean. "I told him I needed some time, and he's been good about giving me space. Maybe too good."

"Oh, my God. You can't fault him for that if you asked him to back off."

"I know. I'm still feeling a little irrational about the whole situation, but I guess we should talk again."

"Yes, you should," Paige agreed. "I know you haven't been dating him all that long, but—"

"We talked about a more serious arrangement, at the very least spending our evenings and nights together."

"You're planning to move in with him?"

"Maybe not officially, but that was the gist of the con-

versation." Nina clenched her hands at her sides. "I've totally fallen for the man . . . and his daughter. I want her in
my life, too, but if he thinks—"

"Stop with the conjecture. Talk to him. Compromise.
You don't need a break. You need communication." Paige
checked her phone. "Yikes, it's time to open the shop.
Are you going to be okay if I leave?"

"Of course. Go do your thing. My hope is I'll be so
busy today I won't have time to think about my personal
life."

She bent to retrieve her purse from beneath the counter.
"In that case, I'm out of here."

"I'll talk to you soon. Thanks, Paige."

"You're welcome."

After her friend left, Nina straightened a stack of business cards as she studied the people beginning to filter
into the event. Maybe now was a good time to call Teague,
before she got busy with browsers and the occasional serious buyer. Pulling her phone from her back pocket, she
jumped when it trilled.

A glance at the display made her smile. Teague was
obviously a mind reader.

"Hi. I was actually just going to call you."

"You were?"

"Paige helped me set up my booth this morning. She convinced me we need to talk." Nina leaned on the counter and
surveyed the thickening crowd. Two women wearing sensi-
ble shoes and determined expressions looked like potential
buyers. "I'm sorry I've been so nonresponsive this week.
Are you working?"

"I went in early, or I would have offered to help load
your trailer. I can stop by when the event is over to give
you a hand packing up."

"Thanks, Teague. I'd appreciate that."

"Then I'll see you around four."

"Sounds good." She slid her phone into the pocket of her royal-blue capri pants. Paired with a sleeveless silk blouse, the outfit was her concession to looking professional. She had a feeling the two matronly women approaching the booth wouldn't appreciate short shorts.

"Good morning, ladies. I hope you're enjoying the art fair."

"Oh, we definitely are. I love that seascape on the back wall. The colors are amazing." The taller woman turned to her companion. "What do you think, Betty?"

"The area rug in your dining room has those exact same shades."

After thirty minutes of debating the price, the potential buyer promised to think about it and return later.

Nina grimaced as the pair walked away. "Story of my life."

By midafternoon, she was feeling a whole lot more optimistic as she wrapped her second sale of the day in thick protective paper and thanked the gentleman who'd purchased it as an anniversary gift for his wife. Resisting the urge to fist pump the air, she scouted the remaining art patrons for potential buyers. A couple pushing a baby stroller caught her eye, and though she suspected they were just lookers, she gave them a friendly smile.

"Look, Oren. Don't you love those roses? How much is . . ." The woman leaned over the counter, then drew back and tucked a strand of blond hair behind one ear. "Oh, wow. We can't afford that." Her smile held an edge of sadness . . . or maybe she was simply tired. When the baby in the stroller fussed and let out a yell, she lifted the child and held him close.

At least Nina assumed the infant was a boy since he wore a navy onesie printed with sailboats.

"He's adorable."

"Thank you."

"I have postcard prints of the roses, if you're interested." She glanced toward the woman's husband, but his gaze was targeted on the side wall where the picture of the fog-shrouded cove hung. "Do you like that piece? I'll admit it's one of my favorites."

"Who's the girl in the painting?"

The urgency in his tone struck a nerve. "Excuse me?"

The hand he raised to point trembled slightly. "The girl standing by the water. Who is she?"

His wife glanced up from shushing the baby and gasped. When her eyes filled with tears, Nina backed up a step.

"Is something wrong?"

"Do you see the resemblance, hon? I'm not imagining it?" He curved an arm around his wife before refocusing on the painting.

"She looks older, but . . ." The woman pressed up against the counter separating her from Nina. "Do you know that girl?"

"I don't. She was down on the beach with her mother the day I painted that piece. Adding her to the scene was a spur-of-the-moment decision since her melancholy expression mirrored the mood I was trying to capture."

"Her mother?" The woman's voice caught.

"Yes. What's this about?"

The man cleared his throat. "Three years ago, our daughter was kidnapped. There was no ransom request, and the police never had any substantial leads."

"She was only five." The woman wiped tears from her cheeks and clutched the baby tighter. "We've never given up hope that someday . . ."

"The girl in the painting looks like Emma." Her husband's voice broke. "Older, but the resemblance is striking. The pointed chin, and the way her brows arch. Those eyes . . ."

"Excuse me. I've decided to purchase the seascape."

Nina tore her gaze from the emotion-ravaged faces of the couple and blinked. The tall woman who'd been her first browser of the day pulled her credit card out of her purse and waved it. Her companion gave the husband and wife an apologetic smile.

"I'm sorry. I need to . . ."

"Of course." The man pushed the stroller out of the way, but the two didn't go far. Heads bent, they spoke quietly together.

Nina forced a smile for her customer. "I'm so glad you changed your mind."

"I didn't change it. I just decided to splurge this one time. My dining room is going to look amazing with that painting hanging over the buffet."

"That's wonderful." Nina lifted the frame off the hook and laid the picture on the back table. "I'll wrap it for you."

The woman selected one of Nina's business cards and dropped it into her purse. "My husband and I intend to redecorate our master bedroom this fall. I'll keep you in mind when it comes time to choose artwork."

"I would appreciate that."

The excitement she'd normally feel at having made a new client faded as the mother of the baby cried softly on her husband's shoulder. When he pulled his cell from his pocket and made a call, grim determination drew his brows together as he stared in her direction. A knot formed in Nina's stomach. With shaking hands, she finished wrapping the painting and taped the provenance encased in a plastic sleeve to the back.

"Here you go." She laid the seascape on the counter and ran the woman's credit card. "The frame is a little awkward to carry." Catching sight of Teague approaching from the direction of the parking lot, some of the tension in her body released. "Would you like some help getting it back to your car?"

"Oh, no. I'm as strong as a horse." After the woman returned her card to her purse and signed the receipt, she hefted the painting. "Thank you very much."

"I hope you enjoy your painting."

"I intend to." She and her friend detoured around Teague and headed back through the row of booths.

"I see you made a sale. Congratulations."

"My third of the day, and that woman promises to be a repeat customer."

"That's great." His gaze held determination as he stepped up to the counter and leaned forward for a quick kiss. "Are you about ready to pack up?"

She nodded as her heart beat a little faster. Apparently Teague wasn't going to let her keep her distance. Relief filled her.

"Are they potential customers?" He nodded toward the couple with the baby. "They keep looking this way, but the woman seems upset. Are your prices too steep for their budget?"

"No, they think—" She stopped speaking when the man and woman approached, pushing the stroller.

"I've contacted the detective in charge of our daughter's kidnapping case. He's been in touch with the local police, and someone should be here shortly." The man held tight to the stroller's handle, and his knuckles gleamed white. "Please don't take that painting anywhere before the officer gets here."

Teague glanced from the man back to her. "Nina, what's going on?"

When she ducked beneath the counter to stand beside him, he slid an arm around her waist. "They believe a girl I painted on the beach might be their lost daughter."

An awkward silence followed before the woman spoke. "We have to know for sure. Even if we're wrong, we have to know."

"I'm happy to share any information about her I have with the police, but it isn't much more than I've already told you." Nina's gaze shifted toward the parking lot. "Here comes Chris now. Let's hope we can get this straightened out."

"Chris?" The man turned and narrowed his eyes.

"Officer Long. He's a friend of mine."

"Isn't that just perfect." The woman's voice rose. "If you had something to do with—"

"I can assure you I didn't."

"Let's not throw around accusations." Teague's tone was hard. "If you lost your daughter, you have my sincere sympathy, but I can assure you Nina doesn't have anyone stashed in her attic."

"I'm sorry, but seeing that painting . . ."

The woman's face crumpled, and she struggled to hold back tears as Chris reached them. When the baby in the stroller started to cry, she picked him up and rocked him. The motion seemed to calm them both.

"Hi, Nina." Chris nodded to Teague before turning to study the couple. "Are you the Herringtons? I'm Officer Long."

When he held out a hand, the man shook it. "I'm Oren Herrington, and this is my wife, Patricia."

"I spoke to Detective O'Roarke down in Medford. He sent me a photograph of your daughter from the time of the kidnapping." Turning, he faced Nina. "Can I take a look at the painting of the girl?"

"Of course." She pointed. "It's the foggy one on the side wall. Would you like me to lift it down?"

"Please."

After ducking back into the booth, she unhooked the painting and placed it on the counter.

Patricia Herrington stepped closer. "Compare this girl to our Emma, Officer Long. You'll see we aren't delusional."

Chris tapped his phone a few times and held it up next to the painting. After a moment he glanced over at Nina. "There's a resemblance, but it's hard to say. You saw this girl in person. What do you think?"

Nina couldn't stop staring at the face of the young girl on his phone. A happy smile curved her lips. So very different from the sadness she'd seen shadowing the eyes of the girl on the beach. She studied the face with the critical eye of an artist. The nose was the same, and the shape of her ear. Emma's cheeks were a little rounder, a chubbiness that may have thinned over time.

"The basic markers are there. I'm an artist, not a forensic scientist, but in my opinion your daughter would look very much like the girl I saw on the beach when she's older."

Mrs. Herrington clutched the counter. "You think she's our Emma? You see it, too?"

"Or maybe she's just a child who looks similar to your daughter. There's a definite resemblance."

"Officer, is there a way to find her, speak to her? If she lives here in town . . ."

Chris lifted a questioning brow. "Do you know who she is, Nina?"

"I'm afraid I don't. Keely spoke to her on a different occasion, and the girl told her she's homeschooled. I remember because we discussed it afterward. I think she said her name is Lynne or Lynda. No, it was Lynette."

The officer crossed his arms over his chest. "Who's Keely?"

"My daughter." Teague stepped forward. "The mother of this girl in the painting approached Keely twice after she met her on the beach, once in the park and once on our street. She asked about a playdate."

"Do you know where she lives?" Oren Herrington's voice rose. "If there's even a chance the girl is Emma—"

"I have no idea. Possibly somewhere in our neighborhood since the woman was on foot."

"Can you give me a description?" Chris spoke sharply.

"I was out of town." Teague met Nina's gaze. "I didn't see her, but Keely said she was old. From the perspective of a six-year-old, that could mean anywhere from forty to eighty."

"What about you, Nina?" Chris took a notebook from his pocket and jotted something down. "If she was on the beach while you painted her daughter . . ."

"I never saw her up close. She wore a scarf over her head and had her back to me, but she moved slowly, deliberately, like an older person. I'm afraid I wouldn't recognize her if I passed her on the street. Keely did mention this woman said she knew me, but I can't think of any acquaintance, middle-aged or older, who has a young daughter." Nina faced the two parents staring at her with hope in their eyes. "I wish I could be more help."

"It seems likely she lives in Siren Cove if she's been seen in the area several times." Juggling the baby, Patricia Herrington gripped the officer's arm. "Can't you check school records or something? Even if a child is homeschooled, there must be an official document somewhere with a permanent address."

"I'd need a warrant to get that information, and I'm afraid a resemblance to your daughter isn't enough to request one. Unless there's evidence—"

"The police failed to find anything useful three years ago." Her voice grew shrill. "If they'd done their jobs—"

"Calm down, hon. We aren't going to simply walk away. If Emma is here, we'll find her." The man turned to Teague. "Maybe if your daughter described this woman to a sketch artist, we'd be able to get a recognizable picture from it. Surely someone local will know her."

The despair in his voice tugged at Nina's heart. He and his wife were more than likely holding on to a thread of hope with no substance, but if she could give them closure, one way or the other . . .

"I'm afraid we don't have a sketch artist on staff," Chris spoke quietly. "Getting one brought in—"

"I'm pretty decent at sketching from a description. I'd certainly be willing to try, but Keely is pretty young to provide accurate details."

Patricia turned to Nina with tears in her eyes. "Anything that might help. I just need to know."

"I'll sit down with Keely after I get home. Where can I contact you?"

Oren handed both Nina and Chris business cards with his cell number. "We're staying at the Oceanside Inn a couple miles south of town."

She slipped the card into her pocket. "I'll be in touch."

"Thank you." When the baby started to whimper again, Patricia turned to her husband. "I need to feed Jack."

He nodded then faced the officer. "I hope you'll do what you can to locate this woman and her . . . daughter. I'm sure Detective O'Roarke told you we're not nutcases.

As much as we want Emma back, I'm not looking for false hope just to be disappointed again. Losing our daughter the first time nearly killed us both."

"I understand, and I'll check into this, ask around places like the park and the pool where a woman and her child might be regulars. I intend to do everything possible to give you answers."

"We appreciate that."

After they walked away with the baby crying louder with each step, Nina slumped against the counter. "How unbelievably awful. I can't imagine what they've gone through."

Teague clenched his hands into fists at his sides. "If there's a psycho woman living in Siren Cove who stole one child and then spoke to mine—"

"It's been three years since their daughter was kidnapped. The chances of finding Emma alive are pretty thin." Chris's gaze was sober. "I fear they *will* be disappointed, but I'd like to speak to the woman in question to make certain."

"I'll work on a sketch." Nina pulled a postcard print of the foggy cove from the rack and handed it to him. "I won't give you the painting, but take this in case you need a picture of Lynette or Emma or whoever she is."

He took it and smiled. "Thanks. Let me know how it goes."

"I will." After Chris left, she turned toward Teague when he raised his phone to his ear. "Who are you calling?"

"Keely. I need to talk to my daughter."

A shiver slid through her. "I don't blame you one bit."

Chapter Twenty-three

Teague sat on one end of the couch while Keely and Nina occupied the other. His nerves were strung tighter than a high wire stretched between two precipices. On the near side was the life he'd carved out as a single father, full of unexpected demands and worries over his daughter. Across the deep chasm was his relationship with Nina, where love and the possibility of a future together existed. He wasn't sure he had the wherewithal to navigate between the two. Failing his daughter wasn't an option, but neither was giving Nina less than 100 percent.

They still needed to hash out a solution, but at the moment, she was occupied with a drawing pad and Keely's sketchy memory.

"Her nose doesn't look right."

"Was it broader or more aquiline?" Nina's voice registered an extreme amount of patience, despite the fact they'd been working on the drawing for over an hour.

"What does that mean?"

"Sorry, thinner. Like this."

"No, it looked better before." Keely tapped her foot against the coffee table. "That kind of looks like her, I guess. Can we be done now?"

"Sure."

Teague opened his eyes. "It's past your bedtime. Go get ready for bed, and I'll be up to tuck you in shortly." When his daughter reached out to hug Nina, his heart squeezed.

She hugged her back. "Sleep well."

"Okay. Night, Nina."

"Good night, sweetie."

He sat up straighter but waited until Keely disappeared up the stairs with Coco following her to speak. "Well, that was fairly painful to listen to. How did the picture turn out?"

When Nina held up the sketch pad, he slid across the worn leather to her side. "Hmm, looks like a cartoon drawing of Mrs. Claus."

Cocking her head at an angle, she nodded. "Describing facial features isn't easy, especially for a child. I'm afraid this won't be terribly useful."

"You don't recognize her?"

"There's something slightly familiar about the gray hair, the only thing Keely was certain about, but it could be because she resembles someone I saw on TV recently. Let's just say I didn't have any *aha* moments while I was drawing this."

"That's too bad. I'd be losing my mind if I were in the shoes of those poor people. If I suspected someone had my daughter, I'd go door to door through the whole damn town if I had to, and raise holy hell until I found her."

"You heard Chris. Chances are their daughter isn't alive three years after she was taken."

264   *Jannine Gallant*

Sorrow mixed with anger tightened his chest. "I don't know what would be worse, having all hope crushed or never knowing what happened."

She reached over and gripped his thigh. "Don't even think about it."

"You're right." Slowly he rose to his feet. "I need to tell Keely good night. Can you stay?"

"Sure. While you're up there, I'll call Chris and tell him the sketch was a bust. He can break the news to the Herringtons."

"Okay." Upstairs, he found Keely in her nightgown with her teeth already brushed. After tucking her into bed, he read two chapters of *Charlotte's Web*, then dropped a kiss on her forehead. "Good night, Keels."

"Night, Daddy." She yawned wide, her lids drooping. "Is Nina still here?"

"Yeah. She'll probably keep me company for a little while."

"That's good. I like having her with us. I missed her when she wasn't."

Teague smiled. "Me, too. Now go to sleep."

When Coco raised her head and blinked at him from the foot of the bed, he patted the dog, then flipped off the light. The night-light cast a faint glow over his daughter's closed eyes as she drifted into sleep. Leaving the door open a crack, he headed back downstairs.

Nina glanced up from her phone and laid it on the coffee table as he approached. "Is Keely asleep?"

"Yes." He dropped down beside her on the couch. "She missed you this week." Reaching over, he took her hand. "So did I."

"I missed you, too. Both of you. Frankly, I've been miserable."

He regarded her steadily. "What can I do to fix the problem?"

"I suppose it all boils down to trust."

"I trust you completely, Nina. Honestly."

She leaned her head on his shoulder. "I guess we both need to have a little more faith in each other and think before we react."

"True." He pulled her across his lap and kissed her. With his thumb, he brushed hair off her silky soft cheek. "Are we good now? I hated knowing you were upset with me."

"Yeah, we're good. I know no relationship is perfect, but I want to try to make this one work for us both."

"Does that mean you'll sleep over?"

She smiled up at him. "I could be persuaded." Cupping his face in her hands, she pressed her lips to his and slowly deepened the kiss. "Make love, not war."

"Always." With a grunt, he rose to his feet, still holding her in his arms, and headed toward the stairs.

Nina clung to his neck. "I'm too heavy."

"No, you're not." When the phone in his back pocket vibrated, he stopped and closed his eyes for a moment. "Please, not a work emergency."

"I can get it out for you." When she slipped her hand into the pocket of his jeans, her fingers teased his ass.

His legs wobbled as his whole body tightened. "Fate couldn't be so cruel." He glanced at the text as she held it out and pressed the display button. "Damn. Damn. Damn."

Shifting in his grip, she slid down the length of him until her feet touched the floor. "I take it you have to leave?"

"Yeah. It's an all-hands alert. Usually that means a structure fire endangering nearby buildings or a multicar crash with injuries."

"Then you need to go." Her eyes registered disappointment, but she released him after one final kiss. "I'll spend the night here with Keely."

"Thank you." In the entry, he grabbed a jacket off the coat tree by the door to combat the heavy fog, then ran out to his truck. By the time he reached the station, he'd settled down enough to focus on the job ahead, whatever that might be. After parking in the lot, he got out and slammed the door. With a nod to a couple of his coworkers who'd also just arrived, he waited for Mateo, and the two walked toward the building together.

"Any idea why we got called in?"

Teague glance over at his buddy and shrugged. "Not a clue. I guess we'll find out when we get inside."

They climbed the stairs to the meeting room and found it crowded with both members of the fire crew and local cops. At the front of the room, Captain Barker stood beside a grizzled veteran of the police force.

Teague nudged Mateo. "Who's the police chief? I've seen him around town a few times."

"Chief Stackhouse. He's a fixture in Siren Cove. I wonder what the hell is going on."

Before Teague could respond, the fire captain cleared his throat. "It looks like most everyone is here, so I'd like to get started. We have an urgent situation, and Chief Stackhouse has requested our help. I'm going to turn the briefing over to him."

"Listen up, people." The chief's deep voice boomed over the crowd. "You all may not be cops, but you're local men and women trained not to panic if a situation turns ugly. Right now I need manpower since I simply don't have the staff or the time to wait for reinforcements to arrive. I appreciate Captain Barker and all of you stepping up to help me out."

"What's this about?" Over against the wall, Rod straightened and spoke with a tinge of impatience. "The ball game was tied in extra innings when I got paged to come down here."

Stackhouse eyed the fireman with lowered brows. "I was watching the same game when the *governor* contacted me. It appears we may have a kidnapping victim living here in town, and this little girl is the granddaughter of one of his old fraternity brothers. His friend called in a favor, and the governor is asking for our assistance."

"Shit," Teague muttered under his breath.

"If my men start asking questions around town, word will spread faster than a flu epidemic," the chief continued. "I don't want this woman getting wind of an investigation and hitting the road with the victim before we can find her."

"You believe a woman kidnapped this girl?" Mateo called out. "How long has she been missing?"

"Three years. A lead turned up just today." Stackhouse turned on a projector, and an image of a young blond girl flashed overhead. "This is Emma Herrington at the time she was kidnapped." A second photo went up beside the first, the postcard print of Nina's painting. "This picture of the cove was painted not long ago, and the parents of the missing child believe the girl in it is Emma." He shifted and crossed his arms over his chest. "Of course there's the strong possibility the Herringtons are just wishful thinking, but there's also a slim chance they're right. If that's the case, I intend to make damn sure we do everything in our power to find their daughter."

"Seems easy enough to locate and question her," Rod said. "If the artist knows the child—"

"She doesn't," Chris Long interrupted. "Nina Hutton

painted that picture. The girl and the woman who says she's her mother just happened to be on the beach at the time. Unfortunately, we don't have a description of the suspect other than the fact she's an older woman, possibly in her sixties, and has curly gray hair." His gaze connected with Teague's. "We have that description from a child who spoke to her, but she couldn't provide enough details for an accurate sketch."

"What exactly do you want us to do?" Teague's stomach tightened as he waited for a response.

"I want a door-to-door manhunt." Stackhouse spoke decisively. "Since the woman and child have been seen in Siren Cove, we're hopeful they live in the vicinity. I want each of you to use the picture of the girl to question household occupants. Tell them she's in potential danger and ask if they recognize her or know where she lives. Hopefully we'll get a few quick leads that will direct us to the suspect's home."

"Sounds simple enough." Rod leaned back against the wall. "And if we should happen on the woman and the child—"

"Do nothing," Stackhouse said sharply. "I can't stress that enough, since I don't want to create a dangerous situation for any of you or for the child. We have no knowledge as to whether this woman is armed. We have to assume she's dangerous."

Mateo frowned. "So we make up an excuse for knocking, then simply walk away?"

"Exactly. Keep watch on the house and call me or one of my men immediately. I'll have officers at the location within minutes to take charge. If the woman tries to bolt with the child, follow at a safe distance if possible and update me on her status."

"And if the parents of the missing child are wrong, and

the girl isn't Emma?" Teague cleared his throat. "Are you planning to tear a child away from her mother just because the governor's buddy is desperate to find his kidnapped granddaughter?"

Stackhouse met his gaze head-on. "When we find her, my department will safely hold the child while we question both her and the woman. I would think proof one way or the other can be produced fairly quickly. This isn't a witch hunt. We simply want to get answers while causing as little trauma as possible to the girl."

"That's what I wanted to know."

The police chief scanned the crowd. "Any more questions?" When no one spoke up, he continued, "Captain Barker has your street assignments and pictures of the girl. Pick them up and head out. If someone doesn't answer your knock and you suspect residents are home, notify me. I don't want anyone kicking down doors. Understood?"

Conversations erupted as the men and women in the room formed an orderly line to collect their instructions. As Teague opened his folder, he noted he'd been assigned streets in his own neighborhood.

Mateo nudged his arm. "Looks like I got the other side of town."

"We tried to assign areas you're each familiar with. People are more likely to be helpful when they know or at least recognize you." Glen Barker raised his voice to be heard. "Each of my people will be working in close proximity to a police officer. Hopefully, we can get this search finished quickly and produce results."

An older man from the department approached Teague. "I'm Art Cantrell. I'll be working the neighborhood near your home with you. We divided it into two sections."

Teague held out his hand. "We met not long ago when Nina Hutton was attacked."

The officer shook his outstretched palm with a firm grip. "That's right. O'Dell, isn't it?"

Teague nodded. "I assume I'm to call you if I run across anything suspicious or get any kind of lead?"

"You bet. My cell number is there on the sheet you have, along with contact information for Chief Stackhouse. Shall we head out?"

Following the officer as he limped down the stairs, Teague pulled out his phone to check for missed calls. There weren't any, but his nerves were strung tight knowing a potential kidnapper could be somewhere nearby. Once he reached the parking lot, he hurried toward his pickup, anxious to get to work. If the child in Nina's painting really had been taken from her family, he'd do his damnedest to see she was returned safely.

Minutes later he parked by the curb near the edge of his neighborhood, one street over from his home. Though it was pushing ten, lights shone from the windows of most of the houses. He approached the first door, his ID badge in hand, but neither the middle-aged man who answered the door nor his wife recognized the girl in the painting. Thanking them, he headed to the next house to repeat the process. As the hour grew later with each successive inquiry, the blur of lights through the fog went out in the remaining homes. After pounding on doors, he had to wait for residents to get out of bed before they responded.

Finishing the first street, he parked at the end of his own, went to the first dark house, and knocked. When no one answered, he rapped harder. After another minute, footsteps sounded inside, and he held up his ID to the window. A dead bolt clicked, the porch light flashed on, and the door opened.

A young woman, probably around Nina's age, held her

robe together at the neck and gave him a nervous look. "Can I help you?"

"I'm Teague O'Dell with the Siren Cove Fire Department. I'm sorry to bother you so late, but we're searching for a girl who may be in trouble." He produced the photocopied image of the painting. "Do you recognize this girl or know where she lives?"

The woman took the paper and frowned. "I've seen her walking in the neighborhood. With her grandmother, I think. An older woman with gray hair. I'm pretty sure she lives down toward the end of Pine, three streets over. She doesn't play with the group of neighborhood kids, but I run regularly in the area, and I've noticed her a few times." Her brow furrowed. "At least I think it's the same girl. I could be wrong."

His heart beat faster, but he kept his voice even. "Do you have an address for her?"

"I'm afraid not. I'm not even sure which house is theirs, but I've seen her in that general vicinity a few times."

"Thank you for your help."

She gripped her robe a little tighter. "What happened to her?"

"Nothing that I'm aware of. We're simply trying to resolve an ongoing investigation."

"Well, I hope she's okay. If it's the same girl, she seems quiet and well behaved."

"Thank you." Teague ran down the walkway as the door closed behind him with a click. When he reached his truck, he called the contact number he'd been given.

"Cantrell here."

"This is O'Dell. I have a lead."

"Give me the details." The man's gruff voice was all business.

Teague repeated what the woman had told him. "I can be there in a couple of minutes."

"I'm actually headed down that street right now. I'll start at the far end and see what I can discover. Why don't you begin questioning in the six hundred block of Pine. Maybe we can get verification from some of the neighbors with an actual address."

"I'll do that. If you need me—"

"I'll call Chief Stackhouse for backup. Stay clear of the scene if we do find this woman. I'll take over from here."

Teague gritted his teeth. "Fine." Irritation simmered as he started the engine, turned on the lights, and made a U-turn. It went against the grain to be assigned a back-seat role, but finding the girl safe was all that mattered. To that end, he'd do what he was told.

Chapter Twenty-four

She arranged the branches over the top of the pit, trying to ignore the pathetic pleading coming from beneath. With each layer she piled on, the weeping became a little more muffled.

"I'll be good. I promise. I'm sorry, Mama. I didn't mean to make you mad." Harsh sobs filled the night, absorbed by the thick fog. "Please don't leave me here."

She hardened her heart against the crying. Each time she was forced to do this seemed worse than the last. Still, she had no choice. She wasn't an unfeeling monster, but if she wanted her own precious Lynette back, she had to get rid of the impostor first.

Satisfied the pit was adequately camouflaged, she cautiously stepped onto the interwoven branches. They held her weight without even a hint of sag. With a sigh of relief she backed off and flashed her light around the area to make sure she hadn't left anything. When a battered teddy was illuminated by the beam, she swore softly. She'd meant to leave it with the girl . . . for comfort. Too late now. With any luck, nothing short of a full-grown black bear would break through those branches. She wouldn't risk disturbing her handiwork.

Scooping up the stuffed animal, she thrust it in her bag and turned her back on the terrified cries. The girl would settle down in a few hours, and after that . . . Well, before too long, there'd be nothing left of her mistake. Shining the light on the forest floor, she headed downhill toward the house. She had a little packing to finish up and plans to finalize.

The holdup she'd encountered getting into the home she'd rented down in Brookings was becoming a real problem. Leaving town immediately after she collected Lynette was essential. Keeping her in a car for several days before she could take possession of her new residence wasn't a consideration. She knew from experience the first few weeks with her daughter wouldn't be exactly pleasant . . . or quiet. But after a time, she'd stop crying and realize she'd finally come home where she belonged.

Sticking around Siren Cove was a risk, but one she might have to take. She slapped a branch aside and huffed a little as she pushed past a manzanita bush. She wouldn't wait a single extra day to claim what was hers. Hurrying toward the thinning trees, she stopped cold as car doors slammed and male voices echoed through the darkness.

What in the world . . .

Snapping off her flashlight, she cautiously felt her way the last few yards and crouched behind a fir tree. Two police cars were parked at the end of her street. As she waited, her neighbor was escorted out of her house and into the back of one of the cars.

"You're making a huge mistake." Stella's voice rose. "I don't care what you think you know. You're wrong."

"Ma'am, if you'll come quietly with us, you'll have plenty of opportunity to talk once we get to the station."

"You can damn well bet I'll talk. Irving Stackhouse is going to get an earful." When the young blond girl she frequently babysat was helped into the second official vehicle, Stella let out a shout. "Don't you dare scare that poor child! I'm responsible for her while her mom is working tonight. If you'd just give me a chance to call her—" Her voice was cut off as the patrol car door slammed shut.

Huddled out of sight, she waited in the dark until the cars drove away and silence resumed. Something bad had happened. Whatever it was, she intended to stay clear and avoid unwanted attention. She'd prepare the safe place she'd discovered for Lynette, just in case, but hopefully she wouldn't have to use it for long. Not more than a day or two at most. Whatever Stella had done to stir up trouble, she'd hunker down and stay away from the commotion. Nothing would stop her from getting her daughter back. Nothing.

"They hauled Stella in for questioning. This whole night has been one huge clusterfu—"

"What?" Nina blinked in the dark, stared at her phone, and frowned. "Teague? What the heck are you talking about?"

His sigh held a wealth of frustration. "The emergency I got called in for was to help the police search for the girl in your painting. Apparently those people who were at the art fair have connections to the governor, and he demanded action from the local cops."

"Oh, my God." Scooting up against the pillows, she flipped on the bedside light. "You're kidding."

"Dead serious. The police chief called out all the stops to put together a door-to-door search to locate her."

"And they arrested *Stella*?"

"Not arrested. Took her in as a person of interest. I'm at the station now, waiting to see Stackhouse so I can assure him Stella isn't guilty of kidnapping. Christ, she's the only older woman in Siren Cove Keely would definitely recognize."

"Why would they think she was involved?"

"Someone in the neighborhood said she'd seen a woman who lives near the end of Pine Street with a young blond girl, and she thought this girl might be the one in your painting. Stella babysits fairly often for a girl who's around the same age at the missing child. So the cops jumped the gun and decided they had their perp. As I said, it was a complete cluster."

"That's crazy."

"Yeah, it is. Hey, there's Stackhouse. I've gotta go. I just wanted to let you know it may be a while before I can straighten this out and come home. Or get back out on the streets to finish the door-to-door search. God only knows how this night will end."

"I'll see you whenever you get here. I hope you find that girl and get her identity settled once and for all."

"Me, too. Good night, Nina."

He hung up before she could respond. Laying the phone on the nightstand, she flopped back down and snuggled into his bed. The sheets smelled like Teague. She pressed her face into his pillow and breathed deep. Not as satisfying as the real thing, but she'd take what she could get. Closing her eyes, she drifted into sleep . . .

The repeated chime of her cell brought Nina out of a dream that included a giant bed of feathers and Teague. He pressed her deeper into the soft down while he kissed her all over, his hands sliding down—

When her phone rang again, she jerked upright. Juggling the cell, she nearly dropped it. "Teague?"

"No, this is Chris. I'm sorry to disturb you so late, or maybe I should say early, but we have a situation."

She glanced at the clock's glowing face. Two thirty-seven. "What's wrong?"

"I don't know if you're aware, but we're searching for that missing girl—"

"Teague filled me in when I volunteered to stay with his daughter."

"Great." Chris sounded tired. "Anyway, last night we had a bit of confusion with a woman who fit the description of the one we're trying to locate. So when I got a call to bring in a second person of interest for questioning—" He broke off and said something too muffled for Nina to hear. "Do you know a woman named Lola Copeland? You were one of the people she listed as a character reference. Despite the fact I didn't ask for any. She's pretty indignant and threatening to sue everyone in sight. I want to question her, but—"

"I know Miss Lola. If there's a young girl with her, she's probably her granddaughter. Lola talks about her all the time."

"That's what she claims."

"Keely met Lola once when she was at my house. She would have recognized Lola if she was the woman who spoke to her at the park and outside her home, the one who said she's the mother of the girl in the painting."

"Are you sure?"

Nina frowned. "I think so. Does the child there with Lola look like the one in the painting?"

"They're both blond and probably similar in age, but since we don't have a photograph . . ."

"The painting I did was damn accurate. You'd recognize her, I assure you." She slid out of bed. "But if it'll clear this up sooner, I'll go ask Keely."

"That would be helpful."

Nina pulled her shirt and capris pants on over her underwear and headed down the hall to Keely's room. A princess night-light cast a soft glow across the bed. At the foot, Coco sat up and thumped her tail on the spread. Sitting on the edge of the mattress, she shook Keely's shoulder. When the girl slowly opened her eyes, Nina smiled at her.

"How come you're here? It's still dark."

"I know, but I need to ask you a question. Do you remember Miss Lola?"

"The lady who took home the robin painting?"

"That's the one. Is she the woman who asked you about a playdate with her daughter?"

Keely yawned so wide her jaw cracked. "No."

"You're positive?"

She nodded her head against the pillow. "The other lady's hair was curlier, and she was taller."

"That's what I needed to know." She stroked the hair off her cheek. "You can go back to sleep now."

"Okay." Keely's eyelids drooped closed.

Quietly leaving the room, Nina spoke into her phone once she reached the hallway. "Did you hear all that?"

"I did. Thanks for clarifying the situation for me."

"You're welcome. Will you continue the search?"

"Not until morning. The chief called it off once this lead came in," Chris answered. "People aren't terribly co-operative when you wake them up in the middle of the night."

"Get some sleep. I'm sure you'll find the girl tomorrow."

"I hope so. Good night, Nina."

Outside, an engine rumbled then cut off. With a smile, she entered Teague's bedroom as footsteps sounded on the front porch and the door squeaked open. After peeling off her clothes, she dropped them in a heap on the floor and slid into bed. Moments later, Teague quietly entered the room.

"I'm awake."

"Sorry. I didn't mean to disturb you." He dropped his clothes on the floor, then pulled back the covers and slid into bed.

She turned and snuggled close. "You didn't wake me. Chris Long called a few minutes ago."

He stiffened before gathering her tighter against his chest. "What the hell did he want?"

"Keely confirmed their latest suspect wasn't the woman they're looking for. Do you remember me mentioning my client, Lola Copeland?"

"The one with money problems?"

"Yeah. I guess her granddaughter was with her last night. Since she's the right age, and Lola is in her sixties with gray hair . . ."

"Jesus."

"Keely met her once, so she was able to confirm Lola isn't the woman they're looking for."

"That's good, but I'm sorry all our leads tonight were a bust. Chief Stackhouse is bringing in reinforcements in the morning from nearby towns, so our services won't be needed."

Nina pressed her cheek against his warm neck. "I wonder if that girl I painted really was kidnapped. I feel sick knowing I was so close to her more than once and simply walked away."

His warm breath brushed her forehead. "Did she look like she was abused?"

"Not physically, but there was a sadness in her eyes I tried to capture in my painting."

"I'm sure they'll find her. Siren Cove isn't that big. Tomorrow the cops will get a lead that'll pan out."

She nodded, her hair sliding against his skin. "You must be exhausted."

"I am. As much as I'd like to make love to you right now, I'm not sure I have the energy."

"There's always morning sex."

"Good point . . ." His voice drifted off into even breathing.

Nina lay awake for some time, enjoying a state of contentment she couldn't ever remember feeling. She loved this man more than she'd thought it was possible to love anyone. Cocooned in happiness, she let herself relax into sleep . . .

Something tickled her nose. She brushed at it with her fingers and encountered the rasp of stubble. Smiling, she wound her arms around Teague's neck as his lips claimed hers.

"Morning, beautiful."

She blinked a few times as dim light streamed beneath the blinds she hadn't remembered to shut the night before. "Is it morning? I feel like I haven't slept."

"It was one hell of a night, but I have to get up for work. My real job this time."

"That's too bad."

"I agree. I wish I could stay, but—"

"Go. I'll be here when you get home." She laughed softly. "Well, maybe not right here in bed, but close enough."

"God, I love you." He pushed up onto his elbows. "Uh, I hate to ask, but when I spoke to Stella at the station last night, she said there's no way in hell she'd be here by seven thirty. Not after what the cops put her through."

"A blinding light and waterboarding to get the information they wanted?"

He sputtered with laughter. "Not exactly. I think everyone involved wished they hadn't been so quick to take her down to the station by the time the night was over. At any rate, can you—"

"Of course. Keely and I'll make pancakes, then maybe we'll take Coco for a walk. I could use some exercise. We'll have fun."

"Stella promised to be here by ten."

"Not a problem."

He pushed off the bed. "You're the best."

Plumping the pillows behind her, she eyed his extremely fine ass as he headed toward the bathroom. "In bed or in general?"

He glanced over his shoulder and grinned. "Both. I'm going to take a quick shower. Suddenly, I feel invigorated and ready to face the day."

While he was getting ready for work, Nina put on the same clothes she'd worn the day before and headed toward the stairs. When Coco squeezed through Keely's partially opened bedroom door and followed her down, she let the dog out and ran across the street. After disarming the security system, she hurried up to her room to grab shorts and a T-shirt along with clean underwear. After resetting the alarm, she headed back to Teague's house.

Coco stood on the front lawn, staring toward the woods. When she growled low in her throat, Nina frowned.

"What is it, girl? Did something spook you?" Picking up the dog, she climbed the steps to the porch and met Teague on his way out. "That was certainly quick. Don't you want some breakfast?"

"No time." He bent to drop a kiss on her lips. "I'll eat when I get to the firehouse. What's wrong with Coco? Her fur's standing up."

"She was staring toward the woods a minute ago. I didn't see anything."

"Probably ravens. When I opened the bathroom window to let out the steam, I heard them cawing. Coco doesn't like them."

"Well, I'll bring her inside with me. I plan to take a shower before Keely wakes up."

"Thanks again for helping me out."

Clutching the clothes and the dog in one arm, she reached up to brush a thumb across his cheek. "You don't have to thank me. I like spending time with Keely. Have a good day."

He smiled, his eyes bright with appreciation . . . and love. "You, too. I'll see you in a few hours."

Nina didn't move until he climbed into his truck and drove away. Then, with Coco squirming to get down, she entered the house, set the dog on the floor, and shut and locked the door. "Geez, scratch me with your nails, why don't you?" Shaking her head as the spoiled mutt pranced toward her food bowl in the laundry room, Nina ran upstairs.

A peek into Keely's room told her the girl was still asleep, sprawled across her bed. The covers were kicked mostly on the floor. With a smile, Nina headed to Teague's bathroom, set her pile of clean clothes on the counter by the sink, and turned on the water. After stripping off her dirty shirt and capris, she stood beneath the hot spray and soaked in the warmth.

Showering with Teague would be a heck of a lot more fun, but with Keely just down the hall . . . Maybe having a child in the house meant they had to be a little more circumspect, but she didn't mind. Having Keely in her life was worth making a few changes. She'd grown to care about Teague's daughter almost as much as she loved him.

When the room filled with steam, she squirted a dollop of shampoo into her hand, then wrinkled her nose. Pine was a good scent on him, but it wasn't her first choice. From a distance, Coco went off in a barking frenzy, faint but still audible.

"What the heck is wrong with that dog?" Nina rubbed the shampoo into a lather as Coco suddenly quieted. She'd just stuck her head under the spray when the bathroom door creaked open. Eyes closed as she rinsed her hair, she called out, "Teague, did you forget something?"

The glass door clicked.

"What—"

Pain exploded in her head. Her foot slipped on the shower floor, and she went down hard as the world dissolved into blackness.

Chapter Twenty-five

Teague was working his way through a plate of scrambled eggs and hash browns when Mateo hurried into the firehouse kitchen. The look on his friend's face made him instantly lose his appetite.

"What's wrong?"

"I was listening to the police scanner to see if there was an update on the girl we were searching for last night when a nine-one-one call came in from an address on Cedar Lane. A missing child. Nina made the call."

Teague dropped his fork as his breakfast threatened to come back up.

"They're sending a response team now."

As he finished speaking, the overhead PA system engaged and the siren blew. "Request for an ambulance at 820 Cedar Lane. An assault victim."

Teague rose on trembling legs as the room swayed around him. He held on to the table with both hands.

Mateo rushed forward and grabbed him by the arm. "I'll drive you."

Before he could move, let alone answer, his cell rang.

Pulling it from his pocket, he stared at Nina's name on the screen for a second before connecting the call. "What happened?"

Hysterical sobbing was her only response.

His gut tightened. "Nina, talk to me."

"Keely's gone." Her voice was so choked with tears, he could barely make out the words. "Someone hit me, and I passed out for a few seconds. I called nine-one-one. I'm sorry. I'm so sorry." She broke down again, crying uncontrollably.

"I'm on my way." He forced calm into his voice, when he wanted to scream and shout and put his fist through the wall. "So are the police. Don't lose it on me, Nina. They'll need to talk to you. Are you hurt?"

"My head is bleeding."

"Hold a towel on the wound." Running behind Mateo, he took the stairs two at a time, his heart pounding so hard he was afraid he might keel over. "I'll be there in a few minutes."

She drew in a shuddering breath. "They have to find Keely. They have to "

"We'll find her. I need to hang up now. Just sit down and wait for me."

"Okay."

He shoved his phone in his pocket and nearly broke down when Mateo put an arm around his back.

"Hold on, dude." He glanced over his shoulder as Rod took the driver's seat in the ambulance. "Captain, can Teague ride with you?"

"Of course. You take shotgun with Rod. We'll be right behind you."

A few seconds later they pulled out of the fire station, sirens blaring. Teague stared straight ahead through the windshield of the captain's truck, too numb to even think.

"Whoever took your daughter only has a few minutes' head start. The police will find her, and based on the nine-one-one report, your girlfriend's injuries don't sound too severe."

He couldn't speak through the burning knot in his throat, so he only nodded. All the horrible memories of getting the call about Jayne and rushing to the hospital rose to the surface in a suffocating wave. This had to end differently. He couldn't live with the possibility of losing his child.

Two patrol cars were parked at adjacent angles in front of his house. The ambulance pulled into the driveway and cut the siren. The captain stopped beside the mailbox and turned off the engine.

When Teague reached for the door handle, Barker grasped his arm. "Let the cops do their job, and let Rod and Mateo tend to Nina. Losing your cool won't get results any faster."

He nodded again and climbed out of the vehicle. Before he was halfway to the porch, Nina ran out the front door. The side of her neck and her hair were covered in blood, and there were dark-red patches on her yellow T-shirt. Tearstains ravaged her face. After stumbling down the steps, she threw herself into his arms, her whole body trembling.

Tightening his arms around her, he held on, never wanting to let her go.

"I'm so sorry."

He stroked her back. "This isn't your fault. Let Mateo take a look at that cut on your head. Did you talk to the police yet?"

"Yes. They're inside processing the scene, but Chief Stackhouse said they'll probably have more questions for me afterward."

Teague guided her over to the back of the ambulance. "Come sit down so we can assess your wound." He kept his voice calm, professional. If he did anything else, he might start swearing—or crying—and never stop.

Nina looked broken . . . destroyed, and it was killing him. But nothing compared to the all-encompassing, gut-clenching fear of knowing some psycho had his daughter.

Teague sat beside her and held her hand while Rod gently cleaned her wound and examined her pupils. Mateo ran through a series of questions to test her responses. He made a few notes on her paperwork then stepped back.

"How long do you think you were unconscious?"

"Only for a few seconds." She tightened her fingers around Teague's. "I was rinsing my hair when the person opened the shower door and hit me. My eyes were closed at the time to keep the soap out, and I thought it was Teague returning for some reason."

"So you didn't see the freak who took my daughter?" He forced the words out between gritted teeth.

"I didn't see anything. I slipped and fell and hit my head against the shower wall. Everything went dark for a moment before swimming back into focus." Her breathing was ragged as she continued. "There was pink in the water washing down the drain. I remember the pink." A shudder ran through her.

"There's a laceration on your scalp." Rod taped a gauze pad over her injury. "Head wounds tend to bleed pretty freely, but the cut isn't deep. The bleeding has nearly stopped. Are you sure you were only unconscious for a few seconds?"

Nina glanced up and nodded. "I'm sure. I was dizzy at first, but I could hear Keely screaming. Then she went quiet, like someone covered her mouth." Her voice broke. "I crawled out of the shower, grabbed a towel, then ran out into the hall. Her door was open, but she wasn't in her room. I heard a car start while I was on the stairs. The front door had been left wide open, and Coco was shut in the laundry room, barking and scratching to get out."

"Did you see the car?"

Her body shook as she pressed against him. "By the time I reached the front porch, it was already gone, so I called nine-one-one. The person I talked to told me to stay where I was and that help was coming. I went back upstairs to put on clothes and called you. The police were here pretty fast."

Teague's pulse pounded at his temples. "Are the cops out looking for Keely? What the hell are they doing inside the house?"

"Chris and another officer left to search the neighborhood, and Chief Stackhouse mentioned setting up roadblocks."

Mateo squeezed her shoulder. "Nina, do you want to go to the hospital to get checked out? Based on your responsiveness, I don't think you have a concussion, but it's always a possibility."

"I don't want to go anywhere." She raised a hand to wipe tears off her cheeks. "I just want to help find Keely."

Teague stroked her blood-soaked hair. "Are you sure?"

"Absolutely. I feel fine, except for tenderness to the touch on my scalp and a headache."

He rose to his feet. "Then I'm going to go talk to whoever is in charge and see what the hell they're doing to find my daughter."

When he reached the front porch, Coco's faint whining hit him like another punch to the gut. He headed straight back to the laundry room and opened the door. His dog cowered in the corner in front of the washing machine, eyes wide with fear.

"Hey, you're okay, girl." Bending, he scooped her up

and held her against his chest. "Are you hurt?" He gently felt her quivering limbs, but she didn't wince. Apparently, whoever had taken Keely had simply tossed the dog in the laundry room and shut the door. Tamping down on the anger roiling through him, he followed the voices upstairs.

His boss stood with his back to Teague, speaking to Chief Stackhouse. When the cop held up a hand and met his gaze, Barker turned and motioned him forward.

"How's Nina doing?"

"Upset, obviously, but she'll be fine." He glanced at the police chief and forced himself to speak calmly. "What's being done to find Keely?"

"We've put out an alert along with her photo. Nina sent me a recent shot of your daughter she'd taken on her phone." The chief ran a hand through his iron-gray hair, looking every one of his sixty-odd years. "Roadblocks leading out of town were established immediately, so chances are the kidnapper didn't get out of the area, but we're sending an APB statewide, just in case. Right now, we're organizing a door-to-door search, using a copy of the photo. We have the manpower already available from the ongoing search for the other missing girl."

Teague tightened his grip on Coco, only loosening it when the dog let out a yip. "Don't you find it beyond coincidental that some woman from Siren Cove may have abducted another child, and now my daughter has been taken?"

Stackhouse lowered his brows. "I'm not completely dense, son. We'll be looking for that woman in connection to both missing person cases. Glen, here, has offered his crew up again to expedite the investigation. Since we haven't found any helpful evidence left at the scene to identify the perp, we're going to get cracking on the search."

"I'll go out with you." Teague breathed steadily, slowly,

determined not to lose his shit and get banned from the search. "I can't sit around here doing nothing."

"If the person who took your daughter calls about ransom—"

"Why the hell would anyone do that? I don't have the kind of cash that would interest a kidnapper. Anyway, I don't even have a landline, and I'll have my cell phone on me."

His boss cleared his throat. "Are you sure you're up to this? You don't look so great."

"I'm not going to pass out or do anything stupid." *Unless I find the bastard—or bitch—who has Keely.* He clamped his lips shut on the final thought.

"Fine. If Nina declined medical attention, head back to the firehouse in the ambulance with Rod and Mateo. They're setting up the task force down at the police station right now. I'll follow with the captain once he finishes up here."

Teague nodded and turned away. His legs weren't quite steady as he descended the stairs. When he found Nina waiting for him in the entry, he handed her the quivering dog. "I'm going out to look for Keely."

After taking Coco, she stroked the dog's head. "What can I do to help?"

"I don't know." He rubbed a hand over his eyes. "Stay with Coco. Maybe call Stella to tell her what happened."

"I will." Nina rose on her toes to press a kiss to his mouth. "Find your sweet girl."

"I intend to. I just hope it's before she loses her innocence."

Nina sat on the front porch, holding Coco in her lap, wondering how in the hell this nightmare had happened.

The police had left, and Teague was out with the task force, searching door to door for a clue—*anything*—that would lead them to Keely. Her nerves were stretched to the point of breaking, and her head throbbed. After a moment, she rose to her feet and went inside. She set the dog on the floor and shut the door.

Staring at the knob, she frowned. How had the kidnapper entered the house? The cops had just assumed she'd left the front door unlocked, but she distinctly remembered throwing the dead bolt before going upstairs to take a shower. After her recent break-ins, she hadn't been careless.

Coco followed when she headed into the kitchen. Searching through the drawers, Nina found one that contained a jar of gummy vitamins and a bottle of ibuprofen. She popped three pain tablets into her mouth and swallowed them with a glass of water. Bracing her hands on the counter next to the sink, she stared out into the backyard. The gate was partially open. Again. Had the police searched out there and gone into the woods from the yard? Leaving the room, she stopped in front of the back door. It was unlocked. Frowning, she bent down and pushed the doggy door. It swung freely, but a piece of blue material was caught on the top hinge of the plastic door. She pulled it loose and held it up. A ripped piece of light cotton, possibly from a dress shirt or blouse.

She glanced from the flapping door to the lock as an idea formed. She went outside and lay down on the stoop. Stretching her arm up through the doggy door, she was just able to reach the dead bolt and flip the lock. On the other side, Coco barked like a lunatic. After switching it back, she turned the knob, and the door opened. She half fell inside.

"Oh, my freaking God." Climbing up off the floor, she

pulled her phone out of her pocket and called Chris Long's direct line.

"Long here."

"Chris, it's Nina. I just figured out how the person got into the house."

"Hold on a second." He returned to his phone a few moments later. "The front door was open, and the back door was unlocked. Either entrance could have been used."

"The kidnapper came through the back door, all right, but it was locked when he—or she—arrived. I found a scrap of material stuck on the hinge of the doggy door. The person lay down outside and reached up through it to unlock the door." Her voice was flat. "I tried, and it worked."

"Damn."

"Yeah. It wasn't my fault the psycho got inside. The cloth looks like it came from a sky-blue dress shirt or blouse."

"Thanks. I'll spread the word that the perp may be wearing a blue shirt. Thanks for calling me."

"You're welcome. Any news yet?"

"I'm afraid not, but we won't stop searching until we find her."

Nina's shoulders slumped. "Okay. Bye, Chris." Glancing at the time on her phone's display, she winced. Nine fifteen. Keely had been missing for nearly two hours. She tapped a few times to bring up Stella's number and held the phone to her ear, dreading telling the woman what had happened.

After a few rings, the call went to voice mail. With a low oath, Nina disconnected. She wasn't about to break the news of Keely's kidnapping to Stella in a message. Possibly, the sitter was still asleep or in the shower.

Glancing down at her feet, she stared at Coco's drooping ears and tail.

"We'll walk over there. We could both use a little fresh air."

After putting the dog on a leash, she locked both the back and front doors before heading across the porch. When her phone rang before she'd gotten to the end of the driveway, she answered without looking at the display.

"Hello."

"Nina, have you heard anything about what's going on in town? Rumors are floating around about a missing child, and there are a bunch of cops from out of the area down at the station."

When Paige paused for breath, Nina broke in. "Someone took Keely out of her bedroom this morning." Her throat burned as she forced out the words. "They hit me while I was in the shower, and I couldn't get to her in time."

"Oh, God. Oh, no." Her friend's voice rose. "Is Teague . . ."

"He's holding it together somehow. They're out looking for her now."

"Are you okay?"

"I don't know how to answer that. My head hurts, but I feel like I'm going to lose my mind. I keep thinking about Keely, alone and scared to death . . . or worse. It's making me sick, imagining what's happening to her."

"Then don't," Paige spoke firmly. "I'll come over. Just sit tight, and I'll be there in a few minutes."

"Right now I'm walking over to talk to Stella, the woman who watches Keely. I thought it was her calling back since she didn't answer her phone a few minutes ago. She only lives a few blocks away and was supposed to babysit Keely today." Nina's grip on the leash tightened. "I didn't want to leave her a message."

"I don't blame you. Fine, I'll be over in a half hour instead."

Nina stepped over a crack in the sidewalk. The last thing she needed was more bad luck. "That would be great. Right now I could use a friend."

"I'll see you shortly."

She hung up and pushed her phone into her pocket. Her head itched from the dried blood, and even though she'd washed most of it off her face and neck, she probably still looked like the victim of a horror flick. When Coco stopped to pee, she waited for her to finish before picking up their pace.

A block from her destination, she passed a patrol car parked at the curb. Two officers she didn't recognize, no doubt part of the out-of-town contingent, spoke to old Mr. Peterson, who waved when he saw her. The cops turned to glance her way as she waved back, then returned to questioning the elderly man. Rounding the corner onto Pine, she arrived at Stella's house a few minutes later. The woman's motorcycle was parked in her driveway, and next door, a white sedan that looked vaguely familiar had been left at the curb with the passenger door open.

Coco strained against her leash and growled.

"Hush." Hauling the dog up the walkway, she knocked on Stella's door. When it swung open, she stepped inside. "Stella, are you here?"

Silence echoed back at her, interrupted by Coco's whining. Uneasiness filled her as she walked farther into the house. When her foot slipped on the hardwood floor, she fell to one knee and put her hand down to press back upright. Something sticky and damp coated her palm. Turning it over, she swallowed hard.

"Stella!" Surging to her feet, Nina rounded the corner into the kitchen and found the woman sprawled on the tile. Blood stained her pink terry-cloth robe.

Dropping the leash, she pushed Coco out of the way and felt for a pulse. Faint and thready. When Stella moaned, she touched her cheek.

"Oh, God. What the hell happened? Who did this?" Pulling her phone from her pocket, she dropped it when Stella opened her eyes and grabbed her wrist.

"Keely," she whispered.

"What about Keely?" When her eyes rolled back, Nina raised her voice. "Hold on, Stella. Talk to me."

"Next door. Go."

Nina didn't argue. Grabbing her phone, she rose to her feet and ran toward the entry. A car door slammed as she reached the yard. Moments later, an engine started.

"No!" Running full out, she reached the sedan as it pulled in a circle to turn around at the end of the court. Coco leaped against the driver's door, barking frantically, as Nina reached for the handle.

When the door opened straight into her, she sprawled against the pavement. Dragging herself to her knees, she met a hard, determined gaze.

"You won't stop me. I won't let you!"

Before she could scramble out of the way, the woman stepped on the gas. Rolling hard to her side, Nina smacked her head against the pavement. Exhaust fumes fogged her brain as the trees above her wavered, and the world faded.

Chapter Twenty-six

When his cell rang, Teague stopped short at the end of the walkway to a white bungalow-style home and yanked his phone out of his pocket to glance at the display. Not Nina. A number he didn't recognize. "Hello."

"Teague, it's Paige. I'm so sorry about your daughter." Her voice was filled with angst. "Nina told me what happened, and I came over to stay with her, but she isn't here."

"Did you try my place?"

"Yes, but no one answered the door there, either, and it's locked. Nina said she was walking over to talk to the woman who watches Keely, but she should have been back by now, and she isn't answering her cell. Did she contact you?"

"I haven't talked to her in the last hour or so. I'm not too far from Stella's house now, so I'll go see if Nina's still there or if Stella knows where she went after she left."

"I'd appreciate that. With everything that's going on, I'm a little freaked out. Are the police making any progress finding Keely?"

His lips flattened, and he had to blink back tears. "Not yet. I'll either call you back when I know more or tell Nina to contact you if I see her."

"Thanks, Teague."

Crossing the street, he waited for Art Cantrell to finish questioning the neighbor and then waved him down. "I'm going over to Stella Lange's house down at the end of Pine."

The officer frowned. "Isn't she the woman we took in for questioning last night?"

"Yeah, she babysits my daughter." He clenched and unclenched his fists. "Nina was supposed to go talk to her, and now she's not answering her phone. I need to find out why."

"I'll finish this block. Check in with me before you go anywhere else, okay?"

"Will do." Teague headed toward his truck and started the engine. A couple of minutes later, he parked in front of Stella's house, got out, and slammed the door. As he hustled up the walk, his gut tightened. It wasn't like Nina to keep her friends waiting or ignore calls.

The front door was wide open when he reached it. "Stella." The hair on the back of his neck prickled when only silence echoed through the house. "Stella!" Raising his voice, he walked through the entry, glanced into the empty living room, then turned toward the kitchen.

"Holy shit!" Dropping to his knees beside the unconscious woman lying on the floor, he felt for a pulse. Faint but detectable. His hands shook as he pulled out his phone and dialed nine-one-one.

"Nine-one-one operator, what's the nature of your emergency?"

"I found an unconscious woman in her home at the end of Pine Drive in the eight hundred block. Her name is

Stella Lange, and she's bleeding from what looks like a serious laceration. Please send an ambulance and the police. My name is Teague O'Dell. I'm an EMT, and this woman needs immediate transport to the hospital. There's a second woman missing from this location who may also be in trouble. I need to go look for her after I get some compression on this wound."

"Thank you, Mr. O'Dell. Help is being dispatched now."

"I'm hanging up." He rose to his feet and pushed his phone back into his pocket. "Nina, are you here?" Grabbing a dish towel off the counter, he peeled back Stella's robe and placed the folded towel against the bleeding wound, then tied the robe belt around it to hold the makeshift pad in place.

Leaping up, he ran from the room. "Nina! Nina!" A frantic glance into the dining room then laundry revealed no sign of her in the front of the house. Tearing down the hallway, he threw open the doors to the bedrooms and bathrooms. Nina's body wasn't sprawled on the floor anywhere in the home. Thankfulness flooded through him, followed by a chill that shook him to his core. If she wasn't here, then where the hell was she?

Teague hurried back to Stella's side as the distant wail of a siren grew closer. Trying not to contaminate the scene, he knelt beside her and checked the towel. She'd lost a considerable amount of blood, but he'd slowed the flow. He glanced up when Cantrell entered the room. The older officer's gaze went to Stella, and his face lost some of its color.

"She's still alive, but barely."

The cop knelt beside him. "I heard the nine-one-one call. Hey, it looks like she's coming around."

Teague turned back and picked up Stella's hand to squeeze it. "Can you hear me, Stella? Where's Nina?"

Her eyelids fluttered, and she blinked twice, but her gaze was unfocused. Outside, a siren cut off, and the roar of the ambulance engine quieted.

"Stella, tell us what happened. Help is here now."

When she mumbled something incoherent, he leaned closer. "What was that?"

"Next door." Her voice was a whisper. "Help Keely."

Before he could respond, her eyes rolled back in her head. Behind him, Captain Barker and Rod ran in with a gurney and a bag of gear.

"Out of the way, Teague." His boss nudged him aside. "Let us see to the patient."

"She has what looks like a stab wound in her side. I tried to stem the bleeding. She was unconscious when I arrived and came around just now, but she's passed out again." He backed out of the way and clenched his fists. "She mentioned Keely, and Nina is missing. If she talks when you get her to the hospital . . ."

Barker met his gaze. "We'll let the staff know she may have crucial information. Let's just hope she pulls through."

"She has to."

"Looks like this is what cut her." Wearing plastic gloves, Cantrell held up a carving knife with a bloodstained tip. "Whoever sliced her threw it into the sink."

Rod glanced up. "What the hell is going on in this town?"

Teague couldn't wait another moment. "I'm going across the street. I'm almost positive Stella said *next door* before she mentioned Keely's name."

"Hold on, son." The cop slid the knife into an evidence bag he took from a pouch on his belt. "You stay back and let me call this in first. Obviously the perp is dangerous, and if there's a hostage situation you could endanger your little girl."

Teague gritted his teeth while the older man spoke into the radio at his shoulder. The urge to run across the street and tear open the front door was overwhelming. If Keely was there . . .

"Backup is on the way. I won't tell you to stay here since I know you won't listen, but keep out of the way and let me assess the situation first. It's possible the injured woman wasn't lucid, and I'm not about to burst into someone's home with guns blazing without more information. Got it?"

"Yes." Teague bit off the word. Time was wasting. When tires sounded on the pavement outside and doors slammed, he followed Cantrell to the door. Chief Stackhouse and Chris Long approached them.

"Give me an update." Stackhouse met Teague's gaze briefly before focusing on his officer.

The man explained in a few brief words.

Long narrowed his eyes on the house next door. "It doesn't look like anyone is around."

"No, but we have enough for probable cause to enter the home." The chief glanced back at Teague. "Stay outside until we know what the situation is in there."

Frustration rose to the boiling point as the three cops headed toward the neighboring house. He kicked a piece of loose gravel and prayed they'd find Keely and Nina both safe. Taking slow breaths, he rounded the patrol car Long had left parked in the middle of the cul-de-sac and frowned when a flat pink object caught his eye. Nina's cell phone case. He scooped it up and stared down at the cracked screen while his heart pounded in his chest.

Ignoring instructions, he ran over to the house as the men disappeared inside.

"Clear."

"Clear."

The words echoed back at him as Teague paused for several long heartbeats in the entry.

"Clear up here, too." Long appeared at the top of the stairs. "Looks like someone packed everything up and left in a hurry without taking all of their belongings. There are boxes stacked in two of the bedrooms."

"In the kitchen, as well." Stackhouse returned to the entry and frowned at Teague. "You don't listen very well, O'Dell."

"I found Nina's phone on the street. She must have dropped it." His hand shook as he held up the pink case. "I don't know why she wouldn't have picked it up again unless—"

"Unless someone stopped her." Cantrell came out of the living room. "There are children's books in here, left out on the coffee table."

"I found adult women's clothing in an open suitcase in one bedroom and a few stuffed animals in another." Long descended the stairs. "Oh, and one of those Disney Princess dresses."

Teague's heart nearly stopped before racing on in a frantic rhythm. "Which one?"

Chris frowned. "What do you mean?"

"Which princess?"

"I don't know. It's yellow and shiny. Plus there's a stuffed cat and a monkey."

Teague grabbed the doorframe and held on tight. "Those belong to Keely. They disappeared from our house a couple of weeks ago. Whoever took her must have planned this well in advance."

Stackhouse cleared his throat. "Could be the neighbor saw the perp with your daughter and confronted her. That obviously didn't end well."

"Maybe Stella sent Nina over here to look for her." Teague pressed a hand to his chest. "Maybe she saw the kidnapper, possibly recognized her."

"Then where the hell is Nina now?" Chris reached the bottom of the stairs and smacked his hand down on the railing.

Teague braced himself in the doorway. "The psycho who took Keely has them both."

Nina woke slowly, feeling a little nauseous with her skull pounding. She let out a groan as she opened her eyes and blinked in the darkness. A single ray of sunlight streamed through a crack in some sort of wooden platform overhead to create stripes on the dirt wall in front of her. Beneath her was hard ground that had a musty smell. A hint of smoke in the air irritated her lungs, and she coughed.

"Wake up." The high voice trembled slightly before a hand touched her cheek.

"Keely?" Nina pushed upright to a sitting position despite the throbbing in her head and pulled the girl into her arms. Her whole body ached as she hugged her tight. "Oh, thank God. Are you hurt, sweetie?"

"No. That mean woman made me breathe something nasty, and when I woke up I didn't know where I was. Anna-Banana, Trudy, and my Belle dress were there, but when she hurried me to her car, she said we didn't have time to take them." Keely pressed her face against Nina's neck, and tears dampened her skin. "She told me Daddy died in a fire. She called me Lynette."

"Sweetie, your dad is fine. He didn't die. He's looking for you right now." Nina's heart ached as the girl broke down, sobbing. "He'll find us soon. I know he will."

"She said there was a big fire and—"

"There wasn't. That woman lied. She's very sick and needs help. I promise your dad is just fine."

Hysteria tinged her voice. "The lady said she would take care of me, but the way she looked at me was creepy. I just wanted my daddy."

"I'm so sorry you were scared and upset, but you don't have to worry anymore. I'll make sure nothing else happens to you." Nina stroked Keely's hair until her sobs quieted and wondered how she was going to make good on her promise. "Do you know where we are?"

"A room in the ground. I was sure you were going to save me, but then that lady hit you with the car. She said bad words 'cause you're heavy."

"How far did she drive?"

"Not very far. She stopped by a burned house. There was a trapdoor and steps. The lady said this would be my safe place until we go to our new home. She was mad about you ruining everything."

"I bet."

Nina's mind raced, processing the information. Hank Murphy's burned-out house was just down the street from Stella's home. It would take nerve to leave them in a cellar so close to the crime scene. Her head throbbed, and her mouth felt like she'd swallowed cotton. Though her stomach churned when she moved, she released Keely and rose to her feet.

"Did you try to open the hatch up there?"

"I did after she left, but it wouldn't move." She rubbed her arms and shivered. "I don't know where the other girl is. The one I met on the beach."

Nina's already queasy stomach revolted, and it was all she could do not to puke. She couldn't think about the blond girl she'd painted. Emma. If this psycho freak had kidnapped Keely, surely she'd taken the other girl, as well. But right now her only concern was getting out of this hole.

Wincing with each step as pain ricocheted along her limbs, she climbed the rickety stairs, feeling the bruises that had surely already formed on every inch of her body. When she reached the top, she pressed her shoulder against the wooden cover and heaved upward. It didn't budge even a millimeter. Clearly their captor had locked it shut from the outside.

Raising her voice, she shouted, "Help! Help us! Help."

"The lady said no one would hear me if I yelled."

Nina climbed carefully down the steps and sat beside Keely again. "We'll have to come up with another plan." She tried to think, but her aching head made concentrating difficult. "Did she tell you her name?"

"No, just to call her Mama." Keely's voice took on a spark of defiance. "I didn't. She couldn't make me."

"Good for you." Nina hugged her close. "I wish I knew—"

She broke off as she struggled to bring a fuzzy memory into focus. She'd run up to the car with Coco at her side, fear giving her speed and strength, then . . . nothing. Reaching up, she felt a second knot on her head. The lump hadn't split the skin, but she'd be lucky if she didn't have brain damage after this hellish day.

Nina let out a frustrated sigh. "If I saw her, I don't remember."

"What are we going to do when she comes back?"

The way Keely's voice shook tore at her heart. "I'm

not sure yet. Did you see anything in here when the hatch was open?"

"There are shelves on the wall over there." Keely's arm swung out to point. "I think something was on them."

"I'll take a look." When she stood, her aching body cried out in protest. Nina pressed her hands to her pounding skull and drew in shallow breaths. One thing was certain, in her present condition outrunning even an elderly woman wasn't an option.

Holding her hands in front of her, she walked in the direction Keely had indicated until her fingers brushed flat wooden planking about a foot wide. Possibly, Hank had stored food down here. Feeling along each board, she encountered a lumpy bag and cringed a little as she folded back the burlap to reach inside. Potatoes. Not the most ideal weapon.

She stretched up to a higher shelf and continued her search. When her hand touched cold glass, she grasped the container before it could fall. A pint-sized canning jar that sloshed when she shook it. Careful investigation revealed five more jars.

"Jackpot!"

"What does that mean?"

Nina glanced in the direction of Keely's voice. "It means I think I know how we're going to get out of here."

Taking two jars with her, she brought them back to a strategic location not far from the stairs. Two more trips completed her arsenal.

"What are you going to do?"

"I'm going to pray I can still throw a decent fastball and that I'm not too dizzy to stand up and take aim." Once she had her jars in place, she sat back down. "Until then, we're going to hang out and wait for that woman to come back."

Keely wrapped her arms around Nina and held tight. "I'm not scared anymore. You make me feel brave."

"I hope so, sweet girl. You'll always be safe when I'm around."

"I wish you could stay with me and Daddy always."

Nina tightened her grip as a fierce, protective urge unlike anything she'd ever felt before surged through her. "I want that, too. But after we get out of here, your dad and I need to settle a few things first."

Keely rested her head on her shoulder. "I love you, Nina."

"I love you, too."

Chapter Twenty-seven

Teague walked out of the house, leaving the cops who were combing the place for evidence to do their job. The ambulance carrying Stella had left a few minutes before. Standing in the middle of the cul-de-sac, he tried his best to hold it together as his entire life unraveled around him. Staring up at the sky, he shook as he rubbed damp eyes with the back of his hand.

The absolute only bright spot was the knowledge that Nina was in all likelihood with Keely. His little girl wasn't alone. Telling himself that Nina was smart and resourceful helped some, but fear that she might be seriously injured . . . He wiped away more tears. At least there'd been no blood on the street near her phone. If the freak had stabbed her the way she had Stella, surely there would have been blood somewhere.

Quiet whining penetrated the fog of worry surrounding him. Turning, he stared toward the trees as Coco crept out of the underbrush.

"Hey, girl." He hurried to the edge of the street and

crouched down to pet his quivering dog. "Where have you been? I'm sorry I forgot all about you."

He checked her for injuries, then smiled when she stood up and shook before wagging her tail. Just scared, not injured. Coco wasn't a fan of noise and confusion. "Were you hiding out in the woods to escape the sirens and loud voices?"

Or did you go after Keely?

Maybe the kidnapper hadn't driven off with his daughter and Nina. There'd been no sign of them at the roadblocks set up on the highway. Teague faced the dense forest behind the two houses at the end of the street. What appeared to be a faint trail where ferns had been flattened and the layer of needles on the ground disturbed led past a big Douglas fir. Had the crazy bitch hidden Keely and Nina in the woods?

Anything was better than standing here, doing nothing. Scooping up Coco, he followed the faint path, not well used but still detectible. When the dog whined to get down, he set her on her feet. She stopped to pee and sniffed a couple of leaves, but she didn't act like she was on the trail of her missing mistress. But then, Coco was no bloodhound.

Still, he kept going, pushing deeper into the woods. After walking for a good ten minutes, his steps faltered. There was no way in hell an older woman could have hauled Nina's unconscious body this far. Unless she was fully lucid and forced to walk at gunpoint . . .

Teague clamped his jaw tight and pushed aside a tree branch. Someone, or something, had made the trail. Possibly animals. He'd seen a couple of deer in the neighborhood. But if the path had been made by a human . . . He came out of the trees into a small clearing and stopped. Some of the grass was flattened in places, and there were broken branches spread out on the ground near the far edge of the woods.

The hair on his neck prickled.

"Nina! Keely!" His shout seemed to be absorbed into the stillness of the forest.

Leaving his side, Coco wandered over to the branches, sniffed, then let out a soft woof. Not the level of excitement he'd expect if Keely were in the area. Following the dog, he glanced around and frowned. What looked like fresh dirt had been scraped off the weeds near the pile of sticks, and mounds of earth had been flung into the bushes and ferns.

"What the hell?" Hadn't Nina mentioned something a while back about finding a hole some kids had dug?

He pushed at the branches with the toe of his boot, then bent to shift them. If someone had been digging in the area . . . Working faster, he hauled the limbs aside until the remainder of the branches crashed downward into the hole.

When Coco started barking, he hushed her. Had that been a cry, or just the dog?

"Keely?" His voice rose. "Keely, are you down there?"

When the branches shifted and moved, he slid down into the pit and piled them to the side. Frightened eyes stared up at him as he uncovered a girl huddled in a tight ball. Not Keely. But something about her was familiar.

"Emma?"

She let out a whimper but didn't speak. Her terror was almost palpable.

"I'm a fireman, Emma. I save people." He kept his voice low and steady. "Don't be afraid. I'm here to take you home."

She shook her head. "No. No. No. Mama will bring me back here." Huge sobs racked her body.

"Okay, not home. Somewhere safe. Let me help you, Emma."

"I'm Lynette, not Emma. I'm Lynette."

"Okay, Lynette. I'm going to pick you up and lift you out of this hole. I'm not going to hurt you. Will you let me do that?" When her only response was to cringe farther away, he tried again. "I have a little girl of my own, Keely. You met her on the beach one day. Do you see Coco up there?" He pointed toward the furry face staring down at them, issuing an occasional bark. "Coco is her dog. I promise you can trust me."

Her uncontrollable crying slowly subsided, and finally she nodded. "I remember her. She seemed nice."

"She is nice. She liked you. Are you ready to get out of this hole now?"

When Emma gave another nod, Teague gazed skyward in relief. Carefully, he bent to take her into his arms and tried a cautious smile. "When I lift you up, you need to scramble out onto the ground, okay?"

"Okay."

Boosting her upward, he held on until she'd crawled out onto the grass. Once she'd moved away from the edge, he stood on the broken branches, then heaved himself up and out of the hole. Coco came over to lick his hand and sniffed the cowering girl.

With a shaking hand, Emma reached out to pet her. Tears slid down her cheeks when Coco rolled onto her back for a belly rub.

Teague stood, pulled his phone from his pocket, and called Art Cantrell since his was the only direct number he had. When the officer answered, he turned his back on Emma and spoke in a low voice. "I found the girl."

Cantrell hesitated for a moment. "Your daughter?"

"No, the kidnapping victim we were looking for yesterday. She was left in a hole some distance into the woods behind the house where that psycho was living. Her mental condition is questionable, but she doesn't seem to have been harmed physically. I've calmed her down to the point where I think I can carry her out of here."

"That's excellent news. I'll let Chief Stackhouse know to expect you with her shortly. Do you need any help?"

"I think we're okay. She's beginning to trust me. Maybe the chief can contact the couple who reported her missing, although the girl may not remember them."

"I'll do that. There's no sign of the perp in the woods?"

"No, the woman must have left her here alone when she went after Keely." Teague glanced over his shoulder, but Emma seemed to be occupied with the dog and not listening to his conversation. "I'm not sure how long she was in that pit."

"All right. Contact me if you have any problems, and make sure you can find the way back to the site again afterward. We'll need to process the scene once you bring the girl down here to safety."

"I can do that. I'll see you shortly." He closed his eyes. "Any word on Keely and Nina?"

"Not yet, but we'll find them. For now, just get that poor child back here."

"I will." Teague shoved his phone into his pocket and turned to face Emma. "Ready to go? I'm sure you'd like to put on some clean clothes and have something to eat."

She nodded but didn't look him in the eye.

"I'm going to carry you, okay? You're probably tired, and the trail is pretty rough." When her hand stilled on the dog's fur, he hurried on. "Don't worry, Coco will be coming with us." When she glanced up, wary caution in her eyes, he smiled. "Are you ready?"

After a moment, she nodded again.

Relieved, Teague bent to pick her up. With Coco running along beside them, he headed into the woods. After a few minutes, her body relaxed, and she rested her head on his shoulder. His heart contracted and tears formed as he prayed he'd soon be able to hold Keely just like this.

And Nina.

He didn't talk as he carefully made his way through the woods, only hoped he was providing a modicum of security for the traumatized child. He couldn't imagine what she'd been through. Didn't want to try. For her, at least, the nightmare was over.

When the trees ahead began to thin, and voices carried through the forest, Emma's grip on him tightened.

He stopped and glanced down into frightened blue eyes. "It's okay. I've got you, and the people waiting are here to help you. Policemen who only want to make sure you're safe."

She clung with one arm around his neck in a stranglehold. When she didn't struggle against him, he moved onward, pushing a tree branch aside to cross the weedy grass to the street.

As he met Stackhouse's gaze, a second car with a county logo on the door rolled up the street and stopped. A young woman with kind eyes, freckles, and red hair got out and approached. She paused for a moment to speak to Chief Stackhouse before continuing toward Teague. When she reached him, she smiled at Emma.

"I bet you're scared and confused right now, aren't you?"

The girl nodded.

"I don't blame you one bit. You've been through a lot.

My name is Kitty, and I help kids. Would you let me help you?"

Emma's grip on his neck loosened. "Kitty's a funny name for a lady, but I like it."

She smiled again. "I like it, too. Would you be willing to come with me? I imagine you're hungry, and we can go get whatever you'd like to eat."

"Pizza?"

"Sure." When Kitty held out her hand, Emma took it.

Teague slowly lowered her to the ground and met the woman's eyes before facing the girl again. "Kitty will take good care of you. I promise."

"I definitely will."

Stackhouse approached as they drove away. He laid a hand on Teague's arm. "Kitty from Child Protective Services is a wonder. She'll make that poor child feel comfortable in no time."

"I hope so. What about the parents?"

"They've been notified, but there are legal channels we have to go through first."

"If I were them, I'd be—"

"They'll get to see their little girl shortly. That story will have a happy ending. I'm sure of it," the chief said gruffly.

Teague pushed his hands into his pockets and clenched his fists tight. "I'm glad. Now I want the same happy ending for my child. For Nina."

"We'll find them both. After what I just witnessed, I have a good feeling this day is only going to get better."

His heart nearly tore apart with fear for the two people he loved most in the world. "It has to."

* * *

The single streak of light through the crack above them had faded some time ago as the sun moved across the sky. Nina shifted slightly on the hard ground, even though it was agony simply to move. At the moment, Keely was asleep in her lap, and she didn't want to disturb her. The longer they waited, the more certain she became their captor wouldn't return until dark provided her some modicum of safety.

After a while, Keely stirred and stretched then sat up. "I have to go to the bathroom."

"You can pee in the corner over by the shelves if you need to."

"Eww."

"I know, but we don't have a lot of choices."

The girl stood and moved away. Overhead, footfalls vibrated, and metal clicked against metal.

"Keely, stay where you are, crouch down, cover your head, and stay quiet." Nina spoke in a sharp whisper.

"Is she coming?"

"Yes. Now do as I say. Please."

Wood creaked and groaned before the trapdoor thumped open onto the ground. Dim gray light filled the empty space before a bright beam flashed down in her face.

"I see you're awake."

Nina reached behind her for the first jar and shaded her eyes from the blinding light with the other. "No thanks to you. I could have broken my neck when you pushed me down those stairs."

"It's just too bad you didn't. Where's Lynette?"

"She's not feeling well."

"What?" Panic sounded in her voice as the light flashed around the chamber and landed on the huddled figure. "Lynette, baby, what's wrong?" When there was no response, she came down the first two steps and glanced at

Nina. "I have a knife. Don't try anything stupid. Do you hear me?"

"I hear you."

The stairs creaked, and the light wavered. Bringing out the jar, Nina hurled it with all her strength. The flashlight flew through the air and landed with a thud but didn't go out as the glass jar shattered against the wall.

"You bitch!"

Nina heaved two more jars in quick succession, then jumped to her feet when the woman tumbled down the stairs. Metal gleamed in the light as her adversary rolled over, knife raised. Picking up the fourth jar, Nina threw hard, and the knife went sailing toward the bottom of the stairs as the jar broke. Behind her, Keely screamed long and shrill when their captor pushed upright. Nina aimed the fifth jar at her head and threw.

The jar smashed against the side of her face with a sickening thunk, and the woman dropped like a stone.

"Keely, go. Be careful of the broken glass. I want you to run to the first house with lights on and tell the people there to call nine-one-one. Tell them to send help."

Keely skirted around the fallen woman and scampered up the stairs.

Nina focused on the figure sprawled in front of her. Reaching past her, she grabbed the flashlight and pointed it toward the foot of the stairs, then scooped up the knife.

"Lynette!" The woman spoke the name on a moan as she struggled to sit, using one hand to hide her face when the light hit her in the eyes.

"I have your knife and more jars. I won't hesitate to brain you or stab you if you move an inch. Is that clear?" Nina's voice was cold, hard, filled with all the anger she'd kept bottled up inside since this freak had first taken Keely.

"Where's Lynette? Where's my baby?"

"Keely's gone, and you'll never touch her again. Where's the other girl, the child that was on the beach? What did you do to her?"

"You'll never find her. Never!" Her voice rose in a shriek. "She pretended to be my perfect girl, but she was an impostor. I did to her what I had to, what I did to all the rest for their deception." Slowly the hand came down, and familiar blue eyes flashed with madness. "You'll never take Lynette away from me. You can't stop me!"

"Marge! Are you freaking kidding me?" When the woman lunged forward, Nina swung the metal tube of the flashlight and nailed her in the neck, knocking her backward. "I said don't move. Next time, I'll kill you."

The soft-spoken, unassuming woman who'd fitted her bridesmaid dress blinked, her lips drawn back in a feral snarl. "This is all your fault."

"What the hell are you talking about?"

"You took my winning lottery ticket and hid it. If I'd had those millions, this would all have been so much simpler. But maybe I should thank you. If I hadn't been searching for the ticket you picked up on the beach, I never would have seen Lynette. My real daughter. Not that sassy fake I harbored in my home."

The woman was crazy, utterly and completely mad, but she was the only one who knew where she'd left the kidnapped girl . . . if the poor child was still alive.

"Maybe I'll let you have Lynette back if you tell me what you did with the impostor. I'll even give you the lottery ticket."

"You're lying! I can tell you're lying."

In the distance, sirens sounded. The woman came at her, hands extended like claws. Nina swung the flashlight, but the metal tube glanced off her arm. When fingers closed around her neck, she grabbed the final jar and smashed it down on her head. It broke in a shower of liquid and glass as the grasping fingers slipped away and Marge crumpled to the ground.

Pushing to her feet, Nina barely noticed the sharp shard that stabbed her palm. When she reached the stairs, she climbed toward the faint moonlight as doors slammed and voices shouted. Booted feet pounded the ground as the authorities raced toward her.

"She's down there." Raising a shaking hand, she pointed. "In the cellar."

"Nina!"

Turning toward the only voice she wanted to hear, she cried out and ran forward. Teague caught her in his arms and held her tight while she finally gave in to the overwhelming fear she'd kept at bay, for his daughter's sake. Her whole body shook.

"Keely's okay. She's fine."

"I know. I saw her and held her, but I had to find you, too." Cupping her face in his hands, he kissed her. "God, Nina, I was so afraid I'd lose you both."

"That's never going to happen." She clung to him, so very thankful. "I don't ever want to let you go."

"Neither do I. It's over, and we have each other. That's all that matters." When she touched his cheek, he covered her hand before turning it over. "You're bleeding."

"I cut myself on some glass. It's nothing."

When lights flashed around them, he held her away from him. "Hardly nothing. You look like you've been through hell."

"A few cuts and bruises. I'll survive." She stared into his eyes. "The other girl, Emma . . ."

"I found her. She's safe."

Nina collapsed against him. "Oh, thank God. What about Stella? I left her bleeding—"

"She's out of surgery and in critical condition, but the doctors think she'll pull through."

Holding tight to him, she kissed him, then pressed her face to his neck. "That's all I need to hear. Let's take Keely and go home."

"We will, right after we get you checked out. I'm not taking any chances." Scooping her up in his arms, he held her tight to his chest. "Then we'll go home, the three of us together where we belong."

Chapter Twenty-eight

Teague slid the lasagna pan into the oven, shut the door, and then set the timer. From the other room, Keely's high-pitched laughter mixed with Nina's lower tone. Relief that both his daughter and the woman he loved had survived the previous day's nightmare gave a lightness to his step as he crossed the kitchen. Just the thought of those panic-filled hours still had the power to induce a cold sweat.

He paused in the living room doorway to simply enjoy the moment. A Candy Land board was spread out on the coffee table between the couch where Nina sat and Keely, who knelt on the area rug with Coco at her side.

Before he could move, his daughter jumped to her feet and danced in a circle. "You lose a turn. You lose a turn. That means I get to go twice."

"Of all the bad luck." Nina's gaze rose to meet his, and her eyes sparkled. "Are you sure you didn't stack the deck?"

"Huh?" Keely took a card and moved to a blue square then drew again. "Red. I win!"

"And so graciously." Teague stepped into the room and nodded toward the dog. "Can you take Coco to the backyard? She hasn't been outside to pee in hours."

"Do I have to?"

"Yes."

"Fine." Keely's pink tennis shoes scuffed against the floor as she moved slower than any turtle.

Teague ruffled her hair as she passed. The need to touch her and know she was safe was constant. He waited until the back door slammed shut to round the coffee table and drop onto the couch next to Nina. "How're you feeling?"

"Like I got caught in a stampede . . . or pushed down a flight of stairs. I imagine I'll be sore for a while, but at least I didn't break anything."

A purple bruise marred the perfection of her cheek and complemented the dark circles beneath her eyes, the result of a mostly sleepless night.

"The concussion is bad enough. I know the doctor told you to take it easy for a few days, but that doesn't mean you have to play Candy Land. If you'd rather just have peace and quiet, I can find something to occupy Keely."

"I'm fine." When he reached for her hand, Nina twined her fingers through his. "After the drama we went through, mindless board games are relaxing. Besides, it makes Keely happy. She needs normal right now, and I'm delighted to do my part."

"Thankfully, she doesn't appear terribly fazed by what happened. Other than being a little clingy last night, she seems to have dismissed her kidnapping." He squeezed her hand a little harder. "Meanwhile, I'm not sure I'll ever recover."

"All we can do is encourage her to talk about her feelings so she doesn't bottle them up inside. Maybe have her see a counselor."

"I already made an appointment with someone the Child Protective Services woman recommended. I asked Kitty about Emma, but she said she couldn't discuss the case. I'm afraid that poor child has a long road to recovery ahead, but at least she's been reunited with her parents. I know they're doing everything they can to help her."

The back door squeaked open then slammed shut, followed by running footsteps and clicking nails against the floor. When several loud raps sounded from the front of the house, Coco barked like a lunatic.

"I'll see who it is." Teague released her hand and rose to his feet. By the time he reached the entry, both Keely and Coco were at the front door. "I'll answer it." Gently pushing his daughter and the dog behind him, he glanced through the glass pane and frowned before opening the door.

Chris Long stood on the porch. When Teague shushed the dog, the officer held up his hand. "Not another problem, I swear. I wanted to check on Nina, but she wasn't home."

"Come on inside. Nina's hanging out with us so I can keep an eye on her."

"I hope she's not—"

"Mild concussion only, but it's the second one she's had recently. The ER doctor we saw last night recommended rest." Teague led the way into the living room.

Nina glanced up from putting away the game and smiled. "Hi, Chris. How are you?"

"Better than you, based on the number of visible bruises."

"I'm pretty much black and blue all over. What's going on?"

He cleared his throat and glanced over at Keely, whose eyes were wide as she stared at the uniformed police officer standing in her living room. "I wanted to see how you're feeling and give you an update. I figured you'd be curious."

Teague rested his hand on his daughter's shoulder. "Now would be a good time to straighten up your room. We'll be eating dinner soon."

"It's not that messy, and you said—"

"The grown-ups need to talk. Please do as I ask."

"Can I watch extra cartoons later if I do?"

"I suppose." When a pleased smile curved her lips, he muttered, "Extortionist."

"What does that mean?"

Teague pointed. "Go."

Chris's smile broadened when her footsteps thumped up the stairs. "Your daughter is a born negotiator. We could use her on the force when she grows up."

"Isn't that the truth?" Nina waved toward the club chair across from the couch. "Have a seat. Thankfully, Keely seems to have bounced back from her ordeal."

"That's excellent."

"I'm beyond relieved." Teague sat on the couch beside Nina after the other man took the chair opposite them. "You have news to share?"

"First, Stella Lange is recovering well from her surgery."

"Thank heavens. I called the hospital, but they wouldn't tell me much."

Chris's smile faded. "Unfortunately, that's the only good news. I thought you'd want to know Marge Glazer has been talking. Actually, once she got to the hospital to have her injuries treated, she wouldn't shut up. It was damn freaky listening to her go on and on about all her *mistakes* and how she had to get rid of the *impostors*."

Nina let out a little cry. "There were other girls like Emma?"

"I'm afraid so. Since the Glazer woman ranted in front of half the hospital staff, word is spreading around town at warp speed. I wanted you to hear the unadulterated version, not that it isn't horrible enough."

Teague picked up Nina's hand and squeezed it. "What did that woman do?"

"From what we've learned in the last twenty hours, Margery Guzman, aka Marge Glazer, was a single mother back in the early eighties, living in Pocatello, Idaho. Her daughter died of unknown causes. Unknown simply because her body wasn't discovered until . . . well, I won't go into details. Apparently Glazer had a mental collapse as a result of her death."

"I can imagine. How heart wrenching." Nina's voice broke.

"Her grief is understandable," Chris continued in a hard tone. "What followed wasn't. Guzman kidnapped a local girl, disappeared with her, then assumed a new identity. She's been going by Marge Glazer for quite some time now. Based on her own admission, after a few years, she came to realize her replacement wasn't her real daughter, probably because she'd grown too old to fit the image in her mind. So she repeated the process. Each time, Glazer left the current girl buried somewhere near her home, found a new *daughter*, then moved to another location in the Northwest."

"How many young girls has she kidnapped and murdered over the last thirty-odd years?" Teague asked. His chest tightened, just imagining all the grief the woman had caused.

"We don't know for certain, but if her account is to be believed, probably at least a dozen."

"I can't—" Nina broke off and pressed a hand to her stomach. "How could she have gotten away with such evil for so long?"

Chris's eyes darkened. "She kept a low profile and brainwashed the girls into believing they were her daughter, Lynette. Since the average age of the victims was five or six at the time they were taken, it wouldn't have been all that difficult to gain their cooperation."

"I might be sick." Nina's face had lost all its color, and she swallowed a time or two. "It's all my fault Keely was on that woman's radar to begin with."

"What are you talking about?" Chris asked.

"She said I picked up her winning lottery ticket off the beach. I don't remember doing it, but I must have. That's what she was looking for when she searched my house."

"She did mention a lottery ticket when she was ranting. I thought she was delusional, but a winning ticket was sold locally and never claimed." Chris leaned forward in the chair. "Do you still have it?"

Nina shook her head and winced. "I must have thrown it away. She was after that stupid ticket when she saw Keely."

Teague slid his arm around her. "Hey, it's over . . . thanks to you. That woman will never hurt another child."

She closed her eyes and took a few deep breaths. "Keely's safe, and you saved Emma before it was too late for her. Thank God for that."

"We have a lot to be thankful for." He met her gaze in silent communication as the seconds ticked by.

Chris rose slowly to his feet. "Unless you need something, Nina, I think I'll go."

She tore her attention away from Teague. "I have everything I want. Thanks for stopping by and filling us in. I appreciate it."

"No problem."

Teague released Nina and stood to follow him to the door. "Thanks for keeping us in the loop." When he held out his hand, Chris shook it.

"Nina went through a lot yesterday, physically and emotionally. I wanted to make sure she was okay."

"I expect she'll have a few nightmares. I know I will, but I intend to be there for her every step of the way."

The cop's eyes darkened. "She deserves that. She's a special woman."

"Believe me, I know."

He nodded and pulled open the door. "Great. Have a good evening, Teague."

"Thank you. I intend to."

Nina dipped her brush in a brilliant azure and added streaks to the softer blue of the sky above the Sirens out in the cove. In contrast to the painting she'd done in this exact spot earlier in the summer, her current work was filled with brightness and light, reflecting the sunny day and her stellar mood. On the beach, Teague built a sand-castle with his daughter while Coco ran in circles, chas-ing seagulls. Keely's happy laughter mingled with gentle waves lapping against the shore.

Lately, Nina's utter contentment had colored her work . . . and her life. After putting the finishing touches on a clump of seagrass, she cleaned her brushes and packed up her gear. When her phone rang, she pulled it from her pocket and checked the number. With a frown, she answered cautiously.

"Hello."

"Miss Hutton, this is Patricia Herrington. Kitty from Child Protective Services told me you were asking about

Emma and left your number. Since she couldn't fill you in on an active case, I thought I'd give you a call."

Nina's frown faded away. "I'm so glad you did. I've been painting on the beach lately, and your daughter has been on my mind. I hope she's doing well."

"She really is. With counseling, Emma's remembering more and more of her old life. Not everything, but enough." Patricia's voice rang with joy. "She loves her baby brother and enjoys helping with him."

"That's terrific."

"We're taking her recovery one day at a time, but I'm encouraged. I'll never be able to thank you enough for your part in bringing her back to us."

"Knowing she's recovering is all the thanks I need. I appreciate you calling."

"I was thinking . . ." Her voice was hesitant. "Maybe you'd like to paint a portrait of my two children next Christmas. If you do projects like that."

A smile curved Nina's lips. "Not usually, but I'd be thrilled to paint them. I'll look forward to hearing from you in the fall."

"I'll be in touch."

She hung up and glanced toward the water. Teague waved as he strode across the damp sand toward her. His bare chest was tanned to a dark bronze, and his abs were clearly defined above low-riding shorts. The devilish gleam that lit his silvery eyes curled her toes.

"I was planning to come join you."

"Did you finish your painting?" When she nodded, he rounded the easel and draped an arm over her shoulders. "Hey, you included Coco."

"Her silly antics seemed to fit the fun mood of the piece."

"I love it, but then I love all your work. If I had my way, you'd never sell a single one."

"Then I'd be a poor, starving artist instead of a moderately successful one. Anyway, I like knowing someone else is getting enjoyment from my art."

"True." After tilting her face up with a warm hand, he kissed her slowly, thoroughly. "But maybe not as much enjoyment as you give me."

"I could respond to that, but then you'd have to hide behind my easel until you cooled off."

He laughed out loud. "Your humor is just one of the dozen reasons I love you."

"Only a dozen? I must be slipping." Nina leaned against his hard chest. "No matter, I'm in an excellent mood. While you were building castles, I talked to Patricia Herrington."

"Emma's mother? How's she doing?"

"Really well."

Teague hooked a strand of hair behind her ear and brushed her cheek with his thumb. "That's terrific."

"Isn't it? The perfect news for such a gorgeous day." When he glanced over her shoulder and grinned, Nina turned around. "What's Keely doing?"

"Kicking down our sandcastle. Looks like Coco's helping, digging like a fiend. She'll be a filthy mess."

"Wouldn't be the first time. Kids and dogs should be allowed to get dirty now and then."

"Agreed."

"Speaking of dirty, I need to go home to do some laundry, maybe bring over more clean clothes. I seem to be spending all my time at your house lately."

"About that . . . I'd like to make a few changes."

Her good mood dimmed as his eyes darkened from silver to pewter. She backed up a step. "Is something wrong?"

"Yeah, something's definitely wrong."

Her heart thumped behind her breastbone. "I thought everything has been pretty great, but if you want a little more space . . ."

His face softened. "Not more space, Nina. Less. I'm tired of you running back and forth between two houses. I want you in mine. Permanently."

One hand crept up to cover her mouth as he reached into the pocket of his shorts. After pulling out a small velvet box, he flipped open the lid. A round diamond set on a plain gold band lay on his palm.

"It reminded me of you. Straightforward. Elegant. Beautiful."

"It's perfect." She could barely speak through the lump in her throat as Teague dropped onto one knee.

"I love you more than my life. I want you in my heart and in my home. I want to share with you the most precious gift I have, my daughter. Will you marry me, Nina, and make my life complete?"

She could only nod as he slipped the ring on her finger and rose to his feet. She threw her arms around his neck, then stood on her toes to kiss him. "I love you, Teague. More than I ever thought possible. And I love Keely. I'd be honored to be your wife."

He swung her in a circle and kissed her again. "God, I love you."

Behind them, feet pounded against the sand. "Did you finally ask?"

Teague grinned and pressed his forehead against Nina's. "Yes."

"Did she say yes?"

Nina turned her head to look down at the beaming, sandy face. "I did."

"Yay!" Keely danced in a circle around them, shouting with excitement, while Coco barked like a lunatic.

Nina couldn't stop smiling. "Is this what our life will always be like?"

He smiled back and kissed her once more. "I sure hope so."

If you enjoyed *Lost Innocence*, be sure not to miss the
first book in Jannine Gallant's thrilling Siren Cove series,

BURIED TRUTH

*Visit Siren Cove, Oregon, for gorgeous beaches, miles of
hiking, delightful small-town shops—and a dark side
none of its residents could have possibly imagined . . .*

Leah Grayson has lived in Siren Cove all her life. It's
where she buried a time capsule with her fifth-grade
class. Where she spent an unforgettable night on the
beach with her first love. Where she married then
divorced her rotten ex.

But there's something ugly going on in her pretty little
town. When Leah organizes a reunion for her fifth-grade
classmates to open their time capsule, they discover a
roll of film no one remembers saving. Afterward, strange
incidents begin happening. Warnings. Accidents.
Random acts of vandalism.

Luckily, her first love is back in town, too. Ryan
Alexander has made it big with a wildly popular social
media startup, but he's still the same sweet, cynical man
she fell for all those years ago. And the chemistry they
felt as teenagers is as strong as ever.

A nostalgic fling turns deadly when someone is
convinced Leah has the key to secrets long buried. With
no way to know whom they can trust, Leah and Ryan
will have to seek out the answers themselves . . .

A Lyrical mass-market paperback and e-book
on sale now!